Night's a Shadow; Day's a Shine

Night's a Shadow; Day's a Shine

A Geechee Tale

BY

Karen Dove Barr

RESOURCE *Publications* · Eugene, Oregon

NIGHT'S A SHADOW; DAY'S A SHINE
A Geechee Tale

Resource Publications
An Imprint of Wipf and Stock Publishers
199 W. 8th Ave., Suite 3
Eugene, OR 97401

www.wipfandstock.com

PAPERBACK ISBN: 979-8-3852-4977-0
HARDCOVER ISBN: 979-8-3852-4978-7
EBOOK ISBN: 979-8-3852-4979-4

VERSION NUMBER 06/23/25

This is a work of historical fiction set in an actual geographic location. Names, characters, and incidents either are the product of the author's imagination or are used fictitiously, and any resemblance to actual persons, living or dead, business establishments, or events is entirely coincidental.

This book is dedicated to my husband, Dr. Douglass Havey Thomson, who upon retirement said, "I'll never have to grade another paper"—then spent two years correcting drafts of *Night's a Shadow, Day's a Shine.*

Contents

Acknowledgments

The members of my writing group deserve heartfelt thanks for suffering through endless drafts and telling me how to make them better. I owe you Lance Levens, Sally Rountree Klein, Laine King, David Holloway, Chuck Eyler, Patty Leone, and Doug Thomson.

Chapter One

September 1856

F aint echoes of ancestral drumbeats drifted past Lizzie on wind from
the incoming tide. Barely noting the distant drum, she rose stiffly
from her crouched position under the endless blue dome of Skidaway
Island's sky. Suddenly, the barren fields of blackened cotton stalks reminded her of the dry fields of Mauretania. She shuddered and tossed
one last ripened cotton boll onto a filthy sheet of canvas. Suppressing
the memory of Africa, she hoisted baby Cass to her hip and turned to
beckon six-year-old Dicie to follow her home.

But Dicie wasn't waiting in the furrow behind her, as her mammy
expected. Fearing the worst, Mammy narrowed her eyes and scanned the
field. Wild hogs, rattlesnakes, and swamp panthers were among the least
of the dangers lurking on this wild island. Finally, she spotted the child at
the far edge, hidden in a patch of goldenrod.

"Lord, help her," she grumbled. "Chile ain't got no sense."

Flittering orange butterflies in the late-blooming flowers held Dicie
spellbound. Even after sweltering in the blazing sun all day, the child had
more spirit than a squirrel full of acorns. She chased down the butterflies
while her mother turned to pick up Cass.

Too tired to run after her, Lizzie cut loose her eerie panther scream.
In neighboring fields, startled women sprung erect. A flock of crows
soared upward from under dying cotton plants. The scream brought Dicie running. Even Daddy stepped lightly when Mammy screamed.

Although Dicie was Lizzie's only living girl child, on hot autumn days like today she felt ungrateful. No telling what the child would get into. She pestered her mother with chatter all day long, wanting answers to everything. Dicie even talked to the animals. If Lizzie hadn't had the baby in her arms, she would have cut a switch.

While hurrying the child back to the compound, mother and daughter lined up outside the open-walled cookhouse. They held out plates for collards, cornbread, and steaming-hot crab. While Lizzie found a bench under a moss-draped oak to sit and feed the baby, Dicie plopped down cross-legged on a pile of dead leaves.

The little girl gobbled her collards and expertly opened the crab. Soon as every crumb was gone, she jumped up and ran across the weed-filled compound to the edge of the marsh.

Like always, she forgot to give her plate back to her mammy, leaving it half buried in the sand for the ants. Cool water and marsh mud were too enticing to resist. Dicie pretended not to hear her mother hollering after her. Maybe Mammy would forget—although Mammy never forgot.

"You, girl! You done forgot yo' plate," Lizzie screamed, to no avail. Soon as she finished feeding the baby, she snatched up her own plate and Dicie's, and rushed off to tend her garden, baby Cass heavy in her arms.

Left behind, Dicie squatted naked in her favorite puddle where the cookhouse women threw dirty dishwater. The water cooled her bare feet and soothed her ant bites after a day spent in the cotton field.

Boom, boom, bam, bam. Distant drumbeats shivered in the hot, wet air. At first the little girl didn't notice. Fiddler crabs waved their over-sized right claws from holes in the salt marsh, while her light brown hands patted and shaped imaginary sweets from mud. A few crabs dared filter the dishwater for bits of food, but Dicie was too engrossed in her work to notice. Spider-like fiddlers scuttled all over the marsh.

Settling into the warm puddle, she dug her hands underwater and grabbed a fistful of gray marsh mud. Flattening the mud ball, she pretended to make saraka, her favorite sesame seed and honey treat. Mammy said her mammy taught her the recipe. She must have learned it before she got kidnapped and hauled out of Mauretania. Mammy clenched her mouth shut soon as she told how she learned to bake saraka. No matter how much Dicie pestered her, she wouldn't tell more about when she was a little girl. Not even how she got stolen.

Further down the edge of the marsh, two almost-grown mink pups chased each other through the wrack, scattering thick piles of rotting marsh grass washed up by last year's hurricane.

Drops of brackish water glistened on the pups' dark brown fur. Stopping in their tracks, the minks made eye contact with the little girl. The bigger one shuffled closer, while the other watched Dicie pick up a strand of marsh grass covered in tasty barnacles. Dicie dangled it toward the braver pup. Pouncing forward, it grabbed the strand in its mouth, and scampered off, but not too far.

Dicie clapped her hands and laughed. Children her age were rare on Skidaway Island, but the young animals filled the gap. Drops of mud splashed Dicie's oval face and her eyes crinkled, revealing a hint of Arabic in her Pan-African ancestry. All day long she sweated in black dirt between rows of cotton plants, minding baby brother Cass and flapping her arms at hungry crows. Still, she had plenty of energy for making mudpies and playing with the minks.

Boom! Boom! Bam! Bam! The rhythmic pulses of distant drums grew louder. Now, instead of wind-blown whispers, the drummer at the next plantation took up the beat. A brisk evening breeze blew his pulsing boom across the forbidden ditch to Dicie. Faraway beats from plantations further south faintly echoed the primeval sound. From the west another echoing boom joined the chorus. The minks stopped chewing on barnacles and lifted their heads to listen. High in the sky, buzzards circled.

As Dicie cocked her head toward the loudest booms, her belly tightened. Too often, the drums beat the message of death.

Splashing her hands in dirty water to wash off the mud, she raced her short legs back to their tabby hut yelling, "Mammy, Mammy, the drum!"

The minks followed her part way, hoping for more barnacles, until the approach of a man sent them scampering back to the water. Iridescent black crows chattered a warning as she neared her home.

Her mammy said children should be seen, not heard, but Dicie was too scared to fret about Mammy reaching for a switch. Hopping over the wooden threshold of their one-room dwelling, she called, "Mammy! Mammy!" Her shouts echoed in an empty room

It wouldn't be any use looking for Daddy. He never came home while the sun was in the sky.

"Get yo'self out here," Lizzie hollered from the garden back of the cabin where she plucked weeds from rows of okra and picked fat green worms off yellow squash. Baby Cass lay in the shadow of the cabin on an old quilt. Pink clouds streaked the sky overhead. Less than an hour of daylight remained, but the heavy wet air hadn't lost its heat.

Dicie jumped up and down shouting, "Mammy, Mammy, the drum."

Her mother turned her good ear, the one on the other side of her face from the scar, in the direction of the drumbeats. "I hear it, chile. I ain't deaf."

Lizzie was thin as the slavedriver's whip, except where her abdomen bulged from birthing children. Nine had been born, not counting the ones she lost. Sweat oozed over the bright red scar on her cheek and dripped down her pale tan skin.

"Where you been?" she said, raising her hand to slap Dicie. "You s'posed to be keeping the gnats off this baby."

BOOM! BOOM! BAM! BAM! A stronger gust of wind off the rising tide blew the drumbeats closer. Lizzie dropped her hand and cocked her good ear toward the loudest beats. Two long and two short. Fast was for good news, slow for bad. One long, three short meant special danger, not that danger wasn't always lurking on the exposed semi-tropical island. Tonight, the beats were all quick, even the two long ones.

"Big Tom," she said. "He telling us a gathering coming. Finally. They need all us's help baling cotton." She counted the drumbeats. "This Saturday night." Her mouth curved up in what Dicie knew was a smile, even though part of her lip was missing.

Batting at the cloud of biting sand gnats swarming around her face, Lizzie grabbed Dicie's hand. "Stay here and mind Baby Cass while I run to the cook house and see what Sampson got to say. Maybe we can git a pass." Sampson, the snaggle-toothed, black-skinned slave-driver would be sitting at the wooden table outside the cookhouse, eating his dinner and counting the workers

She patted her charm, a raccoon penis bone hanging around her neck on blue string. Sometimes it worked its magic, sometimes not. Tonight, she needed its help.

Sampson scared Dicie, even when he wasn't on a rampage. She was glad to stay with Cass. Women bent low in the fields to avoid looking him in the eye and stepped clear of his leather whip. Even though the women never stopped working, he especially liked to crack it when they talked to each other. Unless the woman was one of his favorites. Lizzie, with her scarred face, constant pregnancies, and reputation for witchcraft, was never a favorite.

Dicie seated herself on the quilt next to the sleeping baby. She reached her finger to touch his smooth brown skin. Her hands remembered the soft, hot feel of Stavy, Mammy's next oldest baby to Cass, and how she had rocked him to sleep in her arms. How she had held him burning up with fever before he died. A baby was a gift from God, but God too often took back His gifts.

Big nighttime gatherings never took place on Brisbane where Dicie lived. The quarters were too close to tall marsh grass and deep tidal creeks leading to the Atlantic Ocean. A strong swimmer could escape if he knew the tides and places where hard sand instead of quicksand bottomed the creeks.

The much larger plantation next door, Hibernia, covered the highlands in the center of Skidaway Island. A two-story wood house for buckra, with glass windows, overlooked its main slave compound. More than one overseer kept a close eye on its workers, making sure no one came or went without a pass.

The Geechee workers tried hard to spread any crumb of news all over the island. The buckra tried harder to stop them. Divide and conquer was the slave-owners' motto. Easy enough since the workers had been kidnapped and sold into slavery from so many different African tribes. Few spoke the same languages as their fellow workers. Slaves unloaded on Georgia's sea islands in the watershed of the Ogeechee River came to be called Geechees, reflecting their destination, not their origin. Learning to communicate with each other was an important act of rebellion. Reading and writing were whipping offenses, but messages relayed by tribal drums were largely considered not a threat to slave owners.

Lizzie kept quiet about learning to read and write before she got kidnapped. Since her education was in Arabic, writing did her little good on Skidaway Island, but she recognized numbers and knew how to add and subtract. Signs told her the buckra were now hiding something important.

Absentee owners couldn't entirely keep their human property ignorant. Once they finished their assigned work, slaves like Rosa and Cletis were allowed to paddle a bateau full of fish and produce to City Market in Savannah. Lizzie was hired out to cook for a hunting party. Workers with special skills were loaned to other plantations. Buckra forced slaves to attend prayer services. Whispers flew as workers gathered on the grounds of the praise house. Dicie stood quietly and pretended not to hear, so her mammy wouldn't send her away.

Grownups watched covertly as ships from foreign places unloaded illegally kidnapped Africans on the isolated island. Savannah buckra were in a tizzy about slaves being sold west to Kansas. Skidaway slaves giggled about goings-on of women, not wives, carried to the island by married white men. And now, speculation about why the usual get-togethers weren't happening passed quickly through each plantation.

At a big work gathering even Sampson couldn't stop the flow of information. Colored folks from all over Skidaway Island got passes to shuck corn, bale cotton, or cook the feast. Whispered code words flew as the enslaved workers pieced together what each one knew, while patrollers kept close watch on everybody, especially those who wandered away from the crowd.

Little Cass stirred and let out a hungry cry. Dicie lifted him into her lap and bounced him up and down. "Mammy coming," she sang to him.

Lizzie ran lightly back to the garden. She reached out her arms to take the baby and grinned. "My penis bone done worked. We got passes." Holding Cass to her breast, she patted her good luck charm while he sucked hungrily.

Dicie pictured Daddy with a big smile on his face when he heard the news. He hadn't made it home to eat dinner, but he understood the message of the drum. Daddy loved to dance. Everybody, even Mammy, clapped for him at the last bonfire when he ended up last man standing in the buzzard lope. She barely remembered the steps to the dance, but Daddy's gleaming white teeth shone brightly in her mind.

Dicie loved her Daddy. On cold winter nights when work was short, she sat on his lap with the fire in the cabin chasing the cold out of the one room where they lived. His salty smell blended with pine smoke; his worn flannel shirt rubbed softly against her face as his big arms circled her.

"You my special baby," he said, and she did feel special.

But he didn't come home that night. Mammy sat in the worn willow-weave rocking chair, Cass in her arms. "Wonder where Cuffie be?" she grumbled to herself. "He gotta git his own pass. He ain't here, and I ain't gone git it for him."

Listening to her fussing, Dicie fell asleep dreaming about Daddy dancing.

Chapter Two

September 1856

Since the last of the cotton bolls had been picked, the next morning Dicie and her mammy headed behind the hut to the garden before the sun got hot. Mammy's garden saved the family many ways and many times. Every month Sampson rowed to Thunderbolt for provisions, but the cornmeal, molasses, and salt pork he brought back were never enough to feed all the workers. After long days tending cotton, women grew vegetables and picked wild berries and scuppernongs. When old Master Warren died and his heirs forgot to give Sampson money, and when yellow fever struck and folks in town were sick and dying, the cookhouse pantry stood empty. Their gardens fed the slaves.

More than just food to sustain life in lean times, Lizzy grew life everlasting, hippo root, and golden seal. Anyone could grow them, but only Lizzie knew how to use them. She treated fever, dropsy, and bile, not just for her own family, but for others. She saved lives with her herbs and spells. Word got around.

Hidden salamanders, newts, and frogs burrowed secretly under the garden's deep leafy foliage. Dicie watched her mother gather, kill, and chop up reptile parts for her roots and charms. Seeing the little creatures sacrificed hurt her heart, but she knew to step lightly while her mammy concocted a potion. If interrupted, she was quick with a switch.

The coins Lizzie garnered from slaves desperate for magic bought an occasional sleeve of sugar or skein of wool. Instead of coins, a customer might pay with liquor fermented from the island's wild grapes. She took the shine but folded her lips and barely spit out a word when she handed the liquor over to Cuffie.

Everybody had been waiting for the celebration, especially Dicie's big brothers. She had three, Gus, Rufus, and Isaac. Sampson assigned the brothers their own acres in the cotton fields, but no more huts had been built. Until everyone in an occupied shelter died or her brothers got sold off, the boys would live with their mother.

Her brothers endlessly practiced their buzzard lope. Dicie laughed when Rufus trailed behind the others, pretending he was a big turkey buzzard. Time had already passed for the boys to take their places in the ring, but the buckra hadn't allowed a gathering. A terrifying September hurricane wrecked the low-lying island in 1855, washing away what cotton hadn't already been taken to town, but in 1856 the harvest was plentiful. Grownups whispered they should have gathered for a July fourth celebration, but it never happened. Nobody knew why.

Dicie barely remembered the last bonfire. Mammy and a woman from the south end had shown the children how to do the camel walk. While the children learned to throw their hips side to side and shuffle their feet like camels, men slipped into darkness, one by one, for a sip of forbidden blackberry spirits. Then there were flames leaping and Daddy dancing.

Cuffie, Dicie's daddy, was taller than most, with shiny black skin, and bulging muscles. His movements crackled with energy. When he flashed his grin, women noticed. He was so strong Old Mastere Warren ordered Sampson to make him work three men's sections. He ended up the last one let out of the fields. His family rarely saw him before they fell asleep.

As he trudged to the cabin the next night, Dicie was first to spot him. The sun had disappeared, but she had good eyes like her daddy. Recognizing the faint swish of his tired step in the sandy dirt, she ran to meet him. He bent to wrap his arms around her and lifted her to his shoulder.

"A dance, Daddy. I get to watch you dance," she said, hugging his neck.

Even Lizzie perked up. "I brung you some ham hocks to eat with your greens," she said, pulling from the coals a stone bowl covered by a tin plate.

Daddy sat Dicie on the floor and gave Lizzie a big hug before devouring the leftover food. It wasn't every day slaves got ham hocks.

"Two nights from now, we'll be eating high on the hog," he said. "Sampson done sent men out shrimping. Hear tell they shot a couple of deer and some wild hogs to roast."

Lizzie gave him her lop-sided smile. "Hope you got enough left in you Saturday night to do yo' buzzard lope," she said, settling the baby in her lap.

On Saturday, Dicie helped Mammy haul water, wash clothes, and scrub floors, while her brothers chopped firewood. Later that day, men and women congregated outdoors near the tabbies, telling each other what they were going to do that night.

Everybody was hungry, but the cookhouse was empty. The women who fixed dinner had already gathered their pots and spoons and headed for Hibernia to prepare the feast. Daddy would be there too, hauling wood for the bonfire and stacking it high.

Mammy washed her own and Dicie's hands. She wet a brush, plaited their hair, and hung Cass in a sling across her back. Dicie and her three big brothers followed Mammy and Cass down a sandy path to the forbidden barrier ditch that marked the southern boundary of Brisbane Plantation.

Isaac was fourteen with dark brown skin like Daddy. His big feet were a sign he would grow tall.

At sixteen, Rufus was almost as tall as Daddy, with the same night-black complexion. He was the family clown, teasing Dicie, and coming up with wild schemes, just like Daddy.

Gus, a grown man, was short with skin almost as pale as a buckra. Even though he was much smaller than Rufus and Daddy, he was hot-tempered and quick to fight. He and Daddy had never gotten along. Dicie didn't know why.

Stretched flat on either side of the path, the recently emptied cotton fields lay cooling in the dying sun. Cotton grown and ginned on Hibernia had been gathered into tall piles for the gigantic job of pressing it into tight bales. Slaves from all over were invited to help. Their reward was a feast, with dancing, and home-grown whiskey.

Overhead, chevrons of great blue herons and snowy egrets flew inland from the day's fishing in the salt marsh. A long line of workers snaked back from the ditch. The men chanted a low, musical call and response as they walked.

The man at the front of the line sang out, "Coming cross the island to bale cotton." Those in line behind him sang altogether, "Gone bale that cotton tonight." The leader called, "Gotta bale it tight."

The leader's line changed each time after the others responded, but the men behind him repeated the same chorus. Their voices blended in the night air. In the distance, Dicie heard the songs of gangs coming from plantations to the west.

Before the family reached the ditch, her big brothers sprinted ahead and blended in with the crowd of singing men. The men surged past the lone guard without showing passes.

Dicie, her mother, and baby brother waited their turn to cross the prohibited boundary line with other women and children. A light-brown-skinned guard almost as pale as Mammy checked passes. Clouds of mosquitoes swarmed overhead, biting bare arms and necks, while those waiting slapped at vicious sand gnats.

Dicie watched curiously as her mammy fished three paper cards out of the front of her dress: one for herself, one for Dicie, and one for baby Cass. Each pass had black letters and a big X at the bottom for Sampson's mark. The guard finally nodded and waved her and the two children down into the overgrown, weed-filled ditch.

Once up on the other side the flat fields didn't look much different from Brisbane, but Mammy said, "We is now on Hibernia."

She gazed around and muttered, "Three years done gone by since I got hired to help cook at the big house over yonder." She spat on the ground and pointed to where the land sloped slightly upward to a big wooden house with four red brick chimneys. "Lot more colored folk here."

Dicie stared at the hulking wooden house surrounded by gloomy dark-green bushes taller than Daddy. No buckra house ever got built on Brisbane. The most splendid building was Sampson's two-room wooden cabin with floors raised up off the ground and plastered walls. Dicie couldn't imagine what the inside of the big buckra house looked like. She wanted to run over and peek through the clear glass windows, but Mammy kept a tight grip on her arm. She lived with her parents and brothers in one room of a two-family tabby cabin, built by slaves out of oyster shells and lime. Another three women and one man lived in the other half of the tabby.

Mammy interrupted Dicie's gaping with a sharp tug on her wrist. "Step lively and stay close. We got to find Cuffie."

The setting sun blinded them as they followed the drumbeats for another half mile. The trampled dirt was crowded with strange black faces. Men ran by. Women with children pressed against them on every side.

In the distance, smoke from a bonfire billowed. Drums boomed and rattled. Dicie made out two different drums, one a deep bass and another with a higher, flatter rhythm. She forgot how tired her legs were. Lightning bugs twinkled as she shook off her mammy's hand and raced toward the circle of people around the fire. She forgot about staying close.

Suddenly, Mammy snatched her by the arm and shook her. Dicie bit her tongue and tasted blood. "Girl, they's evil spirits riding here, looking fo' little chillen like you. You want to disappear, and nobody never find you? I'll whip you if you run off again."

While Lizzie held her tight, they penetrated the ring of workers circling the bonfire. Lizzie twisted her head back and forth searching for Daddy. Dark-skinned field hands, but not from Brisbane, surrounded them. Flaming logs blazed high under two iron washpots. Steam rose and boiling water splashed as women threw ears of corn into the washpots. Tin buckets loaded with live crabs waited nearby. Near the edge of the burning logs, sweet potatoes wrapped in green palmetto leaves roasted in the sand. Dicie shrunk closer to her mammy and grabbed her leg.

"Buck up, girl," Mammy said, loosening her hand.

Dicie couldn't help it. All the strangers scared her. She twisted and turned every which way looking for Daddy, but the crowd packed too close. She couldn't see between people's legs or over their heads.

Mammy yanked her forward to where drumbeats sounded the loudest. "Come on, girl," she said. The earsplitting hullabaloo hurt Dicie's head, but her mother wouldn't let go of her arm.

"Most likely we gone find Cuffie in the midst of the worst goings-on," Lizzie muttered. "Hope he ain't got hisself in no trouble."

Chapter Three

September 1856

On the side of the fire away from wind-blown smoke, a tall thin man with midnight black skin beat a raccoon hide stretched over the end of a hollowed-out log. Strips of raccoon hide padded the ends of his drumsticks, giving them a broader thrum. Next to him, a skinny boy child, hardly older than Dicie, beat a little bitty drum. The boy's instrument was simply skin stretched across an empty tin can, the kind that held beans from the cookhouse.

Dicie couldn't help herself. She jerked away from Mammy and plunked down right in front of the little boy. As she stared at his home-made musical instrument, and his big brown eyes, he slowed his hands, staring back at her, messing up the rhythm.

A young girl, a little taller than Dicie, stepped out from behind the man and glared at Dicie. She tapped the drummer's arm and pointed to Dicie.

The tall man cut his eyes at the little drummer boy, then followed the child's gaze. A grin erased his stern look, but he said, "Boy, you mind yo' business."

Mammy rushed forward, baby Cass in her arms and head bowed to deflect punishment for putting herself forward. "Dicie, don't you bother the man," she said. She turned her unscarred cheek, presenting her best side to face him. "They's busy." Her free hand gripped Dicie's shoulder and snatched her backward, but not before the man smiled, and gave Mammy an appraising look.

"I'm Tom and this here be my boy, Little Tom," he said. "The girl here we call Bella." He pointed to the girl, who looked Dicie over without smiling.

Dicie squirmed under Mammy's grasp but was too shy to look directly at the children with both grown-ups watching her.

Mammy lifted her free hand to cover her scar and said, "That's some fine drumming."

A squat dark-skinned man, one of the Hibernia overseers, stepped out of the crowd behind them and growled at Big Tom. "Git back to your business," he said.

Big Tom jerked his arms back to the drum and hit it a hard lick. The squat man gave Little Tom a hard slap on the side of his head, knocking him to the dirt. A drumstick flew out of his hand.

Dicie gasped. Poor little boy. She started forward to help him up, but Mammy snatched her back into the crowd surrounding the wash pots. Over her shoulder she saw Little Tom scrambling for his drumstick. She watched Bella pick it up and give it to him.

"Oh, Jesus," Mammy moaned. "Where Cuffie be? This girl gone be the death of me."

Dicie finally spotted him. "There. Over yonder." She pointed toward a moss-draped oak by the side of the field away from the crowd. Cuffie was talking to a woman. The long hanks of Spanish moss hid the woman's face. Her hand rested on his arm. He had his other arm around her waist

"*Gawad,*" Mammy spat out the curse in her native Arabic, the curse she used when she was mad at Daddy. She wouldn't tell Dicie what it meant. Hoisting Cass higher on her hipbone, she tightened her grip on Dicie and marched toward Cuffie. As they approached him, her face froze into a neutral expression, but she didn't loosen the fist around Dicie's upper arm.

Dicie struggled hard to break free and run to him. "Daddy!" she screamed, wriggling in Mammy's iron grasp.

Cuffie's whole body jerked, startled. He didn't see his family until Dicie screamed. Jumping away from the woman, he said, "Lizzie!" He pinned a broad smile on his face. "I be asking Mary here if she seen you. So many folks milling around and it getting dark, I couldn't find you." He held out his arms for the children.

Something about his smile didn't seem right to Dicie, but soon as her mammy turned her loose, she fell into Daddy's arms.

"I seen the drums," she said. "We talk to the drummers. One little like me. Then a bad man made us leave."

Lizzie stood back behind an overgrown tangle of goldenrod, saying nothing, even when Cuffie took her hand and walked the family back to the fire. She didn't exactly resist, but her eyes glittered and her footsteps drug. The look she cast back at the woman, the one folks called "evil eye," scared Dicie. Looked like it scared the woman, Mary, too. She hurried off in the opposite direction, while Daddy filled the silence by telling Dicie about all the food they were about to eat.

"Yams and boiled crabs and corn on the cob with butter," he said, smacking his lips.

When they reached the boards laid across tree stumps for seats by the fire, Daddy got tin plates and filled them with shrimp, cornbread, and roasted sweet potatoes. Dicie and her brothers dug into their food, but Mammy hardly touched hers.

Cuffie cast a look at Lizzie, but she turned her head away. He headed into the shadows and came back with a tin cup brimming with strange-smelling liquid. He drank it down in four deep gulps.

"This here will get my strength up," he said, striding off toward the drummer.

Two men with fifes made of dried reed joined Big Tom and Little Tom. Another man carrying a long string of raccoon bones tied with deer sinew stepped forward. The two whistled their fifes, and the man with the bones began shaking and rattling in time to the drums.

Cuffie shouted to Big Tom. Dicie didn't understand his words, but Big Tom hit a hard lick and beat his big drum faster and louder. The bone handler whirled and tossed his string of bones over his head and between his legs in rhythm with the drum.

Daddy leaped, then threw his black and white striped handkerchief onto a patch of bare ground back from the fire. Forming a ring around it, Rufus, Gus, and Isaac, and other men followed Cuffie. Bending their heads forward, they shuffled their feet and danced the Buzzard Lope. Each man circled Cuffie's handkerchief, taking little steps closer toward it, like buzzards checking out a fresh carcass. The men quickly shuffled away from it, as if the handkerchief were poison. Their steps matched the timing of live buzzards circling fresh kill.

Cuffie peeked over at Lizzie to see if she was watching, but she kept her head turned, fussing over Cass, ignoring Cuffie. Finally, he stopped casting glances her way, and threw his head back like he didn't care. Bending his whole body forward nearly to the ground, he became the boss buzzard, shuffling closer and closer to his handkerchief. The other buzzards stepped back, except for Rufus, who moved to the edge of the circle, dancing an exaggerated version of his daddy's steps. Gus, Isaac, and the others formed a circle around Cuffie, shuffling in place, watching to see what the lead bird would do. Cuffie crouched lower and lower as he strutted closer to the handkerchief. Finally, he bent nearly to the ground and picked up the handkerchief in his gleaming white teeth. The crowd exploded in cheers.

Cuffie made a deep bow to the ring of watchers and strutted back to Lizzie. She gave her twisted grin and patted his arm but didn't let go of baby Cass to hug him.

After the congratulations died down, Daddy lit a stick of firewood. Holding the flaming torch high to light their way, he gathered Mammy, Dicie, and the boys, and led the family back down the path and across the ditch to Brisbane. In the black darkness, Dicie saw nothing beyond the ring of light cast by Daddy's torch. The back-and-forth "whoo, whoo" of a pair of great horned owls pierced the uneasy silence of their homeward walk.

Chapter Four

September 1856

S oon as they got home Lizzie snatched up the broom and ran outside to sweep away footprints from the front of the tabby. She performed the ritual every night after Cuffie came home and before she went to bed. All Geechee women swept their family's footprints to make sure no one stole them and cast a spell. The night was filled with witches, haints, and evil spirits. Tonight, she wielded the broom like she was smacking down an evil spirit itself.

After Mammy came in, Dicie listened to her parents' low voices arguing as she tried to fall asleep on her quilt under her parents' bed. Later came the soft sound of Mammy's crying, blanketed by Daddy's noisy snores. Her brothers' quieter breathing filled the other side of the room. Her stomach hurt like always when Daddy and Mammy fought.

On the way to the cotton field the next morning with her mammy and Cass, Dicie asked, "Why you mad at Daddy?"

Mammy grabbed her hand and hurried her along to the field. "What goes over the devil's back, got to come in under his belly," she said.

Didn't make a bit of sense to Dicie, but she knew better than to ask. That was all the explaining Mammy would give. If she persisted, she'd get slapped upside her face.

Settling herself in the dirt between the rows, she made sure not to sit on an ant bed.

Mammy dropped Cass in Dicie's lap and whacked her hoe into the mostly weed-free rows like a mad woman. "Don't know why I bother," she muttered. "This whole field fixing to be plowed under."

Dicie shivered and tried to keep Cass out of Mammy's way. Why was the field being plowed under? Planting time wasn't till March. She didn't dare ask.

When they got home that afternoon, Mammy marched straight to her garden, to the far back where herbs grew. Dicie watched her pick stems of sage and another herb whose name she had never taught Dicie. On the way back from the cookhouse, Mammy left baby Cass with Dicie and ran off into the woods toward a chokecherry tree.

Back in the cabin Mammy pounded a handful of cherries into a reddish-black pulp. Sprinkling in crumpled bits of bay leaf, she added water and set the whole mess in a wooden box filled with dried leaves and bones, the box Dicie was afraid to touch.

Was Mammy making a love potion? Because of the red choke cherries? Love potions had to be red. Dicie had learned that much. Or was it something else, something evil?

Late at night men and women visited their hut with hard to come by pennies. When they tiptoed in, their way lit by flickering candles made from suet, Dicie pretended to be asleep. They left with tiny medicine bottles filled with liquid. Small doses, but potent enough when slipped into blackberry wine to overcome the drinker with lust. Mammy's love potions were mighty powerful.

Her face was serious, and she muttered in Arabic, "*ya khara,*" (my piece of excrement), as she mixed the ingredients. The look was not the light-hearted expression she showed her lovesick customers.

Dicie's stomach tightened. Was Mammy mixing a spell that would hurt Daddy?

Later, after the afternoon sun vanished below the horizon, as the last gleam of light showed Mammy the way, Dicie watched her walk to the back of the garden again. Rummaging through the pile of wilted leaves and discarded stalks left to compost at the edge of the woods, she pulled out dried corn husks and dead pokeberry stalks and brought them back to the cabin.

Daddy still hadn't come in from the fields. Mammy squinted through the top half of the double Dutch door, keeping an eye out for him as she twisted the driest husks into a shape faintly resembling a person. With a sharp knife, she viciously cut arms and legs. A noose of poison ivy gripped the top of the husk to separate a head from the body. Lastly, she painted the whole creation blood-red with mashed up dried pokeberries and bacon grease.

"Mary," she muttered under her breath as she stabbed the finished doll with her knife. "Die."

Dicie hid under her quilt in the farthest corner under their bed. Whenever Mammy mixed her potions and started talking in that sing-song voice, everybody in the family, even Daddy, knew to keep out of her way. At least it didn't sound like she was saying Cuffie.

Finally, Mammy stopped muttering and Dicie peeked out from under the bed. Mammy's hands were stained blood-red with pokeberry juice, and a tortured grimace twisted her face, highlighting the purplish scar. Dicie slid her head back under the quilt.

She lay awake most of the night listening for Daddy, fearing what might happen when he slipped into the house. Thankfully, he never came. When the first gray light of late October dawn filtered through the cracks where wooden rafters joined the crushed oyster shell walls, only Dicie, her mother, and her brothers were in the room.

The next day the sky clouded over. As the tide rose for its after-noon high, rain fell, and a cold wind whooshed through the compound. Mammy and the children left the fields early.

When they got close to home, they saw a plume of black smoke trickling from the chimney, then swept away by the wind.

Daddy was home.

Before they reached the tabby, he opened the door. "Evening, Lizzie," he said, taking Cass from her arms, and embracing Dicie.

Mammy scowled at him like she did when she was about to pick up a switch and cut Dicie's legs. Dicie covered her ears expecting Mam-my's holler. Mammy could screech just like a panther. It was a trick she picked up in Africa when she was just a girl. She scared everybody in the compound.

Dicie buried her face in Daddy's overalls, holding on for dear life. He patted her on the head.

Mammy's throat bulged. Then she looked at Dicie, swallowed hard, and gave Daddy a tight smile. "Can you come to supper with me and the chillen?" she asked.

She waited with her lips folded. Daddy let go of Dicie, put his arms around Mammy and said, "Of course, Lizzie. I'm hungry as a pig." Draw-ing her close, he put his mouth over hers before she could say more.

Her love potion must have worked, even though she hadn't had time to slip it into his wine. Gathering the children, they walked hand-in-hand to the cookhouse.

Dicie's stomach stopped hurting. She forgot all about Mary.

The next day as the women gathered their hoes, preparing to leave the fields for the day, the drum boomed again from all the way over on Hibernia Plantation. This time it was the soft, slow beat of the message of death. A young woman named Mary, who lived on a plantation on the far side of Hibernia, had died. No one knew why. She was said to be a hard worker, in good health, and highly regarded by the enslaved men who knew her.

Chapter Five

March 1857–January 1858

F our cold months went by after the gathering. Once cotton was baled and corn shucked, the slaves had more time to spend with their families. Dicie's daddy accompanied the wagons to the Wilmington River to load baled cotton onto big ships bound for England. After the cotton left, he mended fences, plowed fields to keep down weeds, and planted winter rye for the mules and horses. Until time for spring plowing, Dicie often got to sit on her daddy's lap. It was her favorite time

Daddy had been captured off a rice field in Senegal, where his family farmed for generations. He knew the secret to transforming Skidaway's no-good swamps into big money for the buckra. But even though he knew all about growing rice, he couldn't grow it in the salt-encrusted clay east of Brisbane Plantation. Stubborn Master Warren kept his slaves planting rice oceanside anyway, till he died of fever.

"Stupid bastard," Daddy whispered to Mammy in the night. "Ain't got sense enough to plant rice on the freshwater side of the island. Sampson think whipping me gone make rice grow in salt water, but it ain't happening."

According to Cuffie, Springfield, the Greene plantation along the Skidaway River, would be easy to flood with almost fresh water. Rice would flourish in the rich black mud. Master Greene would make a fortune on Carolina gold, the rice everybody loved to eat. Daddy would get nothing.

One night, while Dicie sat cross-legged on the floor in front of the fireplace waiting for him, there was a loud knock on their door. She heard chains clanking, men shuffling their feet, and her daddy's voice.

Every time Cuffie had talked about growing rice on the west side of the island, Mammy crossed her fingers and spit over her shoulder. "Hush yo' mouth, Cuffie," she warned "You tempting fate, luring that day closer."

Now the dreaded time had come.

She never forgot Mammy's wails when the Brisbane slave-driver, Sampson, and a brown-skinned stranger brought Daddy to the cabin. Chains drooped from his wrists and dragged behind his feet.

Dicie went cold with fear. Her whole body shook.

"We letting him say goodbye," one of the drivers said, not looking at Mammy. "He been sold."

"Cuffie, Cuffie," Mammy moaned over and over, sinking to her knees. "How I'm gone manage these boys without you?"

The drivers ducked their heads, staring at her swollen belly. The stranger said, "Woman, we risking ourselves bringing him here to tell you hisself. It ain't so bad. He been sold to Massa Greene at Springfield on the west side. Not far a'tall. He eligible for a pass."

"Massa Warren's sons done sold him," Sampson added. "Just a short walk from here. Ain't like he going off to town."

No problem except that he wouldn't be allowed to cross the boundary line. Without a pass, he might as well have been sold all the way to Kansas. Except by a miracle, he would never again share a cabin with Mammy, Dicie, and his boys.

Dicie burst into tears. Would she ever get to sit in his lap again? She reached up a trembling hand to touch his chained ankle. Daddy looked at her with sad eyes.

Rufus had laid green wood from a bay tree in the fireplace. When Sampson opened the tabby door, the fire blazed up and smoke billowed out into the room. Ever after, Dicie hated the pungent smell of burning bay wood.

Without Daddy, the crowded cabin felt empty at night. Dicie moved off the floor into his place in Mammy's bed. In the middle of the night Mammy's sobbing woke her.

Despite what the Springfield driver promised, Daddy only got a pass to visit Mammy and his children when rice fields were bare for winter. For the first spring and long, hot summer they didn't see or hear from him.

Without him, even Mammy shivered at the creaks and thumps that woke them during the night. Skulls cracked as male deer clashed during deer rutting season, showing off for the does. More terrifying was the occasional screech of a real swamp panther, not Mammy's imitation. Who could tell if the screech came from a panther or an evil spirit? After the screech, the sad whine of an unfortunate deer often followed. Dicie could hardly sleep.

Haints and witches had to be making at least some of the scary sounds. Mammy said, "there ain't no such thing as witches." But how could Dicie believe her when folks said Mammy was a witch, herself?

Late one morning, a month after Daddy was taken, Mammy dropped to her knees, moaning in pain. Since it was too early to plant, everyone was nearby. Rufus and Gus lifted her and laid her on the bed.

"Get the midwife," she gasped. "Rufus, run!"

The boys stared at each other. The only midwife the boys knew was Mammy.

"Hibernia," she whispered. "Baby ain't due for another two months. You, Gus, set the kettle on to boil and git the rags out."

Rufus dashed out the door. No telling where Sampson was or if he'd have his passes on him.

Gus put logs on the fire, while Dicie filled the kettle. Isaac grabbed a bucket and ran to fetch more water.

Nearly an hour passed, but Rufus did not return. Mammy tried to keep silent, but the children could see her contorted face when the pains hit. After an especially sharp pain, she gasped, "Git Miz Sadie."

The children looked at each other. Miz Sadie lived in the compound, but Mammy always scoffed at her lack of knowledge. Dicie grabbed her mother's hand and held it tight. Despite the cold day, Mammy's face was drenched in sweat.

Isaac dashed out the door without his jacket.

The wind from the door slamming ruffled Mammy's quilt. Dicie looked, horrified at the pallet under Mammy. It was bright red. Her legs trembled, but she willed them to work. She had to save Mammy. She and Gus grabbed the clean rags Gus had gathered and pressed them hard against the flow of blood.

Just as Isaac burst into the tabby with Miz Sadie, Dicie saw black hair covered with blood pulse out from between Mammy's legs.

"Git out the way, chile," Miz Sadie hollered at Dicie. She grabbed at the little head and pulled. Mammy groaned and blood gushed. The baby stayed inside Mammy. "Push, Lizzie," Miz Sadie ordered. "Push."

Miz Sadie jerked hard. The baby popped out. Mammy fainted. Dicie rushed forward with more rags. She crammed them against the flow of blood from Mammy, just as Mammy taught her once when Gus was whipped.

The blood stopped coming. Isaac and Dicie let out a sigh of relief. They held Mammy's hands. Her eyes were closed but her chest moved gently up and down. Dicie looked at Miz Sadie, but Miz Sadie was only looking at the baby, who lay still and quiet.

"Poor little thing. Wouldn't been big enough to live anyways," she said.

Dicie burst into tears.

Just then Rufus walked in with his head hanging. "Sampson wouldn't let me cross the ditch," he said. "I done told him what happening, but he just shook his whip at me. Hit me when I kept begging." Rufus turned to show the slit in his jacket sleeve, stained with blood.

They buried the baby behind the cookhouse. They only had wooden crosses for markers, but Mammy knew exactly where she buried her two babies who died of the fever, and her beloved Susie, who drowned in the marsh when she was nine. The new baby was buried close to them. Gus found a blue medicine bottle discarded behind the big house on Hibernia. To ward off evil spirits, he placed it over the cross he made for the grave.

Christmas was sad and lonely. Santa Claus didn't come to slave quarters, but Daddy had always made it special. That year there was no island-wide celebration, but workers were allowed to gather around a fire in front of the Brisbane kitchen and sing carols. Sampson showed up with red and white striped hard candy for the children and dried apples for the grown-ups.

Dicie's eyes widened at the sight of the candy, the same candy Daddy brought to the tabby last Christmas. The memory of his callused hand holding it out flashed into her mind. She couldn't take her eyes off the candy in Sampson's outstretched paw.

Mammy grabbed her and pulled her away. "You ain't touching nothing he got," she hissed, too low for Sampson to hear.

Dicie didn't dare argue with Mammy, but a tear rolled down her cheek.

Mammy stared at Dicie, daring her to talk back. The little girl managed to stay stubbornly silent, but a second tear followed the first down her smooth cheek.

Mammy's face softened. "Just one piece," she said.

Ten days after their first Christmas without her Daddy, Dicie huddled next to the fireplace. Thick fog shrouded the island. Fierce cold from the northwest blanketed warm air over the marsh. The fields weren't yet planted, so women had a rare day to chop firewood and haul water for washing.

Dicie wrapped a quilt around herself and Cass, who was now big enough to walk. Wind whistled off the marsh and down the chimney. Every time a puff of smoke mushroomed out of the fireplace and into their faces, Cass suffered a coughing spell, but it was too cold to take him outside, and the room too small to hide from the smoke.

"Watch them sparks don't hit that quilt," Mammy told Dicie. She had been grumpy all day, frowning and muttering to herself while she soaked kernels of dried corn in lye and water to make hominy. The garden was bare except for collards and onions. They ate salt pork and sweet potatoes every day.

Dicie had rationed her beautiful red and white striped candy, sucking it down to the last hard sliver, one lick a day. Now it was all gone.

Suddenly the tabby door flung open, causing the fire to blaze up

"Daddy, Daddy," Dicie shrieked.

He grabbed her in his big hug while her brothers rushed forward grinning. His warm, smoky smell filled the room. The same smell he had since she was a baby when she slept between him and Mammy.

Mammy sat stiff and unsmiling in her cane-bottomed chair. "Where you been?" she asked.

Daddy kept his head ducked toward Dicie as he reached out to grab her brothers' outstretched hands. "Couldn't get a pass," he mumbled.

"Pass! Everybody git a pass for Christmas," Mammy said, rolling her eyes. "Chillun expected you."

He wiped his brow with his shirt sleeve, even though the day was cold. "Still need a extra pass to cross over to Skidaway Island, Lizzie. They done hauled me off the island. I be repairing a dike on the mainland up Harrock Hall way," Daddy said, still not looking at Mammy.

When she didn't answer, he turned away and pulled up a wooden box to sit next to Dicie. He dropped his voice soft and low and stretched his arms out to Dicie and Cass.

"How my babies?" he asked.

Dicie put her face against his worn wool sleeve and breathed in his smell. A faint sulfur odor of marsh mud combined with sweat.

"See how big Cass be," she showed him. "He walkin' everywhere. I got to really see after him."

"You my best girl," he said to Dicie. "I brung some candy just for you." He pulled a paper cone out of his overalls and showed her a dozen red and white striped balls.

She popped one in her mouth. It tasted sweet, just like him.

"I brung a jar of honey for you," he said to Mammy, reaching into another pocket. "They say I can stay overnight."

Seeing him with her babies softened Mammy. "I done missed you something terrible," she admitted.

That night Dicie slept soundly on her quilt in her old place on the floor under their bed. Nothing could harm her as long as Daddy was in the house.

Chapter Six

February 1858–November 1858

A fter hurricane season passed, leaves on Virginia creeper and trumpet vines turned turkey red, and the slaves gathered in the last of the cotton crop. Everyone said it was the fullest crop they'd ever made. But time passed and the drum didn't beat for a celebration. Folks scratched their heads, but no one could fathom the silence. If a fracas had caused the cancellation of the gathering, everybody would know. Slaves would be whipped, maybe hung. The Negro overseers would have spread the fearful promise of how and why all the slaves were to be punished. Threats would have rained down upon black-haired heads.

But there was only the eerie silence. Two years had passed since the last big cotton-baling festivities. Workers on Hibernia baled their own cotton in 1858, losing many workdays to the task. They again missed their July fourth mid-summer get-together. The underground rumor mill speculated that the buckra were terrified of news passing between plantations. But what news could have scared them? No one knew for sure. Rosa and Cletis, the two slaves from Brisbane who were allowed by Master Waring to boat to Savannah, whispered that the whites feared war, wished for war. War about slavery.

The only times in 1857 that Dicie caught a glimpse of Daddy were when a traveling preacher, black or white, came to Skidaway Island. Springfield and Brisbane workers were allowed to walk to the Hibernia praise house. Now, soon as preaching ended, drivers plied their whips to hurry everyone back to their plantations with no time for a good visit. After service blackberry cobbler and dinner on the grounds faded to distant memories.

Preachers came less often. In the spring of 1858, soon as cotton seeds were safely planted in the rich sandy mud, colored preachers were banned from the island. Only white evangelists were allowed. The buckra-sanctioned preachers promised no reward on this earth for faithfulness in this life. Instead, they urged the slaves to be humble, work hard, and wait till life after death for their prize

Where slave drivers or the white men who escorted the preacher could overhear, folks shouted hallelujah and gave loud thanks for the privilege of coming to church to glorify the Lord.

Back in the compound, when Sampson wasn't around, men grumbled quietly in groups of two or three about what was preached. After a tin cup full of moonshine passed from one set of thick, wet lips to another, the grumbling grew louder.

Through a gap in the unglazed cabin window Dicie heard, "What they doing? Trying to sell us a bill of goods? Where the colored preachers? Why they keeping 'em away?"

A tall, thin man asked Isaac, "Who they think they fooling with that reward after death nonsense? You man enough to know that ain't right. They work us to death, and we get nothing for it in this life? That ain't right."

Isaac nodded cautiously. Mammy trained her children never to say anything that might get back to an overseer with a whip in his hand. Best to pretend you were too dumb to know the answer. Isaac had seen Gus answer back. His wounds from the whip kept him in bed for two days, before Sampson drug him back to work, with his wounds barely scabbed over.

"Fool talk much, wise man keep his mouth shut," Mammy said. Another of her sayings from her old folks in Africa.

But Isaac couldn't help from agreeing. Besides, drunken men were hardly in position to tattle.

Still, everyone who was allowed made it to the services, bowing their heads during the insulting prayers and saying, "Amen." Church was their only chance to pass information, but now the hymns held no secret meaning.

The drinking men never came up with answers to their pointed questions. Just the "ptoo" sound of spitting on the ground, and sometimes an angry "yah!" "War" was shouted many times. Occasionally a man whispered "free."

Mammy told Dicie she mustn't say "free." "Free" was a dangerous word. A body could get whipped just for saying it.

Under cover of night men and women visited Mammy, asking her to read the signs. Were good times coming or would the lurking evil crush their hopes? Rosa and Cletis, returning from Savannah, whispered of slaves being sold out west to a place called Kansas, of mothers being sold away from their children, of slavers heading to Africa for fresh boatloads of captured men and women, even though the law now forbade it.

Dicie watched as Mammy studied her signs. The evening flight pattern of a colony of bats nesting in the chimney of a burnt down hut showed her which way the spirits had gone. Mammy followed a striped black snake zig-zagging back into the woods to see if it went toward water. "He don't know if he a-coming or a-going," she finally concluded.

A full-bodied brown spider, whose long web hung from the closed shutter on their hut, trapped a cricket. Bad luck coming. Somehow, the cricket squirmed its way out of the web. Bad luck turned to good.

"Change is a-coming," she told the visitors, in exchange for a penny. "Can't tell yet if it be good or bad."

By late November 1858, bales of cotton had long since been barged to town. Flocks of ducks and geese flying south no longer filled the sky. Still, the drivers kept colored folks on separate plantations. Time for a gathering had passed.

Finally, Sampson gathered the women in the field and told them the news they had given up hoping for. "Buckra allowing a corn shucking. The rat got too many ears of corn what didn't get shucked last fall. Nyam, nyam, eat 'em up. Watch for the next full moon."

"Full moon" meant special singing, staying out after dark, a bonfire, sharing news, and a feast with the probability of seeing Daddy. Mammy studied the moon and counted up the days until it would be full. Dicie knew for sure the get-together was coming at last when two long drumbeats followed by two short tones echoed over the compound.

Frost coated the fronds of palmetto at sunrise. Too cold for old folks to leave their cabins at night and walk the distance to Hibernia. Way too cold to linger at an outdoor gathering. Was that what the buckra counted on?

Mammy was determined to go. She, Dicie, and her brothers all prayed for Daddy to come. Months had passed since they'd seen him.

Last time they got to cross the ditch for church service, he wasn't there. A hollow spot filled Dicie's heart where he should have been.

Mammy checked her signs again to figure their chances of seeing him. A spider spun a thick web in the space over their door, a good sign. But when they trudged home after getting supper at the cookhouse the night before the gathering, two crows sat on the roof of their hut. Mammy froze, then turned to face her boys.

"None of y'all done thrown anything out of the house after it got dark?" she asked. Nighttime came early in November. With their one room so crowded, it was easy to forget and sweep out mud or leaves after sunset. But throwing something out after dark was the same as throwing out good luck. Crows on the roof could only mean bad luck.

Dicie knew better than to throw away anything. She certainly hadn't.

"Not me," Isaac said.

Then Dicie remembered. Just as they were leaving for the cookhouse, Cass toddled to the threshold. It was Dicie's job to walk with him. In his hand was a dead mouse. Without thinking, she had grabbed the mouse and thrown it out the door. She gasped.

At the sound, Mammy whirled from Isaac to Dicie. Dicie cowered in fear.

"I done told you," she said, raising her hand. Then she stopped. "What's done is done. We got to pray them crows don't mean nothin', and you ain't let no bad luck in."

The next night, wrapped in quilts, they crossed the big ditch onto Hibernia. Mammy scanned the faces of those who gathered around the fire, searching for Daddy. Wind blustering in on high tide kicked up dead leaves and dust, making it harder to see in the already dark evening. When Cuffie was nowhere to be seen, she herded the children into the shadows. "Just like Cuffie to be where he ain't supposed to," she said.

A short, heavy-shouldered man jerked to a stop right in front of them. Where had he come from? Mammy tried to step out of his way, but he shifted his body as she did, blocking her path.

"Hey, girl. Where you going?" His eyes slid up and down Mammy as he moved closer. "Yo' man ain't here."

Isaac had lingered behind the other shuckers to watch out for Mammy. He stepped up next to her protectively. He was taller but half the weight of the older man.

"I done heard he coming," Isaac said, fixing the man with his best glare.

"Git out of the way, boy. You ain't got nothing to do with this," the man growled. The reek of moonshine blasted from his mouth.

Mammy ducked her head and tried to hide behind Isaac, but the man grabbed her arm. "Give him the chillen and you come with me." His voice was low and threatening. He jerked her away from the crowd.

Dicie screamed as the man dragged Mammy toward a thicket of pine trees, wresting Cass from her arms. Dicie's voice hardly could be heard over the beat of the drum and loud songs of the workers. Hardly able to breathe, she ran forward to grab Cass, who had fallen into the trampled grass.

Just as Dicie reached her little brother, Mammy let out a piercing whistle followed by a panther-like screech. Surprised, the man loosened his grip.

A sudden silence fell as the drumbeat abruptly ceased. The drummer had thrown down his sticks. A long, black arm gripped the man's neck from behind.

"Let go! She don't want you," the drummer said.

"She ain't your woman. Girl ain't got no man," the short man said.

The drummer tightened his grip on the smaller man's neck just as Sampson hurried up.

"What going on, Tom?" he asked the drummer, as he locked the heavy, short man's flailing wrists together with a powerful squeeze.

"Cephus trying to mess with Cuffie's woman," Tom answered.

Sampson's fist flew like lightning against Cephus, knocking him to the ground. "That ain't nothing compared to what Cuffie'd do," he said. "He be here soon as he get through working."

Mammy sank to the ground and turned tear-filled eyes to her rescuers. "Thank you," she whispered, first to Sampson, then to Tom.

"Couldn't let him hurt you," the drummer said. "I'm Tom and this be my son, Little Tom, who been staring at your pretty daughter."

Dicie raised her eyes from Mammy to look up at the drummer's son. Cass was still in her arms. She patted his shoulder to stop his whimpering.

Firelight flickered over Little Tom's dark face, lighting his shy smile just like when they first met a long time ago. He was taller than she remembered, but so was she.

The drummer took a step back and the short man slunk off. "I be watching you," the drummer hollered.

Then he turned toward Dicie. "Who this pretty little girl?" he asked. "My boy can't hardly keep his eyes off her."

Mammy let out her breath. "She Dicie and I'm Lizzie. She be my on-liest girl. I got four head of boys." From her seat in the grass, she grabbed Dicie's leg and pulled her forward. "Where yo' manners, chile?"

Dicie bobbed her head at Big Tom without taking her eyes off his son. "Thank you," she whispered. Little Tom had big round eyes and long eyelashes. He set his tin can drum on the ground and stepped away from the fire toward Dicie.

Mammy bent forward over her crossed legs and untied the string of blue wool from her ankle, as the two children stared at each other without speaking. Woven into the thread was half of a perfect cockle shell. "My charm," she said to Big Tom. "I want you to have it."

"I can't take your good luck piece," he said. "You gone need it."

Mammy hesitated. The man was right. Big Tom lived on Hibernia. He wasn't allowed on Brisbane. Neither was Cephus, the man who attacked her. Mammy made the sign of the cross at the memory of his thick black fingers squeezing her wrist.

"Man, get back at yo' drumming," Sampson hollered.

Big Tom turned back to his drum and hit a lick, but first he whispered to Mammy, "I be keeping my eye on you." He closed one eye in a meaningful wink.

Slowly she bent down and retied the blue wool around her ankle.

Little Tom reached his hand forward toward Dicie, keeping his big eyes locked on hers. She raised her hand to grasp his, but before she reached it, Mammy stood, grabbed her arm, and marched her away. Dicie squirmed and twisted herself around toward Little Tom. He was watching her. "Goodbye," she whispered.

Sides were chosen for the shucking competition, the men of Hibernia against the men of the smaller plantations. Daddy should be on the same team as his sons. Springfield had fewer workers than mighty Hibernia. The captains mounted the pile of corn. Cobs of corn and husks flew in all directions.

In the flickering firelight it was impossible to tell one man from the next, but Dicie knew her daddy by the sound of his footsteps, the curve of his back, and his strong and mighty body. Slipping out of Mammy's quick hand, she circled the workers, searching for Daddy. Why couldn't she sense his presence? Wasn't he looking for her?

When all the corn was shucked, and the winning team celebrated, the big brothers returned to Mammy, Dicie, and Cass.

"Where yo' daddy?" Mammy asked, soon as she saw Cuffie wasn't with them.

"We ain't seen him." Isaac held his head down, not wanting to see Mammy's anxious face. "Some boys from Springfield came, but they don't know nothing 'bout him."

Gus and Rufus shook their heads. Gus was spitting mad. "He should been looking fo' us. Been a year since we laid eyes on him. He should have whipped that Cephus' ass. Man wouldn't have had the nerve to look at you if Cuffie been here."

"Daddy ain't here," Rufus said. "We'd of seen him fo' sure. And, we would of won that contest. Winner got a full jar of 'shine. Daddy would of made sure to win it."

Turning to Gus, Rufus said, "Keep yo' mouth shut now, or we all be in trouble."

Rufus and Gus walked away to watch a wrestling match between a man from Hibernia and a man from Springfield. While Isaac stuffed cornbread in his mouth, and Dicie nibbled on fried shrimp, Mammy asked the women ladling crab and shrimp from a washpot next to the fire if they had seen Daddy. Two of the women from Springfield exchanged knowing glances but didn't answer.

A sinking feeling roiled Dicie's stomach as people shook their heads. If Daddy was here, surely she would have felt his presence, even before they spotted him. Daddy was part of her spirit. She always knew he was near when he came home at night, even before she saw him. Tonight, she only felt an empty place where he was supposed to be.

Sneaking glances across the bonfire to where Little Tom beat his drum, she wished she could have stayed talking to him. Why had Mammy pulled her away? Not many children were born to the men and women who toiled in the harsh, insect-ridden climate of Skidaway Island. Hardly any lived to be as old as her. Of Mammy's eight children, two died before the age of two and one, a girl, drowned in quicksand in the marsh when she was eight years old. Besides her surviving brothers, Dicie's only play-mates were the spotted deer born each spring and the gray marsh rabbits, who were so timid she could hardly get close to them.

She didn't find Daddy that night. He wasn't there. Nobody could say why.

When Mammy returned, her shoulders slumped, and tears formed in her almond-shaped eyes.

Glancing back over her shoulder just before she slid down into the ditch, Dicie saw the stocky black man staring after them with a scowl on his face.

She shivered from more than the cold as they trudged down the ditch, and up the other side on the dark, freezing walk home without Daddy.

Chapter Seven

October 1859

Nobody knew it at the time, but the disappointing 1858 bonfire was the last get together Skidaway planters allowed their slaves to attend. Ever.

During the long hot summer of 1859, Sampson acted meaner than usual. "Y'all can forget about partying. Ain't gone be no more of them heathen bonfires. No more imbibing and sinning, neither. Y'all's gone be a God-fearing community if I got to beat the devil out of you," he said, brandishing his whip. Nobody knew why. In the past, they always celebrated.

Where was Cuffie? Mammy cried when she got the news. Now Dicie's only hope for seeing her daddy was a big church gathering. Mammy, Dicie, and Cass never missed a service.

After the drum announced an approaching service, Dicie asked Mammy, "Wonder if Little Tom'll make the preaching?".

"What you want to know for, chile?" Mammy said. "You ain't gone hardly git to know him. Plenty young girls over where he stay. You too little."

Dicie sighed. Nobody could win an argument with Mammy. Still, she would be happy if Tom only smiled at her.

Each time they trudged down and back up the Hibernia ditch for church service, Mammy searched for Daddy or anyone with news of him. Without letting on to Mammy, Dicie also kept a lookout for drummer

Tom and his young son. So far, she got to see him every time. Little Tom smiled at her, but Mammy barely let her stop to speak to him.

Used to be every month slaves walked to the Hibernia praise house, and her daddy got a pass. When Dicie spotted him holding out his arms, her heart filled with joy. After service, folks used to share dinner on the grounds. If Daddy was there, he filled her plate and Mammy let her sit next to him.

In the old days, an ordained free Negro from First African Baptist Church in Savannah got a pass to preach, or a mainland slave owner rented out a pious slave to lead. Skidaway folks loved that. Those preachers always found a way to pass on codes and secrets from the outside world.

All that changed in 1859. Negroes who didn't live on Skidaway Island were forbidden to come to the island. Those who stayed on the island weren't allowed to mix with slaves from other plantations. Nobody said why. More patrollers were hired to catch those who dared to roam at night. Slaves kept their heads down, working in fear, not knowing which way the wind would blow.

"Lord, look like Sampson be happy when a poor soul git beaten," Mammy said. "Even if it's one less person to work." Whenever Sampson wasn't around, Mammy pulled out her little wooden cards, and turned them this way and that, trying to figure out the future.

Dicie's grown brothers endlessly speculated about a reason for the change. "Is they thinking we gone find a way to git to freedom?" Rufus asked.

"Naw, they just got meaner," Gus said. He had felt the whip more than once.

Mammy disagreed. "Got to be something 'bout money," she said. "If them abolitionists sets us free, gone hurt buckra bad in they pocketbooks." She whispered the word "abolitionists."

Surely Rosa or Cletis, who traveled to City Market twice a month to sell fish and vegetables, would have told if a preacher had been caught slipping hints about escape into the hymns.

Even before they were banned, Black ministers had to be careful about what they preached. Hymns like *Swing low sweet chariot, coming for to carry me home,* and *Where the morning is bright and the Lamb is the light, And the night is fair as the day* held secret messages. Preachers would be lynched if buckra suspected the services passed on codes for slaves planning an escape.

Savannah's First African congregation was a vital link for prospective runaways. By the light of a full moon, desperate men risked drowning in Runaway Negro Creek. Once in Savannah, the church hid them under floorboards and directed their next steps toward freedom.

The first Sunday in March 1859 was the last time Brisbane slaves got passes to cross the plantation border to listen to even a mealy-mouthed white preacher telling them what the buckra wanted them to hear. Everybody went.

The day was unseasonably cold, but the island was already a-flower with ropes of bright yellow Carolina jasmine. Freezing wind howled across the flat, treeless marsh and raged onto the low-lying island. A gust knocked the hat off the white preacher. The two soldiers who brought him to the island buttoned their heavy gray coats.

From her seat on a rotting tree stump outside the praise house, Dicie watched a flock of snowy egrets struggle to fly inland from the grey-brown marsh. The wind blew their v-shaped formation higgledy-piggledy. Once the big white birds finally reached dry land, the formation fell apart, and the birds settled into the piney treetops surrounding the praise house like clumps of white laundry. They squawked so loud, she hardly heard Mammy tell her to stop fidgeting.

Hibernia Plantation's praise house was so tiny only ten worshippers could squeeze in with the preacher. Big logs and planks balanced on tree stumps next to the graveyard served as seats for the rest.

During the preaching, churchgoers propped open the door to the praise house, even in winter, so those outside could hear. Sometimes the preacher stood outside, but not on this cold day. Dicie wrapped herself in a quilt.

When colored preachers came, folks formed a ring and stepped lively to the rhythm of the shouts. Ring shouting wasn't dancing. Dancing wasn't allowed at church. The ring shout would have warmed her, but shouting wasn't allowed by buckra preachers. Too African.

Dicie huddled close to Mammy, a far piece from the praise house door. She tried to sit quietly ,but she squirmed and twisted till she spotted Little Tom and his father. Mammy said Little Tom's mother died when he was born. His daddy raised him himself with help from the women who worked in the cookhouse. Despite being a fine-looking man, Big Tom never came to church with a woman, just with Little Tom. When they passed through the crowd, plenty of grown women turned their heads his way.

Tom and his son took a seat on one of the benches up front, the good seats reserved for Hibernia slaves. It had been summer when Dicie last saw them.

At ten she was still short and thin, but Little Tom had grown tall and good-looking like his Daddy. When he passed her, he turned and smiled. His thin cotton trousers clung to his muscled legs. Just seeing him gave her a shivery feeling. If Mammy hadn't been holding her arm, she would have stood and followed him.

Near the back of the bench sitters, a plump dark-skinned girl from Hibernia sat primly with her mother. When Little Tom took a seat up front next to his father, the girl broke from her mother and ran forward to squeeze in next to him. Dicie gasped. How could she be so bold? At the same time, Dicie wished she could be so brave. The girl had to be older than Dicie, maybe older than Little Tom. Her breasts pushed against the top of her dress. Dicie's bodice was flat against her chest. The girl's braids were thick and glossy. Mammy still kept Dicie's hair in five babyish pigtails.

Dicie watched Little Tom smile at the girl. He squeezed over to make room for her on the already packed bench. When she sat down, wind whooshed into the crowd and blew her skirt above her knees. A secretive smile curved her lips as Little Tom reached over to help her smooth it back over her legs. It seemed like he took more time than he needed to. Even Big Tom patted her shoulder to comfort her. It didn't look to Dicie like the girl needed comforting.

The wench had broken off a stem of yellow Carolina jasmine and threaded it through her braids. Who was she? What was her mother thinking to let her change her seat? Mammy would never allow Dicie to run up front to sit with a man.

While watching her, Dicie's chest tightened. She had hoped to talk to Tom after the preaching. Now she wasn't so sure. Last year, he walked over to speak to her after service ended. His father didn't mind. Dicie had been too shy to think of much to say besides hello, but Tom was braver. "How you like the sermon?" he asked each time they met.

On that cold March day, the preacher used as his text Ephesians, VI, Verse 5: "Servants, be obedient to them that are your masters according to the flesh, with fear and trembling." He shouted those words so slaves at the very back of the clearing could hear him over the squawking birds. Nobody in the congregation gave an "Amen." Most of the rest of what he said got blown away by the wind.

Her mind drifted. What could she say back to Tom to keep the conversation going? She thought of interesting words she'd like to say, but her tongue froze every time he stepped beside her.

"I like it fine," was all that usually came out, even though she had rehearsed much more. And how could she say that today? Nobody liked what the preacher said.

Instead, she longed to ask him if he listened to the egrets squawking today instead of the words of the awful preacher. Did the minks on Hibernia birth pups this year, like they did on Brisbane?

"Stop your squirming," Mammy said. She was upset. Cuffie hadn't come to the service.

After the buckra preacher mumbled a prayer for the last time and folks stood up to walk back to their compounds, Dicie dragged her feet, hoping Tom would step over to her before Mammy herded her and Cass away. She fixed her eyes on his back as he reached over to help the pretty girl stand. He held her shawl as she rewrapped herself in it. His hand grazed her shoulders. Dicie bit her lip to keep from protesting. Surely the hussy could put on the shawl without him.

Mammy paid no attention to Little Tom or the wench. "Hurry up, girl," she snapped at Dicie. "Bet one of them loose women over there making eyes at Cuffie, keeping him from his chillen."

Where was Daddy? How could he stay away? Mammy was cold and sad and anxious to get herself and her children home and out of the wind. No way to know if he was sick or dead, or sold somewhere far away. What if he remained on Springfield, and some woman had caught him in her spell?

But Dicie couldn't be hurried. Little Tom walked the girl back to her mother. Dicie watched her reach out her hand and pat his face. She prayed Tom wouldn't linger with the wench.

The overseers prodded stragglers with the handles of their whips to hurry them along. Big Tom motioned for Little Tom to come on. As Little Tom hurried away with his father, Dicie caught a glimpse of the girl patting the face of a smiling man older than Little Tom.

Tom and his father headed toward the back of the graveyard where Dicie shivered in the freezing wind. Cold as she was, her face broke into a big smile as he veered left toward her.

"Hey, Tom," she said, ducking her chin to hide her smile.

His face lit as he reached Dicie. "How you doin'?" he asked.

The two children stood close, not caring about the wind, just grinning at each other until Mammy snatched Dicie away.

Whip raised, the Hibernia overseer lurked close to where Dicie and Tom had stood. With her eyes fixed on Little Tom, Dicie hadn't seen the threat. She almost got hit.

"Don't you be messing with no boys," Mammy scolded. "You just about got yourself in trouble already, and you ain't but ten years old. Lord help us."

Dicie obediently followed Mammy home, her thoughts focused on the next service at the praise house and what she would say to Little Tom. Bad as she missed seeing Daddy, she barely gave him a thought as she trod the path toward Brisbane. She could hardly wait to see Little Tom again.

Chapter Eight

June 1860

Blam! Blam! The clash of iron sledgehammers echoed across the ditch separating Brisbane from Hibernia. Grim-faced slaves hit blow after blow shattering the carefully nailed boards of the little praise house, then threw the broken boards into a wheelbarrow. Soon nothing was left on the worship grounds except tree stumps and shards of blue glass marking some of the graves. Word trickled throughout Brisbane from the slaves who worked closest to the boundary. Their humble place of worship had been desecrated. It no longer existed.

In the field of rapidly growing cotton, Sampson gathered the women on Brisbane close to him. The stench of his unwashed body perfumed the air. Dicie cowered in the dirt behind them, half-hidden behind a stalk of cotton. She watched fearfully.

He scowled and, brandishing his whip, shouted, "Ain't gone be no more crossing the ditch off this plantation. Not for nothing. Buckra 'specting trouble. Got to stop it before it start."

What trouble? No one knew of any trouble. The women looked at Mammy. Many feared her. Even Sampson stepped lightly around her. He knew she conjured and cast spells. She was the least likely to get licks from him for speaking up.

Mammy was careful to hide any semblance of disrespect for the man. Keeping her head bowed, she asked, "What if'n a white preacher show up on Hibernia?"

Glaring balefully at her, he lifted his whip handle. "Ain't gone be no more preachers. Now git back to chopping them weeds." He spat in the freshly turned dirt, then turned and strode to the edge of the field, circling the long tail of his whip in the air.

The women stood there in shock. The carefully constructed praise house, built decades ago by the slaves of Hibernia in their free time and consecrated by years of traveling clerics, was no more. How could this be? White preachers always said the buckra wanted their slaves to know the word of God.

Even Mammy muttered, "It ain't Christian."

With no real preacher allowed on Skidaway Island, prayers were led at the cookhouse by a slave who knew how to recite verses from the Bible. None of the slaves were supposed to know how to read. Anyone caught drawing letters in the dirt got ten lashes from Sampson's whip. The same verses got repeated at each service.

Daddy couldn't be there. Tom and Little Tom weren't allowed to come. So, church on Brisbane wasn't much to look forward to.

"I said git back to work," Sampson hollered, brandishing his big whip.

The women shuffled their bare feet back to their positions in the field. The cotton was growing as it should, but weeds sprouted under the young leaves and between the rows. Constant hoeing callused every woman's palms. If they eased off, weeds sprung up like a bull in a pen full of cows and brought down Sampson's wrath on the women. So despondent today, all they could do was slap at the dirt between rows of cotton plants. They mourned the bitter loss of their last chance to see loved ones.

Where was Daddy? Was he even on Skidaway Island anymore? Weeks had passed since anyone on Brisbane had word of him. Dicie missed him so hard it hurt. Seldom seen tears ran down stoic Mammy's face, wetting her scarred cheek.

But the banishment from Hibernia meant even more to Dicie. She might never again get to talk to not-so-Little Tom.

Back inside the tabby Mammy shuffled her cards. "Spirits done got unsettled. Good and evil fighting each other out there. Where Cuffie be when I need him?" She threw a pinch of precious salt over her shoulder for luck.

Chapter Nine

April 1861–January 1862

N ews carried over the water that Charleston buckra shot cannon
balls at federal troops and ran them out of Fort Sumter. Bad news
for slaves. Next the folks on Skidaway Island learned Georgia seceded
from the United States of America to join up with the Confederacy. Was
this why the buckra had been so edgy, these past many months. To keep
their slaves from knowing how serious was the threat of abolition?

That summer, Rosa and Cletis, who still had passes to sell oysters,
shrimp, and tomatoes at City Market in Savannah, brought glum news.
"White men going off to war. War to keep us slaves. They women cheer-
ing 'em on; selling they jewelry, buying guns. Partying like you never
seen. They sure think they gone win."

Shoulders slumped and mouths pulled down as the men and women
remaining on Skidaway Island sweated in the cotton fields, any sliver of
remaining hope for a change too weak to penetrate the burning sunshine.

Mammy said, "Done told you something be wrong. Too many owls
hooting the sound of death."

Hulking iron-clad warships steamed into Wassaw Sound from the
Atlantic Ocean and dropped anchor near the north end of Skidaway
Island. From her perch in her favorite oak tree on the edge of the island,
Dicie watched distant men in blue uniforms pace the deck between
huge guns aimed her way. The ships flew stars and stripes. Yankee ships
and Yankee men.

"More of the same anchored down in Ossabaw Sound aiming at the south end," Cletis reported. "Ain't letting no ship from Savannah out. They got 'em parked in the Savannah River, too. Buckra cain't get cotton over to England, and they is mighty riled up about it."

The big guns pointed at Skidaway Island terrified Dicie. The cannon could easily destroy her home and kill all the slaves on the island. But did the warships mean good news or bad? She tried to listen to the grownups.

Mammy wasn't any help. "Wait and see, chile. Wait and see," she said. "Don't you be wandering 'round on the beach. You stay hid behind the trees or in a ditch." How could the ships be good if she had to hide?

Rosa said, "Here tell South Carolina niggers swum out to them ships and got free."

Others whispered war meant salvation. They would be free. Mustn't say it out loud. No telling who might snitch.

Like Rosa said, it was rumored that if somehow slaves managed to row out to the United States ships, they might be taken up as sailors and given freedom. But what if they got there and the sailors rejected them?

"I'd drown before I'd go back to be whipped to death," Isaac whispered one night as Mammy and the children settled down for bed.

"Me too," agreed Gus. He knew.

"Pro'bly most of 'em drowned trying, or got shot," Mammy said. She frowned, drawing her scar down her cheek. "Ain't seen no bateaux leaving them ships, and no niggers on deck. We gotta bide our time."

Sampson acted jumpier than ever. He was everywhere cracking his whip. "Look like he got worms," Mammy said.

Sometimes he was strangely absent. No one knew where he went.

Dicie stayed close to Mammy while they tended the master's cotton.

"Why we growing more cotton if'n they can't sell what we growed last year?" she asked. She wished somebody could tell her what was happening. Even the grown-ups didn't seem to know.

Mammy fixed her with a piercing glare. "Hush your mouth, girl," she said. "You see Sampson right there with that whip. He say plant the cotton. Ain't none of our business to ask why."

Mammy bent over and smoothed the dirt around a row of plants. She muttered to herself as she worked.

"What you say?" Dicie asked, afraid Mammy was angry with her.

"I say, wonder what become of that cotton what was stacked behind Sampson's house? They ain't never moved it to the dock, but it ain't there no more."

Dicie shrugged. At least Mammy wasn't mad at her anymore.

That night when the boys came in, Mammy asked them about Sampson's cotton.

"Sampson had it, last I seen it," Gus said.

The boys looked at each other. What did happen? They frowned. Was Sampson up to something?

Rufus grabbed a tin plate and ladled greens and shrimp. After he took a bite, he said. "I seen him leaving the other day with a big pile in his bateau, covered up with canvas. Something not right. That the canvas he covers our provisions with when he coming back. Bateau s'posed to be empty when he leave."

"Reckon that could have been the massa's cotton?" Gus asked. He had the most reason to not trust Sampson.

Mammy looked at him thoughtfully. There was no way of knowing. That cotton should have gone to Savannah on the big ferry with the rest of the bales. She tucked away the information.

Big guns on the decks of the Yankee ships fixed their sights on Skid-away Island. Rosa and Cletis rowed cautiously west, close to the shoreline in leaky wooden bateaux to haul their catch to market. Often, they were too scared to venture out.

Once the big warships steamed into the sounds, Sampson ordered, "Massa say no mo' sitting outside the cookhouse 'round the fire, running yo' mouths. Yo' ain't going to meet for church no mo'. Pick up yo' own dinner and take it home to eat."

Talk between workers never stopped but had to be carried out in whispers or by hand signals when Sampson was far on the other side of the field. Late at night, when clandestine nightwalkers were sure he was asleep, desperate men whispered, "Think them Yankee soldiers gone set us free?"

Then gray-uniformed rebel soldiers swarmed onto the island. Carrying muskets, they disembarked from over-sized row boats.

Mammy stared at the childlike white faces. In her hut at night, she muttered to Dicie, "Them little Confederate boys crazy to think they can take on them big ships from a rowboat." Her hands shook as she studied her signs.

The Yankee ships still lurked menacingly. So far the Yanks aboard held off firing cannons at the rowboats or at the Johnny Rebs on the is-land, but who could say when they might attack?

Rufus watched the incoming troops. "Love to get my hands on one of them muskets," he said. "Look how easy they take down a deer or hog. We be eating good with one of them things."

"Humpf" Mammy answered. "Where you gone get bullets to go in it?"

News from outside was scarce. Plantation owners cancelled hunting parties. No slaves got hired out to wait on them. The buckra's already infrequent inspections on the island ended. Their great houses stood empty. White-skinned women and children boated out no more, scared off by the looming war ships.

Gangs of the gray-uniformed white boys shoveled piles of dirt into mounds along the Wilmington River near the compound. Johnny Rebs shot their rifles from time to time, but nobody saw bullets reach the giant ships.

In the sweltering fields on Skidaway Island black-skinned laborers swatted swarms of vicious sand gnats, and endlessly cogitated in whispers about what might happen.

Since talking wasn't allowed, workers sang as they hoed:

> "*Way down in-a dat valley*
> *Praying on my knees*
> *Told God about my troubles,*
> *And to help me ef-a He please.*"

Men grinned and whispered to each other as they exchanged dull hoes for sharpened ones or passed filthy canvas sheets loaded with pulled-up weeds down the rows of cotton. Dicie couldn't figure how the men were so brave. Even she knew not to sing that hymn in church. Mammy told her it was part of the code. The chorus line went "*Slavery chain done broke at last.*" Church goers had been whipped for singing it. Sampson had to know what that song meant. Dicie hunkered down in her section distancing herself from the singers as far as she could.

The noisy pale-skinned, gray-uniformed boys scared Dicie as much as the bold singers. Sometimes, for no reason, white boys aimed pistols at people or animals. Other times they shot at the sky for the fun of seeing the workers run. She feared for all the little animals.

Whenever Dicie made the short trip to the outhouse, Mammy warned her to hide if she spotted a soldier. Even if he didn't have a gun. Strangers, especially buckra, always meant danger. Even Daddy, who once saved her from a bobcat, couldn't have protected her from a buckra soldier. And Daddy wasn't here.

Despite Mammy's stern warning, Dicie couldn't abandon the newborn animals she watched over each spring. One day as she walked her favorite forest path behind Mammy's garden, bullets ricocheted off tree trunks, bouncing randomly. She crouched her skinny body on the ground, hugging the trunk of the biggest tree she could find.

"There's one on that tree," she heard a boy yell. Peeping around the tree trunk, she saw the yellow-haired soldier pointing right above her head. A squirrel chatted loudly from an upper limb. "Bang!" The squirrel fell off the limb, on the other side of the tree from Dicie.

Heart beating, she turned and ran as fast as she could toward the compound, praying the soldier wouldn't mistake her for another squirrel.

Horrified as she was by the careless gun play, she couldn't stop tip-toeing along the edge of the marsh below the bluff. She had to check the otters' dens for newborn pups concealed between exposed tree roots. One evening she had almost reached a likely cranny when a dark brown, humped-back otter passed her on the sand, fish in its mouth.

Blam! The report of a rifle startled her. The otter's body jerked and fell. Blood oozed from a bullet hole in its side.

Two soldiers jumped off the bluff and grabbed the dead animal. "I know where I can git fifty-cent for this skin," one of them said. He hoisted the otter. The dead fish dropped to the beach. Without seeing Dicie, the boy jumped back up to the top of the bluff.

Soon as their footsteps faded, Dicie grabbed the dead fish and stepped carefully along the sand, listening for scuffling and tiny, hungry whines. It didn't take her long to see the cranny full of pups. She tore the dead fish into pieces and set them on the edge of the den. Throughout the next weeks, she fetched and carried dead fish, snakes, and lizards to the growing pups.

When Mammy found Dicie was feeding them, she scolded," how you got time for that foolishness? Them pups ain't gone make it anyway now they mammy's gone."

But Dicie stubbornly fished or begged food from her brothers. When an otter pup tried to follow her home, she carefully carried it back to the den, so Mammy wouldn't see. By the end of summer, the pups hunted on their own.

Sampson grumbled and spat and forced everybody to work even harder. He cracked and snapped his evil bull whip. Either way it went, war would be the ruination of the drivers. If the United States won, the great plantations would cease to exist. Sampson would lose his bullwhip and the right to use it. How would he live?

On the other hand, if the Confederates won, Sampson would still be enslaved.

Rumors from the city spread dire news. The South was going to win, and slavery would spread to a place called Kansas and maybe further west. Families would be torn apart. Even now mothers were being pulled off Skidaway Island and sent to Savannah to work in the town houses of the buckra. Their men were left to labor in the fields without women to comfort them. If men were sold to the far west, their children would never see them again.

While Mammy listened to the war talk, her fingers twitched back and forth over the carved iroko-wood charm she brought from Africa. When Dicie asked her questions, Mammy's tan forehead wrinkled, and the jagged scar on her right cheek oozed into a crooked line with just the swollen points visible.

That scar was part of the reason folks said Mammy was a witch, the scar and the story about how she put the spell on Mary, who was caught with Mammy's man Cuffie. Dicie didn't know how she got cut so bad. Mammy would never tell.

The only answer she gave Dicie about the war was, "Trust in the Lord with all your heart."

What was Dicie supposed to make of that?

Still nothing from her daddy, Cuffie. It had been so long, the hurt in her heart almost dried up, even though it popped up at odd times, like when smoke blew in her face. Last she heard, he was tending rice on the other side of Skidaway Island, but that couldn't be. If he was still on the island, he would have shown up for the last praise meeting. Dicie couldn't sense his presence like she used to. Had Master Greene carried him inland to work? Or sold him to somebody far away? Dicie got chills just thinking about it. It was bad enough when he was sold to another planter on Skidaway Island. Nobody would answer her questions, especially Mammy, who muttered, "Hush up, chile," whenever she asked.

In December of 1861 Cletis and Rosa brought back a hopeful story. "Niggers say the United States army done freed all our people on Hilton Head. They letting colored men join the United States army and pay 'em cash money." Good news for South Carolina colored, but not so certain for Skidaway Island folks.

Rosa, a talkative gray-haired woman, who paddled her bateau good as a man, added less optimistically, "Savannah buckra in a panic. They can't git the cotton past them ships to sell it. They ain't got no money, ain't paying no bills, and 'specially ain't buying us no provisions."

Hilton Head Island, South Carolina! Less than ten miles by water from Skidaway Island. Gus and Rufus were burning to go. But the penalty for escaping was death. No one knew for sure how the Yankee men on the warships, who occasionally blasted Skidaway workers with cannon fire, would respond to an escaping slave.

"Hold up, boys," Mammy said. "I done lost one man. Can't do without you."

More and more gray-clad soldiers tramped across the rebuilt bridge over the Skidaway River. They pitched their tents on top of cotton seedlings, carelessly trampling newly plowed ground. A few rode horses, doing more damage to the fragile island.

A harried soldier who seemed to be in charge gave money to Sampson to rent the Brisbane master's workers. The white boys couldn't pile up enough dirt to protect the island.

"Git them niggers digging," the soldier told Sampson. "We got to raise these barricades another three feet. Captain Pritchard wants mounds across the whole island to keep Union boys out."

One of the men drafted to dig was Isaac.

"Keep a eye out fo' yo' daddy," Mammy told him.

Used to hard work as he was, Isaac staggered home after dark, covered with dirt, and with blisters on both hands. Mammy brought him a plate from the cookhouse. He was too worn out to walk the short trip.

"Mammy, they took me in the woods and wanted me to dig up a big mess of dirt. Roots so thick I couldn't hardly get my shovel through. Sampson cracking that whip on me didn't help none." He pulled up his shirt to show Mammy the welts on his back.

Tears rolled out of his eyes and tracked through the mud on his cheeks. Dicie put her arms around him. Her big, strong brother who never cried was hurting, and she couldn't help him, adding her tears to his.

"Didn't see Daddy nowhere," he said, wiping his face with the back of his hand. "Lucky for him."

Before sunrise the bell rang for him and the other men to shovel for another twelve hours. Pulling himself stiffly off his mat, he grabbed a piece of hoecake. Together Mammy and Dicie weeded his untended acre of cotton after they finished their own.

More Johnny Rebs marched willy-nilly onto Skidaway, rolling wagons loaded with heavy iron mountings for the cannon. "Git them niggers to haul these up the earthworks," the soldier in charge demanded, while the white boys plopped on the ground to rest.

"Cannons coming soon. You got to finish the mounds," Sampson said, cracking his whip at his exhausted workers. "Then you gone roll them cannons to the top and set 'em up."

Back in the compound, even Sampson seemed worried. "Them piles of dirt ain't gone stop no Yankee cannon balls aimed at us," he said, shaking his head.

Every evening during Sampson's inspection, he tramped from cabin to cabin in the compound muttering, "No news today."

Suddenly in January, 1862, Sampson ordered Isaac and the other men piling up dirt to drop their shovels and go back to the empty cotton fields. The soldiers collected the shovels, even though the mounds only reached part way across Skidaway Island. Instead of pulling cannon to the top of the piled dirt, the soldiers dismantled the recently installed iron mountings and made the slaves haul them back across the bridge to the mainland.

A few days later Isaac, now twenty-one, thinner but taller and stronger from the weeks of hard labor with the shovel, burst into the tabby in the middle of a cloudy windswept afternoon. Mammy, Dicie, and Cass had just come in. He pulled his head scarf down and wiped the sweat off his face but was too excited to take a seat on the old wooden bench inside.

"Guess what I just seen!" he said, out of breath from running. He gasped for breath before he could say another word. "I hid behind a clump of palmetto down by the river, watching a pack of white boys march across the new bridge, off the island. Then I smelled smoke. Last two of 'em come back with torches and held 'em to the struts."

Dicie stared with her mouth open. How could they? The soldiers had just rebuilt the bridge. More than one slave dreamed of escaping over it once the soldiers left it unguarded.

Mammy handed Isaac a cup of water, and he continued, "Didn't take long in this wind for the whole bridge to go up. Marsh grass caught fire. Bridge is gone and we is cut off again. What you think it mean?"

Mammy closed her eyes and turned her face to the blue-painted ceiling. "Rosa done said soldier boys packing up. That crowd from the south end done been gone." She thought for a minute. "Maybe Big Tom know something? We ain't heard the drums."

Isaac grabbed a poker and stirred the fire as he listened to Mammy. Sparks shot out and landed on the floor.

"Boy, you gone set this cabin on fire, too," Mammy yelled. "I better go see what Sampson's got to say."

"No, you ain't," Isaac said. "They done took Sampson and the overseers from Hibernia with 'em."

Chapter Ten

January 1862

Mammy's mouth dropped. No slave driver? Were they free? Nah! Couldn't be. Abandoned was more like it. And why were they taking Sampson? Without a bridge, how could he bring provisions to the people left on the island? She grabbed her shawl and hurried outside, not waiting for Dicie and Cass.

A crowd had gathered in the muddy clearing by the row of two-family huts. Workers dropped their hoes and rushed in from the pointless job of clearing the barren fields. A plume of black smoke hovered over treetops to the west and gusts of wind carried the burning smell to the compound.

"We been cut off," one of them hollered.

"Let's go," sounded from all directions, countered by "Where? To get locked up downtown by the paddy rollers?"

When Mammy stepped to the center of the compound wrapped in her tattered black shawl with the scar on her cheek glistening red, all faces turned to her. A hush came over the shouting people. Those who lived in the slave compound knew Mammy had the gift of second sight. What did she foresee?

Raucous cries of a pair of crows pierced the silence.

Gathering her children close, she raised her skinny light-tan arms at the crowd. "*Rabbana lakal Hamd*," she whispered in Arabic. Then louder, "Have patience. First, we find out what happen to the buckra soldiers. Is the Yankee ships coming closer? Is we 'bout to be 'tacked?"

The crowd muttered restlessly. One man spat on the ground when she said the word "patience."

Mammy fixed him with her good eye, the one on the unscarred side of her face. Then she addressed the rest of the gathering. "It early times yet. Do folk down island know what happening? Do they still be down there? Hear tell they ain't had but one overseer for a goodish piece. They take him, too?"

No one answered. No one knew. The restless men quieted, pondering the possibility of an agent of the buckra left behind to spy. Almost certainly he would be armed.

Mammy turned to Isaac. "You boy, see if the way's clear for you to run over to Hibernia and get Big Tom to beat the drum," Mammy's deep voice rang loud enough to be heard by the old woman hanging back by the cottage furthest away.

Dicie watched, her eyes wide and scared to death. Long-legged Isaac grabbed his hat and ran off through the woods along the side of the weedless cotton field towards Hibernia. Without a pass. Would he dare cross the forbidden ditch?

It wasn't long before slow, bone-chilling drumbeats sounded all the way from Hibernia plantation south to the slave quarters on Brisbane. Isaac had reached Big Tom. Slaves south of Hibernia and west to Springfield, maybe even Daddy, would hear Tom's message. Drummers on other plantations took up the beat.

The reverberating bass tones passed from drummer to drummer for more than eight miles down the island to the mouth of the Ogeechee River. Dicie felt the foreboding of events beyond knowing. She had never seen for herself, but she knew the river met Ossabaw Sound, still full of Yankee warships. She pictured the sailors hearing BOOOM, BOOOM, booom on the Yankee ships. What would they make of it?

All the slaves on the plantations and the sailors on the ships would know something momentous had happened. But the drums couldn't tell them what. For the slaves to know the details, young men like Isaac had to risk their lives crossing forbidden barricades. But every slave believed the young men would find a way.

When the deep cadence of drums rumbled through the folks assembled at Brisbane, Mammy lifted her arms and called out in her loudest voice, "Now we pray."

The abandoned slaves knelt down and prayed to Jesus. They prayed no cruel drivers with their stinging bullwhips had been left behind. They prayed they could survive without food from the outside, without tea or sugar or shoes in the winter. That they would find a way to live without new iron tools to replace broken ones.

Within twenty-four hours every person enslaved on Skidaway Island knew all the white people and their negro overseers had fled. What they didn't know was what the future held for them. Hope and fear warred in their hearts and minds.

Chapter Eleven

February 1862–January 1864

A ll who were left on Skidaway Island were those who remained as slaves, bound to the island with no master, no place to go, and no one to give them a pass to get there, if a safe place existed. Bales of valuable long-staple Sea Island cotton mildewed in rain-soaked, shrinking piles where ferry boats used to load. The United States steamships of war remained anchored in Wassaw Sound to the north, and Ossabaw Sound to the south. Blockaded Confederate ships could not get in or out of Savannah to carry the precious cotton to England. Savannah was filled with citizens anxious to keep the Geechees enslaved as property, and to throw them in jail if they ventured to town.

No more rations of food, or tools, or slave cloth came their way. None of the buckra seemed to care if their slaves lived or died. The long hot summer passed quietly, but always with twinned uncertainties of hope and fear hanging in the wet, sweltering air. Like all islanders, Dicie read the clouds and felt the direction of the wind. Then came the hot, breezy fall with its perpetual threat of an island-destroying hurricane. Rains came, winds blew, and trees fell, but in 1862 the good Lord kept the flooding killer storms offshore.

Sacks of cornmeal and dried beans that used to fill a lean-to behind the cookhouse were distant memories. Folks grabbed the empty cotton sacks to replace the disintegrating rags they wore. Spiders spun webs in the vacant space.

Whenever Dicie passed the deserted cookhouse, a skinny woman, a few strands of white hair on her mostly bald scalp, and well past the age of productive work, squatted in the weeds outside, futilely awaiting a meal that never came. Her bony legs were pocked with mosquito bites. Wringing her gnarled hands, she wailed a high-pitched lament, "Please give me something to eat. I's hungry, I's hungry."

Dicie flinched each time she saw the poor old crone. A few times she brought her a cup filled with scuppernongs from vines in the woods. The old woman snatched the cup and greedily stuffed the green tough-skinned grapes into her mouth, chewing seeds and all with toothless gums.

When Mammy walked by, she made the sign of a cross. "Left to die except for the kindness of us, who ain't got nothing," Mammy said. Sometimes she sent Dicie back with a piece of corncake hidden from the boys, who scarfed down everything Mammy or Dicie cooked.

Without direction, Mammy and Dicie continued their same old rituals of work for the master, lest the buckra return in full force, infuriated by the lack of production. Without Sampson pacing the field to threaten her, Dicie minded her little brother Cass. Now twelve years old, Dicie was a real help to Mammy in harvesting her assigned acre of cotton, planted the spring before. The buckras' hopes of a quick, easy victory were dashed, but the cotton seed that had been left behind had been duly planted by the workers the spring before. The buckra's financial future was in good hands.

Mammy slipped as many of the ripened cotton bolls as she reckoned wouldn't be missed into a makeshift sling fashioned from long strings of Spanish moss. None but other slave women were there to watch, but habits of caution were deeply ingrained. The bulk of the newly harvested crop sat unloaded and abandoned on the dock with last year's rotting crop, but the possibility of buckra returning loomed darkly over the workers. The woven moss carrier could be easily jettisoned if a suspicious stranger appeared. Once Mammy made it to their cabin with the purloined bolls, she showed Dicie how to clean, comb, and card the fibers.

Mammy borrowed a broken spinning wheel from the shed at the back of the cookhouse. hoping to spin enough thread to weave into cloth. "That wench what used to do the spinning ain't here no more. Hear the massa come got her and the good spinning wheel and took 'em both to Savannah. They ain't had nobody else what knew how to spin," she said.

Mammy could do anything. "This here wheel be old, but it still works once I get Isaac to fix this broken pedal. No sense in letting it set. Course I done watched the girl enough to learn how. Ain't much to it."

Often now with no overseer to stop her, Mammy and Dicie finished the invisible master's work early and hurried home. Behind the dilapidated compound where Brisbane slaves still sheltered, they tended extra rows of corn, turnip greens, and okra.

Like the starving old woman, Dicie worried about what they would eat with no food coming from the cookhouse. The day they shook the last crumbs out of the sugar sack for a final cup of hot, sweet tea terrified her. The cooks had rationed her favorite sugar sparingly, but now it was gone. Maybe forever. And now there were no cooks. Each family was on its own.

On that sad day all that was left to give a little sweetness to cornmeal mush was bitter black strap molasses, dregs left from squeezing the sweet syrup out of the cane. The dregs were considered fit only for slave food. Even that gooey black syrup had been low in the barrel. Now it was gone.

Isaac and Rufus planted rows of sugarcane, but cane took time to grow big enough to cut. Dicie longed for the boiled down sweet syrup, but Mammy hushed her. "Don't hollow out your fried fish till you catch 'em," she said. "Just cause them boys planted cane don't mean it going to grow."

Mammy fretted about her boys. Dicie's older brothers reveled in their new-found freedom. With no slave driver to watch them, Gus, Isaac, and Rufus barely harvested the ripening cotton in the two acres assigned to each. "Lord, I never saw such feckless boys," she said. "Old folk say,' hard head makes a soft back'. Them boys got hard heads. They don't know if we seen last of the buckra."

Gus scowled. "Ain't nobody picked up the cotton we made last year." He spat in the dirt. "What makes you think they gone pick up what we make this year? Wish we had some place to tote it to sell ourselves."

The brothers' hair and beards had grown wild and unkempt. Frizzled curls bounced when they shook their heads. Long sideburns and beards covered their faces like lean, feral animals. All the razors on Skidaway Island had been sharpened until the thin, rusted blades fell apart.

Instead of picking cotton, they went hunting and fishing, paying no more attention to the weed-choked ditch separating Brisbane from Hibernia than did the masked raccoons. They caught possums by hand at night, chasing the fat lumbering creatures through blackberry thickets, and handing them over to Mammy to clean and roast with sweet potatoes.

During the day Cass and Dicie dangled the legbones of the ill-fated possums over the bluff at the edge of the island, tempting blue crabs swimming in the shallows.

In an abandoned barn, Isaac found a supply of string. He knotted a net and cast it after shrimp in the manner of his ancestors. Mammy boiled the shrimp with okra and tomatoes for a tasty gumbo.

Of all Dicie's brothers, only Cass, now aged seven, went to the field with Dicie and Mammy.

"Lord, protect them idiots," Mammy said, wringing her hands. "They don't heed the evil what surrounds them. Back in Mauritania, I got seized when I be safe to home, praying to Mohammed." She clamped her thin lips shut.

No matter how much Dicie and Isaac and Rufus begged her, she never would tell them how she got from Mauritania to Skidaway Island. It had to be how she got her face all scarred up, but even Daddy didn't know. "Hush up, chillen. Can't change the past," she told them, squeezing her eyes shut to hold back tears.

The older boys didn't stop their roaming, even when they spotted two gray-clad soldiers landing a rowboat near where the bridge used to be.

"We watched them for a while," Isaac said. "Looked like they trying to see if the Yanks done took over. We ain't seen no blue coats. If we had, we'd of tried to join up with 'em."

"Where the Johnny Rebs now?" Mammy asked.

"They done left," he said. "Ain't hardly nobody over on that side of the island anymore."

Mammy wrung her hands and asked like she always did, "You seen any sign of yo' daddy over there? Any of them women what's left know where he be?"

"No, Mammy," they mumbled, same as always. Isaac hung his head instead of looking at her pained face. The once bustling slave compound on Springfield Plantation was almost empty.

Who was left on the island? Fewer slaves remained on Brisbane. Some had died. Some disappeared in the night. Occasionally a body washed up on shore, along the river. Who knew whether Cephus, the man who had grabbed Mammy, was still on the island? Dicie saw his fat, determined face in the shadows every time a branch snapped in the night.

She often pictured the boy from Hibernia. The one whose father saved Mammy. Little Tom, that was his name. Fear and excitement rippled through Dicie as she remembered his long, nimble fingers beating the drum in rhythm with Big Tom, his daddy. The last time she saw him was when he left his daddy after service and stopped to talk to her. Just before the praise house was destroyed. He had grown tall and handsome. He must have grown even more since then. Just like her.

With slave drivers absent, nobody but Mammy would stop her if she walked off the plantation and down the island to where he lived. He could cross the ditch separating Brisbane from Hibernia, same as her brothers did. He wouldn't need a pass to come see her. If he were still alive. If he still stayed at Hibernia with his daddy. And if the wench with the yellow flower in her hair had kept her claws off of him.

"Why can't I cross the ditch?" She asked Mammy. "I ain't been over there in more than three years. Isaac say ain't hardly nobody there no more. He go every night to see a girl he likes. I see goldenrod blooming on the far side. So pretty. Why can't I pick some?"

"Cut out that kind of talk, girl," Mammy said, even though her big brothers slipped over the boundary most nights. "You want to get whipped? Nobody know what might be going on to the other end of the island. Buckra could of come back. Even if they ain't, they still got soldiers coming and going. Ain't no reason to send 'em out here, 'cept to snitch."

Despite her scolding, Mammy was easier to live with. She didn't get in a pucker so often without Sampson around to aggravate her. Even when she was missing Daddy, she hardly cried any more.

While reading her signs at night, Mammy's face smoothed. The webs of long-legged spiders foretold the future if you knew how to interpret them, and she did. She counted the paths raccoons took going to the marsh and the thickness of the fall carpet of acorns. The signs gave her hope.

After dark, the hoot of the owl and the eerie cry of the gray fox told her "Change is a-coming."

Her mouth curved in the ghost of a smile when she heard the fox. "Get ready," she said.

"Look like change done already come," thought Dicie. Was Mammy still hoping for Daddy to come home? Sometimes Dicie dreamed about him. The smell of pine smoke always brought back the soft feel of his flannel shirt as he lifted her in his arms.

She had grown so tall her old, torn Negro-cloth dress barely covered her. Two years had passed since Sampson brought dress goods to make a new one. When all the empty cornmeal sacks had been snatched up and sewn into dresses, shirts, and trousers, Mammy found an old loom in a hut where the occupant had died. She promised to teach Dicie how to weave once they twisted enough thread from the stolen cotton bolls.

Through the long winter nights Dicie twisted white fibers on the old spinning wheel that Isaac had fixed. Even after the suet candle burned out, her fingers twisted in the dark. Someday, maybe they would have enough thread to weave. Mammy would show her how, and she could sew a new dress. Except when the blustery winter wind chilled her, she didn't much care about clothes. Younger children ran around naked.

"Mammy, my shoes hurt," she said, one coolish fall day when she tried on the ones she had worn the past two winters. The soles had fallen off, but Mammy had sewed them back on with heavy string twisted from dried palm leaves. Now she couldn't get her feet in them.

"Don't you never mind, child," Mammy said. "You and Isaac fetch me a pile of Spanish moss."

Mammy twisted and shaped the moss around her feet and Cass's feet, until the curly piles of enduring fiber tightened and hardened into a dense cushion. She tied the moss to their feet with vines.

All summer they ate tomatoes, beans, and okra from the garden. In the fall, corn, cabbage, and sweet potatoes ripened. Women no longer hoed blackberry vines out of the edges of cotton fields but let them flower. They shared the sweet, juicy berries. By fall the sugar cane the boys planted was six feet high. Dicie peeled and chewed until sweet juice ran down her chin. Nobody in this fertile, temperate forest by the ocean would starve.

As she hoed weeds out of muddy, barren cotton fields without being threatened by Sampson, Dicie dreamed of the harvest celebration six years ago, the first time she saw Little Tom. Back in the time when the plantation was running full bore and buckra were a common sight. A time when Dicie was six and Tom eight. Now she was twelve and Little Tom must be fourteen—a man grown. Would she ever see him again?

When a cool breeze blew away mosquitoes, men working unsupervised in the next field sang:

> *"I've got peace like a river in my soul.*
> *I've got a river in my soul*
> *I've got joy like a fountain in my soul*
> *I've got a fountain in my soul."*

Chapter Twelve

February 1864

Dicie's brothers roamed freely over the almost deserted island. Why couldn't Daddy come to visit? The least he should have done was to get word to them through some of the men who roamed the island. If he were still on the island. Or through Rosa, if he were in Savannah. Rosa said she always looked for him in City Market, but he was never there. Could he be further away from them than Savannah?

As for Little Tom, where was he? If her brothers could cross the ditch to Hibernia, why couldn't Tom cross the ditch to Brisbane? Dicie listened for the metallic beat of his empty tin-can drum. She hadn't forgotten the exact sound it made, a high-pitched echo of his father's. But she never heard it.

Now, even the big drum was silent. Bad as the slaves needed news, none ever seemed to come to the steadily emptying island. Or none worth beating the drum for. Could it be that Tom and his father had left Skidaway Island?

That evening her brothers came home and ate the food she and Mammy cooked. Afterward, she surreptitiously followed them over to the fire in the center of the compound to listen to their talk. What did men say when women weren't around? Crossing forbidden boundaries, mixing with each other, men had to learn more than women who never ventured far from home.

Crouching in deep shadows just outside their circle, she watched twelve sweaty, dirt-stained men sitting around a low, smoky fire, sipping moonshine from a tin cup and swapping stories. The full moon threw their shadows on the ground, although their faces were hidden in the dark.

Gus was bragging about going over the ditch, across Hibernia, and further down the island.

"There a sweet girl, big"— he gestured toward his chest, "— real friendly, lives over on Orangedale, t'other side of Hibernia. She like company," he said, grinning.

"Boy, that be over two mile," another man whistled admiringly. "How you get down there?"

Gus exchanged a conspiratorial look with Rufus. Did her brothers know the wench he was talking about?

"Ain't telling," said the man who admired the girl's chest.

"That ain't nothing," a third man said. A stick of dried out pine in the fire flared and revealed he was short and wiry with medium brown skin. Since most of the men returned to the compound later than the women, Dicie didn't know his name, but she knew he stayed with a skinny woman and had a child. "I made it over to Springfield. They ain't even planted rice this year. Nothing but red rice growing. The wild stuff. Ain't no overseers there and hardly no niggers neither. Nice deep creek on the other side and nobody hardly to watch, iff'n you don't mind a little mud." He winked.

"Springfield." The word struck a blow to Dicie's heart. The plantation where Daddy was sold.

Rufus stared at the man. "How many times you been over there?" he asked.

"Ain't none of your bidness, boy," the man said.

"My Daddy got sold to over there, back in 1857," Isaac answered. "We ain't heard from him since they knocked the praise house down."

The brown-skinned man's frown faded. "I'm sorry, son," he said. "I ain't seed nobody but old women, but I can ask. Who yo' Daddy?"

Dicie listened intently.

"Cuffie. He a real big, black-skinned man. He know all about growing rice." Rufus looked down at his over-sized bare feet.

"I can see he'd have to be a real big man to be your daddy," the man said. "They ain't growing no rice over there now. Here tell they moved some of them workers to the mainland south of here, winter of 1862. Lot of them's done run off. That why they moved 'em. If you put a boat in the creek there, you might make it over to Hilton Head where our folk been set free. So many swam out that way, buckra on Isle of Hope call it Runaway Nigger Creek."

Would Daddy have run away? Dicie shivered thinking of the danger he would face. He couldn't have told anybody, even Mammy, what he was planning. Too dangerous, even with no buckra around.

But where would he run to? Even if he were alive, once he left Skidaway Island, she probably would never see him again. Tears gathered in her eyes.

Still, that shadowy feeling of being connected to him persisted, same as it did on the nights he came home after the sun went down and Mammy had given up hope. She was always first to see him. He must be alive. If he were dead, she would have felt his passing. She forgot she wasn't supposed to be listening to the men.

If Daddy was lost to her forever, she needed to know about Tom. Springing from the shadows, she faced Gus and asked, "When you cross Hibernia does you ever see a boy a little older than me called Tom? His daddy beat the drum." Suddenly, she had to know if Tom was still on the island.

Moonlight reflected off her pale tan forehead as she jumped out of the shadows into the clearing. Conversation stopped mid-sentence. The chirping of crickets and crackling of the fire sounded loud in the silence. The half-drunk men turned away from examining the fire and stared at Dicie. What was a little girl doing here, interrupting men?

"Isaac, you take that child home," said the man who told the story about Runaway Nigger Creek. "She ain't s'posed to be here."

"Sorry," Isaac said to the man, grabbing Dicie's arm and pulling her away from the smoldering logs.

To Dicie he said, "You know you gotta keep quiet. I shouldn't never have let you follow us. Little girl oughten be 'round man talk."

Dicie couldn't keep quiet. "Was it true what they said? You think Daddy would of run away?"

Isaac stopped dragging her. Brother and sister stood close on the well-swept earth outside their hut. Lightning bugs flickered on and off in the wet night.

"Don't say nothing to Mammy," he said. "She git real hurt. Nobody ain't seen him in a long time. People say the massa over there went back to Savannah before the bridge burned and took a lot of his slaves with him. Maybe he took Daddy. Ever since soldiers first come three years ago, they ain't planted no rice. If he still be on this island, he would of found a way to come see us."

She nodded her head. Men went wherever they wanted to, now that all the buckra and drivers had left. The last of the family who used to live in the other half of Mammy's tabby were gone from the island. Not all at the same time, but one after another. The oldest and youngest were the last two to leave. Would Daddy have left if he had a chance? Of course, he would. Her daddy was the most fearless of all.

"Don't say nothing to Mammy 'bout me asking 'bout Tom, neither," she said. "Mammy done told me not to study no boys."

Isaac smiled at her. "You growing up, girl? She right, you know. Most of them men can't be trusted. I know that boy you asking about. I hear them girls over to Hibernia got they eye on him. Women, too. You be careful."

Dicie reached out and hugged him. Now she knew Tom was still on the island. She spit on her finger and pressed it to her heart.

Chapter Thirteen

April 1864

Dicie turned fourteen that spring when she and Mammy would have planted cotton if there had been seeds to plant. Most people didn't know what day they were born, but Mammy knew the exact day and year for all her children. She didn't let on about it, but she could read and write in Arabic.

In the days before the slave drivers left, when Dicie was supposed to be asleep, she watched Mammy carve letters on the sticks she kept with the herbs she used for making spells. Sampson wouldn't know the marks were Arabic letters. The buckra's inspectors never set foot inside the quarters. Even if they had, Dicie never heard of one who could read Arabic. After all the overseers had been gone for a while, and no white folks came to Skidaway except for an occasional soldier boy, Mammy wasn't so careful about hiding her marks.

One hot day, more than two years after the bridge burned, Mammy reached into the sack where she stored her herbs and pulled out a bundle of nine dried sticks. Each stick was a different length. She showed Dicie knife scratches on the fifth from longest one.

"April 9, 1850," she said. "and your name, 'Dicie.' Mean woman of strength. Today you fourteen years old and a woman. I made a stick for each my babies the day I birthed them. This next to littlest one is Stavie. Now you be fourteen, I don't want to see you messing with no boys."

Dicie stared at the pieces of wood, squeezing back tears at the reminder of her baby brother Stavie, whom she had cared for in the rows of cotton before Cass was born. Mammy had scraped off the bark and flattened a section of the round stem on the stick she said was for Dicie. Wavy lines were scratched into the peeled part. Mammy pointed to the lines and said, "Them's your name and the day and year of the Lord when you was born."

"Can you teach me how to read them marks?" Dicie asked.

"Nah, nah," Mammy said. "Ain't no good. This Arab writing. Nobody can't hardly read what you write like this. Besides, writing be a whipping offense."

Dicie wanted to cry. Why wouldn't Mammy ever teach her anything? She tried to memorize the marks.

"Mammy, please. For my birthday," Dicie begged.

Mammy sighed. "You the worst chile for asking questions. I ain't gone teach you to talk Arabic, and I don't know no English letters, but I hear English and Arabic use the same numbers. Might come in handy, but you got to keep it secret. We go out to the garden and keep a look out. Anybody come near, you tell 'em we pulling weeds. Lemme hide them sticks first."

Dicie took another quick look at her stick before Mammy snatched it. Mammy pointed to 4 and 9 and 1850.

"Them's the numbers," she said. "Look at them good. Ain't but ten of them. We start you learning them. Then I teach you 'nother day how to put 'em together."

In the shade behind the house, Mammy brushed aside dead leaves and drew the ten numbers, 0 1 2 3 4 5 6 7 8 9, in the damp dirt with a sharp stick. She carefully said the name of each one as she drew it and showed Dicie how many fingers each number stood for. Eying her intently, Dicie squatted in the leaves, holding out her own fingers and whispering the numbers. Mammy looked around. No one was near. The tabby hid them from the sandy road through the compound. On another square of dirt closer to the garden, Mammy brushed aside leaves.

"Now you take this stick and copy them numbers yo'self," she said. "I gotta cover 'em soon as you copy 'em. Can't leave 'em for nobody to see. Even with hardly nobody on this island, we got to be careful."

Whispering the names on the numbers to herself as she scratched each one in the dirt, Dicie sensed their power. She copied each number twice before Mammy swept away the first set.

Meanwhile, Mammy weeded the garden for real, keeping one eye on her surroundings. After a few minutes she stepped behind Dicie. "You done wrote 'em twice," she said, pointing to Dicie's two. "That there number saying you copied 'em two times. You fast." She took her bare foot and erased the first set. "You learning good. Just make sure nobody see you."

Dicie could have sworn Mammy smiled at her. She smiled back at her mother.

"Now you a woman," Mammy said. "You fourteen and got a grown-up secret what can get you killed. Won't be long fo' you taking care of yo' time of the month."

Dicie looked at her The only time of the month she knew was when it used to be time for Sampson to bring provisions. That hadn't happened for two years. "What time? What month?" she asked.

"When you get the blood," Mammy said. "You know it when you see it. Now you got to be careful around them boys."

Her words didn't make sense. Dicie had more questions, but Mammy turned away to stuff the sticks in the bag. Her back stiffened like it did when Dicie asked her how she came to be on Skidaway Island, or how she got the scars. It was no use to ask. She wouldn't answer.

Blood. The word churned and twisted in Dicie's mind. It wasn't fair. Mammy hinted at what Dicie needed to know, but never told her what she meant. Today was the ninth of April. Which day was the time of the month Mammy was talking about?

As they walked back into the tabby, Dicie stood straighter, just like her mammy. Once inside, she picked up the iron spider Mammy used to cook cornbread. Last year when she turned thirteen, the spider was so heavy she could hardly lift it. Now the weight of it in her hand felt solid, not too heavy.

Setting the spider back on the hearth, she walked out the cabin door and around back to the garden. Okra and tomatoes sprouted. Little white flowers popped out on the wild plum bushes between the garden and the woods. Birds chirped. Long ropes of orange trumpet flowers circled the tops of pine trees. Change was in the air and not just because of the warm, salty breeze. "I'm a woman today," she whispered.

While Mammy was inside, fussing with her herbs, Dicie slipped back into the woods. Six deer, four females, and two little ones with white spots, browsed for mushrooms through pine straw covering the forest floor. She knelt behind a thicket of yaupon holly to watch. The fawns ran to their mother and grabbed her milk teats. The doe stood still while the fawns gulped milk. Then she shook them off and moved to a fresh outcrop of mushrooms hiding in the detritus of the forest.

Dicie had watched newborn fawns emerge from their mothers, just as she had watched little pigs and gray marsh rabbits. Did that have anything to do with what Mammy said? And how did the babies get into their mother? She had asked before, but never gotten an answer.

Without seeming to notice Dicie, the herd moved a few yards away. Dicie tiptoed in their direction, choosing her steps to keep from snapping a dead stick. Sometimes a young deer allowed her to pat its soft brown fur, but it wasn't likely a vigilant mother would let her get close today.

Lost in thought about Mammy's mysterious reference to blood and without paying attention to direction, she followed the female deer and their babies until she reached the ditch separating Brisbane and Hibernia. It was the first time she had ventured so near the dividing line since the praise house was destroyed. Her grief at losing the church and the chance of seeing Daddy still burned bitter in her chest. Weeds filled the ditch and saplings had taken over the tops of both sides. No reason for her to cross it now, even though there was nobody to stop her.

As she inspected the forbidden boundary, she spotted a tramped down trail through the tall grass and seedling oaks. Did deer make the trail to hunt for food on the other side? Limbs from yaupon bushes as high as the top of her head had broken off on both sides. Surely a deer path would be a low tunnel? Was this the path her brothers used at night?

Forgetting to follow the deer, she walked to the edge of the ditch looking for human footprints in the path. Sure enough, big human toes had mashed round dents in a line in the exposed black clay. Dents as big as Isaac and Rufus's toes. Keeping an eye out for poison ivy, she followed the prints down into the ditch where light blue flowers bloomed. Then she climbed up the opposite side.

Once at the top of the far side, she straightened her back and caught her breath. The fields of Hibernia spread out into the distance, closer than she remembered. Someone had planted tomatoes and pole beans next to the ditch. Someone who had his back to her, hammering stakes on the far side of the garden for the beans to climb. His ragged shirt exposed muscular arms and a powerful waistline. He reminded her of Daddy, but even though she glimpsed him from the back, she could tell he was young. A dark-skinned man who reminded her of Little Tom.

Her heart jumped. She turned and started back into the ditch. The man with the hoe lifted his head and looked in her direction. Dicie froze. Little Tom stared. A crow cawed raucously from the top of one of his stakes.

"Dicie?' he asked "What you doing here?"

Her knees shook. I'm fourteen now. Almost a woman grown, she reminded herself. Ain't no need to be scared. Still, she took a step backward toward the edge of the ditch.

He was taller than she remembered, and the shadow of a beard covered his cheeks, but the same crackling vitality he used to beat a rhythm on a tomato can shone in the way he lifted his hoe.

"It's my birthday," she answered. What a stupid thing to say. Nobody on the plantation cared about birthdays.

He dropped his hoe and strode toward her, his bare feet digging deep indentations in the plowed ground.

Her heart pounded, and not just from climbing up the steep bank of the ditch. Forgetting the mud on her hands, she reached up to brush her hair out of her face, painfully aware of how far her scratched up legs stuck out beyond the hem of her dress.

"It's been so long," Tom said, fixing his eyes on her face. "I hardly knew it was you. What you been doing?"

She took a deep breath. "Helping Mammy and hiding from them soldier boys. I be happy they mostly gone. Little raccoons done come back to where them soldiers used to camp."

He stood so close to her she felt his breath blow by her face and smelled the hot sweat rising from his skin. She forgot to be scared. Even the faint sound of Mammy hollering didn't get her legs scurrying back home.

"Yeah, little fawns eating my okra," he said. "Better the deer than them buckra boys stomping all over it."

Dicie scowled, thinking about the soldiers who drove a wagon right through the acre of cotton Mammy was planting. Sampson made her and Mammy stay out till dark trying to save the seedlings.

He saw her frown and instantly wanted to make it go away. Trying to cheer her up, he said, "Hey, I remember you saying you got mink pups. I thought about you last week when a mink birthed four of 'em over by our cabin."

Her frown melted. "We got 'em again this year. They mammy won't let me near, but soon as they get a little age on 'em, they gone be running everywhere."

Instead of answering, he smiled at her. "You the prettiest girl I ever seen," he said, breaking the silence.

She felt her face heat up. Nobody had ever said that to her. What was she supposed to do? Unexpectedly tears formed in her almond-shaped brown eyes.

"I'm sorry. I didn't mean to get you all upset," he said. "Your eyes just so pretty, I couldn't help myself." He twisted his foot and looked down at the weeds brushing his ankles.

He looked so sad, Dicie's tears vanished. She wanted to comfort him like she did Cass when he was hurt. She reached out her hand to touch him.

He looked up and slowly smiled. Lifting his hand, he wiped the smear of mud off her cheek. Her whole body tingled. He took a step back and studied every inch of her face.

"You got some mud in your hair, too," he said.

Dicie took a step closer to him so he could brush the top of her head.

A loud "Gronk!" broke the silence. A great blue heron shot out of its nest in the top of the tree above where they were standing and sailed off toward the marsh.

Both jumped backwards, startled. Dicie had forgotten the time. The sun had fully risen. She looked back the way she had come. Women were already in the field on Brisbane. Mammy must be throwing a fit.

Her legs trembled and she whirled back toward the ditch. "Mammy don't know I come here. I got to run."

"You got an overseer on Brisbane?" he asked.

"No." She shook her head. "Not any more. Nobody but us."

"Same over here," he said. "Mind if I come see you sometime?"

Dicie shook her head no, but gave Tom one last look, then turned and slid down the ditch. She didn't mind for sure if he came to see her.

But Mammy would.

What would Mammy say if Tom showed up asking for her? Would she grab a switch? Mammy told her not to cross that ditch. She disobeyed and now she was late.

She shivered as she ran toward the field she was supposed to be weeding. Mammy said she better not find her with no boy. But it was too late to tell him not to come.

Chapter Fourteen

April–August 1864

"Where you been?" Mammy demanded. "Ain't you heard me calling you?"

Dicie struggled to breathe as quietly as possible. Making Mammy even madder was too dangerous. No telling what she might do. "I done brung you into this world, and I can take you out," she often said.

Dicie had sprinted straight to their acre. "I done followed the deer and forgot the time," she said, panting. She stared at the dirt, afraid to look Mammy in the face while she told that lie. Mammy would have known. To keep from looking up, she dug her big toe in the sand, making a doodlebug pit.

"Girl, you lucky ain't no overseer. You be working your own acre, not just helping me, and better keep it weeded, even if there ain't no cotton. No telling when them massas be back; Sampson cracking his whip. Can't just let it go."

At least Mammy didn't pick up a switch, maybe because there wasn't anybody in the field checking to see how much work they got done. Nothing grew in the field now except weeds and an occasional wild cotton plant, springing up from last year. But without constant vigilance, the sandy field would be quickly overrun by palmetto and oak saplings.

Cass ran toward them from the big oak at the end of the row. He stopped short and stared at Mammy, her face twisted and angry.

Dicie reached for Cass's hand. He was only eight. No sense in Mammy scaring the bejesus out of him on account of her. "Yes, Ma'am," she mumbled.

"And another thing. You ain't after looking at no boys, is you?"

Blood rushed to Dicie's cheeks, and she stared at her toe.

Mammy gave her a sharp look. "Just because you fourteen, don't be thinking you can do whatever you want. You stay away from boys, you hear?"

"Ain't no boys, but my brothers," Dicie mumbled. She should have known better than to back talk Mammy. Even Sampson was afraid of her.

Mammy glared at her for another moment like she was fixing to break out in one of her fits. "You looking for trouble, girl," she said. Her scar wrinkled as she frowned, making her look even more like a witch. "You know you can make a baby now?"

Dicie trembled. Any minute Mammy might strike her with the hoe handle she held in her hand. No, she didn't know how she could make a baby. Mammy would never tell her and there was no one else to ask. She was afraid to open her mouth. Why hadn't she told Tom not to come? If Mammy caught him walking over to see her, she'd whip her for sure.

Finally, Mammy stopped screaming and smacked a clump of weeds with a mighty blow. Dicie scuttled down the row as far away as she could and began snatching stubborn little three-leafed clovers out of the dirt. Last year there wasn't any way to get the roots of the clover out without disturbing the cotton shoots. In the absence of cotton, clover tried to take over. Jerking it out was a never-ending job until hot weather drove the weed underground. There it spread its roots to pop up with a vengeance next spring.

"Tom ain't gone come looking for me anyway," she mumbled under her breath. She didn't know which she felt the most—sad or relieved. Most likely, both.

By May, five-petaled white flowers with yellow centers festooned the blackberry canes. Next, green berries formed, grew round and fat, and turned red. When the berries ripened to dark purple, Dicie battled the crows for the sweet fruit. Her hands were stained purple. A deep indentation marked her palm from the weight of the wire handle of the tin pail, filled to the brim with sweet, delicious blackberries.

All the while she picked, Dicie scoured the woods with her eyes, looking for any sign of Little Tom. Day after day passed. The island became emptier and lonelier as folks died or disappeared. Tom didn't come to see her. She remembered the pretty girl from Hibernia with a flower in her hair, the wench who forced her way past worshippers to sit next to Tom in church. Far as Dicie knew, he could be with that hussy every day.

Back at the tabby, Mammy dribbled honey over each bowlful of berries. After Dicie passed bowls to her brothers, she fixed one for herself and collapsed on the front stoop to savor the sweetness. As she spooned honey-covered berries into her mouth, she dreamed about Tom. With her free hand, she twirled the feathery leaves of wild indigo growing around the stoop. What did he mean when he asked to come see her? If he meant it, why hadn't he come? Was it just his way of saying goodbye? She wished she knew more about boys. Her brothers weren't any help.

On a hot August day after the blackberries had all been picked, Mammy sent her out with her pail to find scuppernongs. The purplish grapes dangled from vines wound around pine trees. The bare trunks of the pines towered over a sunny spot near what used to be a field of cotton, now overgrown with yaupon holly scrub. More grape vines sprouted from the center root in all different directions, intertwining with yaupon branches. She stepped into the tangle, reached up, pulled a vine toward her, and plucked all the scuppernongs she could reach. Yellow and black striped wasps buzzed, fighting her for the ripest grapes.

Over the musical pling, plang of grapes hitting her tin pail, another strain of music caught her ear. Somewhere in the woods, somebody whistled a hymn. The tune sounded familiar, even though there hadn't been much singing in the half-secret prayer services since slaves were forbidden to meet.

She remembered some of the words:

> "He got the wind and the rain in his hands,
> He got the wind and the rain in his hands,
> He got the whole world in his hands."

Who would be whistling? Had to be someone brave enough or stupid enough not to worry about being overheard.

Footsteps crunched louder than the chatter of birds. Yaupon swayed as a young man brushed the branches aside. "Isaac told me I'd find you here," Little Tom said.

A small shriek escaped her. She slapped her hand over her mouth to muffle a louder scream. "You scared me," she said.

"Sorry. I been meaning to look for you sooner. Hope you ain't forgot you said it be alright if I come see you," he said.

Dicie had forgotten how tall he was, or maybe he was taller than he had been last spring. Mammy's words thundered in her head: "Don't go messing with no boys." Now he was standing next to her, plain as day, with only thick woods and an overgrown field nearby, and no telling where Mammy was.

He saw her tremble. "Don't be scared. I ain't come to hurt you. You so pretty, I wanted to see you again. Ain't nobody now to stop me from crossing the ditch."

At least he stood a decent piece away from her. Not like last time they met when he walked straight up to her.

"Mammy don't want me talking to no boys," she said.

He grinned. "We better go find yo' mammy and see if we can get her to say something better than that."

She looked down at her feet and mumbled, "You don't know my mammy."

"Bet I do. Just made her acquaintance again when I went up to the tabbies, looking for you," he said. "'Course I remember the first time I seen you. Yo' mammy was fighting to get away from that ugly man, Cephus. My daddy helped her, but he don't think she needed much help. Daddy say she probably would have hurt Cephus real bad if Daddy hadn't pulled him off her."

"Mammy know you was looking for me?" She couldn't believe it. Her foot trembled. When she was afraid, she could never keep it from shaking.

"I asked her if I could see you," he said. "She say yes. She be real nice."

"What you say?" Dicie couldn't believe him. Mammy, nice?

Tom gave her a cocky grin that reminded her of Daddy. "She hoeing her garden back of the house. I done seen Isaac with her and knew she must be yo' mammy. I say, 'good afternoon.' Isaac say, 'You finally decide to cross the ditch.' He know I like you. I been asking 'bout you every time he come by."

Dicie's mouth hung open. Why hadn't Isaac told her? She'd give him a talking to later.

"So, I say I got to cross the ditch 'cause I be looking for the prettiest little girl I ever seen. She look just like her mammy."

"Mammy didn't jump on you after you told that lie?" Dicie never heard anybody say Mammy was pretty. Although she could have been before her face got messed up. "Mammy always say 'pretty is as pretty do.'"

Tom kept smiling. "You do favor her with your light skin and turned up eyes."

Dicie stared at him in wonder. "What she did when Isaac say where I be at?" she asked.

"She asked where my Daddy be and told me to bring you back home if your pail be full of scuppernongs."

That really didn't sound like Mammy. She wasn't sure she believed him, but she said, "The pail could hold a few more. If you help me reach the high ones, I think we can fill it right quick."

Obligingly, Tom stretched his arm to the branch beyond her reach and pulled it down. Quickly, she plucked the high-hanging grapes. Tom grabbed the full pail. They turned back toward the compound, Dicie still uneasy about their reception from Mammy.

"Hey, Miz Lizzie," Tom sang out as they emerged from the woods and approached the garden, Dicie behind him. "I brung Dicie back with a full pail of scuppernongs, just like I promised. With your permission, I'd like to set with her on this here bench and eat some."

Dicie held her breath. She couldn't tell from the look on Mammy's face what she would do. She half expected Mammy to reach for a switch. In the treetops, blood-red cardinals and a Carolina wren chirped their encouragement.

Mammy didn't say anything for a minute, just stared at Tom. Then, she gave her lop-sided smile. "Well, I reckon since Dicie fetched them, you should be 'lowed to do just that. Be sure to save some for the rest of us. You two have a seat and tell me more about how yo' daddy been doing. Reckon he might be able to visit, now ain't nobody stopping him?"

Dicie gingerly took a seat on the splintered wooden bench by the door to the tabby. As she listened to Mammy and Tom, she pulled little purple flowers off a stalk of wild indigo. She was afraid to look at Mammy's face.

"My daddy busy teaching me how to beat the big drum. I know most all the codes," Tom said. "Folks been slipping up from both ends of the island to let him know what's going on. He gotta pass the word fast if'n one of them big ships lands. He stay close to home."

Mammy looked disappointed. "Tell him anytime he want a cup of tea, he be welcome."

Tom took a seat on the bench next to Dicie. Her skin quivered at his closeness. She wished he would touch her, but he kept his eyes on Mammy and his hands to himself. "Thank you, Miz Lizzie." he said. "Ain't nothing much happen since them soldiers left. Daddy got a touch of the misery, so that keeping him home, too. He heard 'bout a few bateaux of Johnny Rebs checking to see if soldiers from the other side done landed. Nobody seen them Yanks. Word be they ain't letting us on them big ships, neither. Got too many of us already."

Listening to him, Dicie couldn't help but long for her own daddy. What would Daddy say if she could talk to him?

Unexpectedly, Mammy stood and said, "I got to see 'bout some business. Reckon you two young'uns want to set here a while and eat these scuppernongs. Dicie, soon as you eat enough, say goodbye, and go start supper. Tom, you tell yo' daddy to come with you next time, and I'll see if I can cure him."

Dicie's mouth dropped again as Mammy disappeared around the corner of the cabin and headed back to the shady part of her garden. It was quite a day of surprises. She closed her mouth and said, "Never know about Mammy." She smiled at Tom, "How your garden?"

"Good, good. I got lots of butter beans if you need some."

"We'd love some," Dicie said. Mammy's garden had plenty of butter beans, but she'd never let him know.

"You a real pretty girl," Tom said, fixing his eyes on hers.

Dicie's face got hot. He already told her that. She didn't mind hearing it again, but she didn't know what to say back to him. She hoped he hadn't noticed the bumps swelling her chest. To change the subject she said, "Maybe Mammy will let me pick scuppernongs again with you. It real easy when you grab the high branches for me."

"I'll ask her," Tom promised. He touched her hand. "When I come back."

Her hand tingled where his had been. She touched the spot. It looked the same, but it wasn't.

Chapter Fifteen

August 1864

L ater that evening, after Tom had gone, the family feasted on scuppernongs, along with tomatoes and okra. Dicie missed the rice they used to eat. After she gathered the empty bowls and fetched dishwater, Mammy called her back to the garden.

"I been working on a potion for you," she said. "To keep you from having a baby till you gits older."

"Mammy, I don't know how to make a baby," Dicie said. Just the thought of raising up another child like she raised Cass made her sick. Too much work and worry.

Mammy took a deep breath. She turned her head back toward the garden, so all Dicie could see of her face was the scar on her cheek.

"Some women gits baby and don't never know how it come about. That ain't right. You got a man looking at you," she said. "You old enough to know."

"I seen baby deer drop out of their mammy and mink pups drop out of theirs. Do it be the same with us?" Dicie asked, feeling blood rush to her cheeks.

"It be," Mammy said. "You got a hole between your legs that the baby come out, same as the animals."

Good to have her theory confirmed, but she still didn't have the answer to her real question. "How the baby get into the mammy?" she asked. Her mother never answered, no matter how many times and ways she asked. Maybe this would be the day. She stood there waiting.

"The man does it with his peepee," Mammy said.

Ugh! Wish she hadn't asked.

"Ain't as bad as it sounds," Mammy said. "Men can be mean or real sweet about it. The sweet is what I worry about with this boy. Either way, you don't need no baby, not with us not knowing from one day to next if we still be alive or where we gone lay our heads. I mixed a potion to keep you from getting one. Don't let that boy be touching yo' privates."

"Yes, Ma'am," Dicie aid, turning the words over in her mind. The thought of Tom touching her privates was both thrilling and disgusting.

The next day she watched Mammy cut palmetto leaves and squeeze juice out of the stems into a little tin can. She showed the juice to Dicie. It looked like green water. She motioned to a cluster of drying weeds. "This here be pennyroyal from the garden. I grind it fine."

Mammy had never let Dicie help when she mixed potions. The old metal grinder fascinated her. Mammy had polished it to a dull silver. As she twirled the handle, limp pennyroyal weed poured out of the spout as green powder. She dumped the green powder into the palm oil and stirred.

"You was too young then, but I had to keep a whole jug of this when them soldiers be on this island. Some them wenches ain't knowed how to hide. I'm making it fresh in case this here boy gets your head spinning."

Dicie said, "I want to learn how to make it."

"All in good time, chile. All in good time. First, you got to know how to look out for danger. You got to get yo' head out of them animals what won't hurt you and learn to guard against people what will. I weren't much older than you when I got stole. My mammy ain't taught me nothing 'bout evil."

Mammy set down the spoon she was using and looked Dicie over from the top of her head to her bare feet.

Dicie held her breath. This was the most Mammy ever said about how she got kidnapped.

"Ain't nobody hardly know how to root anymore. You is a bit flighty, but maybe I can learn you. Back in Mauretania, my mammy learned me the roots. You my only girl, so I have to show you. The critters trust you. That a good sign."

So, she wasn't going to explain about the kidnapping, but her half kind words warmed Dicie. Mammy wasn't one to say much of anything good about Dicie or anybody else. Would Mammy be easier on her now that she was almost a woman?

No chance of that. Mammy scowled, "We'll see if you smart enough to learn. First, I show you the good roots. Don't want you hurting yo'self or nobody else."

Mammy pulled out a handful of dried yaupon holly berries, still faintly showing their original red color "Now these here are for a different kind of spell. If you studying that boy, we can make him forget 'bout them girls over on Hibernia and just want you. You keep a lookout for something a brighter red than these, like ripe chokecherries."

Dicie's heart pounded and she grabbed Mammy's hand to inspect the berries.

"Hold your hosses," Mammy said. "First, we got to see if he come back. If he ain't, we don't do nothing."

Dicie's heart pounded as she remembered Tom's smile and his words, "when I come back." She hoped he meant it.

Chapter Sixteen

January 1865

Wind whistled down the Skidaway River, blowing the shrimp net Tom cast away from its intended landing place. Dicie dangled her legs from the top of the low bluff as she watched him struggle. Ever since he first came to visit her, Tom had shown up once a week with Mammy's blessing. Dicie counted the days between each of his visits and made sure she set aside time to spend with him. If only he came every day. She was afraid to ask what became of the pretty girl who used to sit with him in church. Were they still friends? Or had she left Hibernia?

Once Tom started coming regularly, Mammy showed her how to crush the red choke cherries and mix them with dried and powdered bay leaf. Teaching Dicie how to make the love potion was proof of Mammy's approval.

Dicie shivered, then crossed her fingers for luck. Each time Tom stepped outside with her brothers, she said a little prayer and dropped a pinch of the root into his cup. Mammy said it was hard to be sure if it worked.

"Time will tell," she said.

Dicie kept her fingers crossed so much they had little dents in them.

Once, when she and Tom gathered goldenrod, he grabbed her hand and gently placed a sprig of the brilliant yellow flowers in her hair. That was the closest he had come to touching her. What would it feel like if he kissed her? Was this love? She imagined his arms around her, even though the wind blew her hair and made her nose run. His touch felt like love.

"Got to fill this net today," Tom said, interrupting her daydream. He fought the wind to spread the net evenly into the river. "Shrimp be heading out to deep water any day now. This probably the last catch till warm weather."

Dicie shivered. She hoped he caught plenty. Food was scarce in winter. She hated the slimy oysters, but Mammy said they were lucky to have them. What sweet potatoes they saved from the garden were dwindling fast. Mostly she ate collards greens and a little meat if the boys were lucky enough to kill a raccoon or possum. Deer and wild hogs were plentiful, but hard to kill with homemade bows and wooden arrows. Shrimp would be a welcome change if Tom caught enough.

Now that Tom came often, they had plenty of hot tea. He scavenged the leaves from the hedge of overgrown camellias ringing Hibernia's abandoned big house.

"Massa had them bushes brung from China," Tom said.

Dried and steeped, the leaves made tea as good as any Sampson used to bring.

The splash of incoming tide against the bow of a flatbed ferry caught her ear. Launching from Burnt Pot Island near where the old bridge to Skidaway used to be, the wobbly raft rode low in the river, overloaded with people standing shoulder to shoulder.

"Uh, Oh!" she screamed. "Soldiers coming back. We better hide."

Tom jerked his head up, and dumped the net, shrimp and all, into his bucket. He stared at the approaching raft, poled by two black men. "Ain't even high tide yet. Hope they don't get stuck," he said, scrambling up the bluff to Dicie. Once on top, he glanced back at the river.

"Look! They all colored. Can't be soldiers. What . . . ?"

Tom and Dicie scrambled downstream to a thicket of wax myrtle, where they crouched under feathery branches, and turned to watch.

"Way too many people on that raft," Tom said. "Look how low it riding. They like to git stuck on a sand bar 'fo they gits here."

"Lord, the noise!" Dicie said. "They ain't afraid of nobody knowing they here. Don't see no buckra and no soldiers with them. Wonder why they all come to Burnt Pot? Ain't nobody stay there."

The two watched anxiously from behind the scanty leafed wax myrtle. Creeper vines that would have concealed them were bare in winter. Men, women, and many young children crowded the rickety flatbed, straining against the weathered wooden rail. Most carried heavy-looking bundles. There was no space to set their parcels.

Who were these people and why would colored children ride the ferry to Skidaway? The only children on the island had been born here, destined to be enslaved for life. Few survived.

The polemen maneuvered the perilous craft to the landing by Big Ferry Road. Before they could tie it tight, men jumped into the river, climbed the bluff near where Tom and Dicie hid, and boldly tramped down the overgrown ferry road toward the middle of the island. Some were singing. Dicie looked for fear in the dark faces but saw none.

After the last group disembarked, the polemen untied the ferry, pushed off, and headed back toward Burnt Pot Island, where Tom and Dicie saw another group of colored people gathering. Soldiers in blue uniforms waited behind them.

"We better warn our folks," Tom said.

He and Dicie cautiously climbed out of their hiding place, and avoiding the road, ran as fast as they could over downed branches and exposed roots through the winter-bare woods.

"I'll see you soon as I tell Daddy," Tom hollered when they reached the border of Brisbane Plantation. He headed straight across the ditch without waiting for Dicie.

She found Mammy in her garden. The dirt was clean and bare except for onions and collards.

"Mammy, Mammy," she called breathlessly. "Folk be coming. Hundreds of 'em. Colored folk. What happen? What we gone do?"

Mammy whipped around and leaned against her hoe for balance. "Hundreds? You sure, girl? You smell smoke?" She lifted her head and sniffed for fire. "Where they coming from?"

"Hurry, we got to hide." Dicie's heart raced. Mammy's fear fueled hers. "We saw them getting off the ferry. They coming from Burnt Pot, headed this way."

Big Tom's drum began its message. Boom, boom, **BOOM**, boom. Fast, Fast. Harder. Quicker. The code for danger.

"Rufus, get in the house. We gotta bar the door," Mammy called. "Where yo' brothers at?" She shooed Dicie and Cass into their half of the tabby and gathered a couple of hens in her apron, while Rufus latched the wooden shutters.

Once inside, Mammy put her finger to her lips. Everybody strained to hear the sound of footsteps in between the beats of Big Tom's drum.

Nothing outside but birds whistling and chattering as they fought against the wind. A house finch, cardinals, and same as always, crows.

A second drum from Hibernia joined the first. Little Tom beat with his daddy. Dicie grabbed Cass's hand. Even though her little brother had turned eleven, she couldn't lose the habit of protecting him.

"Listen to them crows," Mammy said. "They'll kick up a ruckus if strangers comes near."

Half an hour of panicked waiting went by. Faint drums from plantations further away took up the beat. A single pair of footsteps crunched leaves behind the hut. The repartee between the two crows didn't change. Couldn't be a stranger.

"Y'all in there?" Isaac hollered.

Mammy cracked open the door. "Hush yo 'mouth," she said. "They's strangers on the island."

But Isaac wouldn't hush. "Lots of 'em. I seen 'em. They singing fit to wake the dead. I had to listen. They singing:

> 'Free at last, free at last,
> I thank God I'm free at last.'

You think they fo' real?"

Dicie looked at Mammy. She raised her eyebrows so that the scar of her cheek drew upward into almost a straight line. Her face settled into a crooked, puzzled look. Reaching into the bag where she kept her signs, she drew out three worn wooden squares painted with black lines.

"'Free at last, free at last, I thank God I'm free at last,'" she whispered. "Fool talk much, wise men talk less. They ain't scared if they singing that."

As Mammy studied the squares, the rhythm of the drumbeat evened out. Boom, boom, boom. The code for caution. Faster than the drumbeat of death. Slower than the danger code. Big Tom had gotten news.

Dicie loosened her grip on Cass's hand.

Isaac pushed Mammy aside and opened the door. "I'm going out. If'n I cut through the woods, I can see how close they gitting, and where they going," he said. "I'll stay hid so they don't see me. Don't get yo'self in a pother, Mammy. Ain't no buckra with 'em, 'cept a Yankee soldier."

Mammy shrugged and turned back to her cards. "Sign of the sun," she muttered. "A powerful sign." She held up one of the squares and squinted at it.

Another hour passed. Dicie kept picturing all those people. More than she had ever seen in one place. All those folks pushing and shoving to get off the boat scared her. She remembered the troop of young soldiers who came four years ago, shooting guns. There hadn't been nearly as many.

The tabby door burst open. Dicie almost passed out from fright, but it was only Isaac with Gus. "We Free! We Free!" he hollered.

Mammy looked from Isaac to Gus.

"Yes, Mammy. It true," Gus said. "We talked to Tom. Some them colored folks what landed be reaching out to all the plantations. United States soldiers helping them. Soldiers followed Big Tom's drum to Hibernia. They say Yankee army done took over Savannah. Tom say it true. He changed the code to the drum."

Isaac jumped in. "Reverend Ulysses Houston, hisself, with 'em. He the head preacher from First African Baptist Church in Savannah. He coming to tell us, soon as he tell everybody at the big plantations. You remember him at the old praise house. Him the one give us a bit of code to help runaways. They ain't never let him come back after that. He be here now."

"Praise God! Thank you, Jesus." Mammy let out a scream that scared Cass. Tears ran down her scarred cheeks. *"Bismillah Hir Rahman Nir Rahim. Shukran li Allah daeeman!* Allah the most gracious and merciful. Always thank God." She knelt on the wood floor with her head to the ground, chanting in a language Dicie had heard her use before, but didn't understand.

Finally, she sat up and said, "It rain, and every man feel it some day."

Chapter Seventeen

January 1865

"What do it mean, we be free?" Dicie asked, looking at her big brothers. She wasn't sure what was happening. Mammy had turned back to her weeping and praying.

Isaac and Rufus looked at each other.

"No more Sampson," Gus said.

"No more whippings," Rufus added.

"We can leave this God-forsaken island any time we want," Isaac added.

"Can Daddy come home?" Dicie asked. Daddy coming home would be the best thing about freedom.

Mammy lifted her head. "If Allah see fit." She leaned over to put her forehead back to the floor and resumed her prayer.

"What we supposed to do now?" Dicie asked.

Mammy lifted her head again and said, "Wait and see."

The family slept fitfully through the night, the grown boys, Gus, Rufus, and Isaac, taking turns listening for the sound of strangers entering the compound.

Next morning Big Tom's drum woke them with the same rhythm of caution from the afternoon before. Isaac grabbed a wedge of cold cornbread and stuffed it in his mouth, dribbling crumbs as he let himself out of the tabby. Rufus and Gus stayed behind to protect Mammy, Dicie, and Cass.

Despite Mammy's command to stay inside, soon as she turned back to praying, Dicie let herself out of the cabin. She couldn't stand being cooped up anymore, like a pullet in a flock of chickens. Outside the air was sharp, but she was able to breathe without the stink of sweat and the odor of the overflowing slop bucket.

From Springfield and plantations further south, resonated the faint echo of Big Tom's loud drumbeats and Little Tom's sharp, tinny ones. From the tops of the sweetgums, noisy pairs of songbirds called to each other. The garden was just as they had left it the day before, except the leaves of potato plants were fuller and a raccoon had left tracks in the collard patch.

Dicie wondered, "Does plants and animals know we be free?" They probably wouldn't care as long as they got tended. What would happen to the garden if strangers forced her family out? She plucked out tiny new sprouts of weeds peeking through the dirt and patted down a collard stalk a raccoon had uprooted. Best to let the garden know she was still there.

Hours later blasts of a bugle startled folks hiding warily in their huts. Nobody knew what would happen next. Following the jarring notes, buckra soldiers tramped into the compound. Peeking through the shutters, Mammy sighed with relief. "Blue uniforms. That a good sign."

"Hear ye, hear ye!" The first soldier yelled. "Everybody gather up!"

Another soldier beat a drum. The frightened slaves remained in their cabins.

A colored soldier hollered, "You dumb niggers, git yo'selves out here."

Isaac cracked open the door. Gus and Rufus had taken to sleeping in the deserted other half of the tabby. They peeked out their door. Seeing the colored soldier and the blue uniforms, they opened the doors wider. Dicie peered under Isaac's outstretched arm. Everywhere, dark heads protruded from doorways.

"Git yo' black asses out here," the colored Yankee soldier yelled again.

Either from curiosity or habit of obedience, the frightened slaves crept out, murmuring to each other. Dicie clung to Mammy's skirt, hiding behind her.

When everyone had taken a place in a circle around the soldiers, the officer signaled to the bugler. Three triumphant notes resounded throughout the compound, startling the crows who increased their warnings.

"You people are no longer slaves. You are free, by order of General William Tecumseh Sherman." His voice resounded throughout the compound. A drum boomed at the end of each sentence. An osprey screeched and circled overhead.

The people all looked at each other, afraid to believe his words. What were they supposed to do?

As if reading their thoughts, the soldier said, "You must now organize a settlement and prepare a government for yourselves within this settlement."

The residents of the compound stood there in stunned silence. It had to be true. But how?

A crowd of newcomers formed behind the soldiers. "You dumb Geechees!" One of the newcomers yelled. "Ain't you hear what the man said? We got work to do."

"Praise be to God," a Brisbane man yelled. Others from the compound cheered, "Free! Free!" Some leaped high in the air, performing a ritual African victory dance. One of the newcomers grabbed up a flattened piece of tin and beat it with a stick like a make-shift cymbal.

The soldier lifted his arms for silence and continued his message. "The sea islands from Charleston south to the St. John's River are set apart for the settlement of the Negroes now made free by the acts of war. Any Negro male of good character, formerly enslaved, may apply for title of up to forty acres of tillable, confiscated land. Reverend Houston here will tell you all about it."

The bugle played again. A Negro man a little older than Daddy stepped forward from behind the soldier. Like Daddy, he was a good-sized man, but unlike Daddy, his thick head of hair had turned white. He wore a full white beard. Both hair and beard were neatly trimmed, unlike Dicie's memory of Daddy, who had little time to worry about his looks. Even though Reverend Houston was colored, he wore a matching coat and trousers over a collared black shirt, same as white preachers. Dicie had never seen a colored man so finely dressed.

The man's voice rang out in the cold air. "I am Reverend Ulysses Houston from the Third African Baptist Church in Savannah. I bring you good tidings. The Lord said, 'I am the Lord. I will bring you out from under the burdens of the Egyptians and I will rid you out of their bondage. I will bring you in unto the land and I will give it to you for an heritage.' The Lord has done so. One thousand of our brothers are here to make it happen. Let us pray."

Mammy and Dicie's brothers stared at the man, hardly able to believe what they had heard.

"You reckon what he say be true?" Gus whispered to Isaac.

Dicie looked at Mammy as the man continued to pray.

"Signs point to it true," Mammy said. She stared at the reverend. "He the last colored preacher over to Hibernia praise house back in 1858, 'fo Sampson chopped it down. He had a full head of hair back then, but it weren't solid white like now. That why, at first I didn't know who he be. After him, the buckra never let another colored man preach on Skidaway Island. Him standing there now be a powerful sign. We blessed to hear him again."

"I done told you," Isaac said.

Reverend Houston finished praying. A sudden stiff breeze blew the clouds away. Sun beamed down on his aureole of white hair, reminding Dicie of a halo. He told the bewildered ex-slaves that they must form a colony of free Negroes. They must elect a colored mayor for Skidaway Island, and they must choose a council of Negroes to run the colony.

Dicie didn't understand all what he said, but Mammy kept nodding.

Soon as he finished praying and stepped back, a sea of black faces moved out from behind the trees and swarmed into the compound. The one thousand black men, with their women and children, had followed the soldiers to Brisbane.

"Hallelujah! This be our promised land," several of them shouted. "We ain't leaving till we get our land." A tall, thin, ragged newcomer armed with a stick rushed toward Dicie, who had moved out in front of her brothers. She jumped behind Mammy.

"Look here," Gus shouted at Reverend Houston. He grabbed the stick and struggled to push the man back outside the ring of Brisbane residents. "This be our home. Our crops. We live here all these years. Took care of this land ourselves, with no help from nobody since the war started. We ain't giving it up."

The crowd pressed forward. A woman from the compound fell as a newcomer pushed her out of his way. Instead of helping her up, two men stepped on her body. She screamed in pain.

Seeing the raging crowd, Mammy ordered Dicie and Cass, "Get back in the house and bar the door. Isaac, you, and Rufus grab me the axe."

While Dicie pulled Cass back into the tabby, Mammy turned and raised her arms at the oncoming crowd. "Halt, Halt! *Tawaqqafa!*" she screamed the panther-like screech Dicie always feared. Mammy then put two fingers in her mouth and gave an ear-splitting whistle as she snatched the axe from Rufus and waved it above her head.

The skinny newcomer fighting Gus for his stick looked up to her disfigured face, contorted with rage. When she whistled her shrill, terrifying notes, he dropped the stick and stumbled backward. The screaming mob froze in mid-frenzy.

Two buckra soldiers, guns drawn, hesitated for a moment, mesmerized by her otherworldly glower. They tiptoed cautiously toward Mammy, who was still swinging the axe.

A startled soldier quavered, "Stand back, woman! Order! Order."

From the crowd, voices whispered loudly, "Witch!'

As everybody watched, Reverend Houston raised the large wooden cross chained around his neck and stepped between the frightened soldiers and Mammy. Holding the cross high in front of him, "Peace," he roared. "We come in peace. Woman, put down that axe!"

When Mammy didn't move, Reverend Houston continued, "It is not our purpose to dispossess newly freed slaves. Surely there are empty dwellings on this big island."

"There and there. Not my house," Mammy's voice rang loudly, matching Reverend Houston's tone. She still held the axe over her head with both arms. She waved it toward two nearby decaying tabby cabins whose residents had died or disappeared.

"Big houses of the buckra all over the island be empty. And the old overseer's little wood house." She pointed to where Sampson had dwelled. "We ain't got no big house here, but there are many on the island, all vacant, or so I been told. Hampton Place over yonder had a big house, till them soldiers burned it. They's plenty of room without yo' folk putting us out our homes."

Still holding the cross high for protection, Reverend Houston stared at her as she spoke. The mob fell silent.

"And another thing," Mammy said. "We ain't got no real food, only what we can gather for ourselves. No flour, no sugar, no salt, no beef. How they gone eat if they stay here?"

"Never mind that," Reverend Houston said. "The soldiers will bring provisions."

Turning back toward the crowd, he pronounced, "We come in peace. She is right. We will continue to move across this fruitful island looking for empty houses and fields not being tilled."

Cautiously, Mammy laid the axe within easy reach behind her on the doorstep.

Reverend Houston directed the soldiers to move the throng away from the Brisbane tabbies and across the ditch.

In response to Reverend Houston's command, the lead soldier motioned to the other two, who marched to the front of the throng and hollered, "Let's go! Move on!"

The ragged, hungry ex-slaves formed a haphazard column between the soldiers and reluctantly began the trek to the next plantation. Keeping his pistol pointed at the crowd, the commander assumed a position at the rear of the newcomers and yelled, "Forward march!"

A few black faces turned toward Mammy as they passed. Peeking through a crack in the shutter, Dicie couldn't tell if they were merely curious or still hostile. Some almost appeared to admire Mammy's stand.

Soon only stragglers remained. After inspecting the filthy abandoned tabbies, they too followed the soldiers south toward Hibernia and the main part of the island.

But would the homeless mob be back?

Chapter Eighteen

January 1865

That night the exhausted family barred the door to the tabby but un-latched one of the shutters. They took turns keeping an eye on the moonlit clearing, should any of the interlopers return. Dicie moved her quilt under Mammy's bed, so she would be hidden while she slept.

"Wonder if we git any of them provisions?" Rufus asked. He was always hungry.

Dicie was too busy worrying about Tom and his daddy to care. What if the mob turned ugly again and tore up Little Tom's garden? Tom said they lived in half a tabby, same as she did. With only the two men sharing the room, would a desperate city family try to move in with them?

"We ain't seen the last of them," Mammy said. "Better sleep with one eye open." She stowed her roots and powders back in the sack, pulled out two bricks from the corner of the hearth, and poked the sack inside.

The family slept fitfully through the night. All was quiet except for the soft sound of water as Dicie rose to use the slop bucket. The black sky was barely lightening the next morning when Mammy rose, stirred the fire, and added kindling.

Lying wrapped in her quilt under Mammy's bed, Dicie dreamed that Daddy had risen before dawn to get to the fields when the great orange sun popped out of the marsh. The fire caught hold, and the smell of the smoke roused her. Half asleep, she imagined it was the smell of Daddy. Even after she woke, her nose was full of his scent.

Leaves crunched outside. Mammy turned from the fire and reached her hand to open the shutter.

Dicie stood and tiptoed to peek out. The smell of sweat blew through the crack where Mammy opened it. A man headed straight for their door. A tall man who walked like Daddy, but was thinner, with gray in his hair and a full beard.

"Lizzie, you in there?" the man asked.

Daddy's voice.

Dicie pushed Mammy aside and lifted the heavy piece of wood holding the door shut from its iron bracket. She flung the door open wide. She hadn't seen her father since winter of 1860.

"Dicie?" the man asked. He sounded like he wasn't sure. She had changed a lot in the last five years.

"Daddy," she screamed, throwing her arms around him. He smelled the same. What did it matter if strangers were lurking? Her daddy was home. He would keep them safe.

He hugged her tight, then lifted his face to look at Mammy. "Lizzie," he said.

Mammy stared, shocked; then her face softened. She put down the iron spider she was about to place on the coals. "Cuffie! Where you been?" Her voice was shrill in the small room.

Tears welled up in his eyes. Wet tracks glistened on his cheeks. "Long ways away. Down the coast, almost to Florida." He took Mammy in his arms. "I missed y'all so much. They took me to a plantation near a town called Darien, but out in the country. Soon as I heard the soldiers done freed Savannah, I walked all this way to git home to my family."

Mammy wrapped her arms around him. Her tears wet his shirt sleeve.

Daddy patted the back of her head and said, "We ain't slaves no more. Not sure the buckra know about it down at Darien. They ain't told us, but the drums was beating. I took a chance on leaving, hoping we be free. Nobody tried to stop me, but nobody saw me.

"Once I got to Savannah, I knew it true. They's burnt out houses outside Savannah and Union soldiers inside. Colored folk in town celebrating in churches. White folk hiding in they houses. Buckra want us out of the town. Us coloreds s'posed to git out to this island and start our own colony. You know 'bout it?"

Cass stepped over to Mammy and put his arms around her protectively.

"It's alright, Cass," Mammy said. "You don't remember yo' Daddy?"

"No," whispered Cass. "A boy say I ain't got no daddy."

"Well, you do now," Cuffie said. "I'm hoping I be home for good." He patted Cass's shoulder.

Rufus, Gus, and Isaac heard the voices and came in from the other side of the tabby. They looked on shyly, until Isaac stepped forward and gave Daddy a hug. Rufus followed. Gus stared at Daddy warily, then shook his hand.

"You boys take care of yo' Mammy?" Daddy asked.

The boys nodded their heads.

"Least me and Dicie had our men," Mammy said, smiling at the boys.

"Tell us about Savannah," Isaac begged.

"Full of people what got no home and short on food. That the reason they sending us out here. What y'all heard? Is they sending help, or just sending out starving, homeless niggers?"

"We ain't sure," Mammy said. "A preacher come by here yesterday talking about his thousand colored men getting land and provisions. He brung them out here, not expecting us. Good news—we be free. Bad news— he mean to take our home and land and give what we got to them people. We don't know what we gone do. Some trying to put us out."

Daddy stood there shaking his head for a minute. "Good thing I come home. Times bound to get better. The Lord has set us free."

Both of them bowed their heads for a silent prayer. Dicie grabbed hold of her daddy and prayed he never leave them.

Daddy let go of Mammy and reached into the sack slung over his shoulder. "You know I never come empty-handed." He handed Mammy a small blue glass bottle with liquid inside. "Go ahead. Open it."

Mammy unscrewed the stopper and lifted it. A sweet smell like Dicie never smelled before filled the room. Mammy stared at Daddy in disbelief.

He shrugged his shoulders. "I stopped at a empty house on my way up here. Most white folk done run away. I be looking for food but found this. I wanted to give you something if'n I made it here."

Tears rolled down Mammy's cheeks. "I ain't smelled scent like that since I left my home in Mauritania," she said. "My mammy had some just like it."

Mammy had a mother? Dicie was stunned. Never before had Mammy said a word about parents. Did she have a daddy too? Dicie inhaled the exotic odor. Questions flooded her head, but she knew better than to ask. Mammy kept sobbing.

Daddy pulled a paper sack out of the breast pocket of his overalls. "Don't cry, Lizzie. See what else I brung you. Salt. You gone need it to replace them tears."

Gus and Rufus jerked around. Mammy stopped crying and let out a loud hiccup.

"Salt?" Dicie said wonderingly. She reached out a finger to touch the sack. "We ain't seen salt since 1863. Where this come from?"

"Same place I got the scent," Daddy said. "I looked through the cupboards. They was mostly cleaned out, but I found this."

"Can't wait to sprinkle it on them 'taters we been eating without nothing on them," Rufus said.

Usually serious Gus sported a wide grin. "You ain't gitting it 'fo' me," he said.

"Hush!" Isaac whispered.

Outside the tabby wall, a twig cracked.

Chapter Nineteen

January 1865

Another stick snapped. Footsteps tramped outside the unbarred door. A second set of footsteps swished dead leaves near the threshold. After Dicie let Daddy in, nobody had returned the plank to its bracket.

Isaac rushed to bar the door. Too late. As he lowered the plank into its iron holder, the door smashed open, knocking the heavy piece of wood into his stomach. Mammy grabbed the axe. Cass dived under the bed. Dicie sprang to the door, pushing it backward with all her might. She was the one who opened it for Daddy.

Two strangers grabbed the edge of the door, wresting it from her hands.

"We looking for that witch what wouldn't let us stay here last night," the taller one said. "This gone be my forty acres and my house."

The short, heavy-set man behind him said, "Brung my own axe case you want to give me trouble." A spark from the fire illuminated the gleaming blade of a small hatchet in his hand. He used his free hand to grab Dicie, who was still trying to close the door. "If you don't git out my way this girl gone be the first to see I mean business."

Axe in hand, Mammy froze. "How we gone get out yo' way when you blocking the door?" she asked. The crowded room where they all cooked, ate, and slept was packed with Mammy, Daddy, the four brothers, Dicie, and two intruders.

The intruder scanned the inside of the tabby. Only one door for the whole hut. "Me and her gone back out the door. If all y'all ain't out by the time I count to ten, she gets it," he said.

He squeezed Dicie against his body, half lifting her as he dragged her over the threshold and out the door. She could hardly breathe. Her mind raced. She struggled to escape, but he only held her tighter.

Mammy and the boys filed out of the door, Mammy carrying her axe. Cuffie was the last one out, the sack slung over his shoulder. He kept an eye on Dicie, who squirmed.to get loose.

Soon as Daddy cleared the doorway, the tall, thin man ran inside the tabby.

"OK, we out now. Let her go!" Daddy said.

The man looked down at Dicie, still struggling in his grip. He raised one hand to pinch her breast. "I might just keep her," he said. He shifted his hold on the axe as he reached for Dicie's leg to lift her and carry her back into the tabby.

A blinding rage came over Dicie. Now she knew why Mammy used her spells to kill.

Feeling his grip loosen as he reached for her leg, Dicie struck a mighty blow against the man's throat. To avoid a second blow from her clenched fist, he turned his head and struggled to get a better grip on the axe. Dicie slipped out of his arms to the ground. She tried to roll away.

Enraged, the man bent over her, the axe now firmly gripped. "You gone be sorry," he growled, planting one filthy bare foot on her chest. She could barely catch her breath.

Kaboom! An acrid smell filled the cold air. Blood squirted from the man's back as he dropped to the ground on top of Dicie. Warm body fluids and oozing flesh covered Dicie's chest. With all her strength, she squeezed out from under the weight of the dead body and tried to stand.

Mammy whispered, "Well done, Cuffie."

As Dicie tried to catch her breath, the door to the tabby burst open. The tall, thin man rushed outside, one of Rufus's prized fishing nets clasped in his hand. His eyes lit on the gaping hole in his accomplice's back.

"You ain't getting away with this," he yelled. "We got a thousand men with us. We got the United States Army." He reached down and snatched pieces of paper from the dead man's pocket, while keeping an eye on Daddy.

Dicie scrambled to her feet and ducked around the edge of the tabby. Her chest ached from being stomped on. She remembered the man's hand on her breast, and her face burned. Daddy had saved her. But what were they supposed to do now?

Daddy still held the pistol in his hand. It looked like the ones buckra soldiers wore in their belts when they forced Isaac to shovel dirt for the barricades that were never finished. Where had it come from? It didn't matter. When the thousand men heard about the killing, they would all be dead.

"They ain't gone care about one dead nigger," Daddy said. "Specially, if nobody tells."

Blam! He fired a second shot straight at the man.

Dicie stifled a scream. The blast hurt her ears.

Daddy aimed good. The bullet pierced the man's shoulder. It knocked him backwards and blood spurted, but from her vantage point around the corner, Dicie could see he wasn't dead. Yet.

The man struggled to his feet and charged at Daddy. The blade of a knife glittered in his hand.

Mammy watched, frozen, still gripping her axe. Then, when the man charged, she sprung like magic. Raising her arms, she swung the axe from side to side. Like a dead chicken's, the man's head rolled on the ground separate from the rest of him.

Dicie's stomach wrenched. Gagging, she grabbed the rough tabby wall and vomited. Through the roaring in her ears, she heard the repeated blows of Mammy's axe and the crack of bones breaking.

"Step lively boys," Mammy commanded, keeping her voice low so the neighbors couldn't hear. Although they must have heard the gunshots, so far no one else had emerged from their tabbies.

Rufus, Gus, Isaac, even Cass clustered around her. "We got to hide all this quick. Don't know who might be coming. Rufus, fetch the shovels. Gus, get the wheelbarrow. Isaac, empty the slop bucket and bring it to me now. Rest of you, git out of my way."

After removing the dead men's clothes, Mammy swung the axe over and over cutting them into bits. "Tide just turned. We gone feed these two to the sharks."

Daddy stood there, mouth open, splattered with blood, staring at Mammy.

"Cuffie, if you run, they'll suspect us. We got to clean this up and mind our business same as usual," she said.

Mammy turned to Dicie. "Girl, you git down to the bluff and wash yo' whole self in deep water. Leave your clothes on and see if'n you can get the blood out. Don't get stuck in the mud. I know it January, but water ain't that cold.

"Cass, you go with her and make sure she don't pass out. Take a quilt with you."

Icy water. Just what she needed. Dicie couldn't scrub hard enough to wipe out the memory of the man's arm strangling her waist, his fingers on her breast, and the upheld hatchet aimed at her.

Mammy seized a shovel and began loading the remains of the two men into the slop bucket. Cuffie grabbed another shovel and followed suit, filling the wheelbarrow and a washtub. He signaled the boys to turn under the blood-soaked dirt around the door to the tabby and rake it smooth like Mammy did every night. Anyone who came by would expect fresh broom marks.

Daddy pushed the laden wheelbarrow toward a deep cut in the marsh. High tide had filled the cut with salt water and wrack. Soon the tide would ebb, rushing back through the marsh into the Atlantic. By the time the sodden bits of flesh and bone reached the ocean, a hundred tiny sea animals would have sucked nourishment from the chopped bodies.

Before she followed Cuffie, Mammy scooped up the papers the second man had pulled from the first one's pocket. The words on them were English. "*Laen*," she cursed in Arabic, hiding the papers down the front of her dress.

Dicie sprinted the quarter mile to the edge of the marsh. Even though the air was freezing, her body poured sweat by the time she squeezed through yaupon saplings and sharp-edged palmetto to the bluff. Plunging through the wrack into cold water froze her very innards but forced her to concentrate on getting clean instead of what had happened. Strangely, the saltwater felt warmer than the air. Knowing that any minute she could writhe with shivers or pass out, she gritted her teeth and sunk up to her chest. Bloodied clothing ballooned around her. She swished it clean as best she could.

Daddy stepped through brown, frost-bitten cattails and into salt water up to his waist and dumped the remains of the two men out of the wheelbarrow. A flock of hungry buzzards circled as the current bore decaying blood and flesh out to sea.

Behind him, Mammy stood amidst yaupon saplings on the bank. Dicie watched her lips moving as she uttered an incantation: *"They compassed me with words of hatred; and fought against me without cause. So let it come into his bowels like water, and like oil into his bones."*

Dicie reached for Cass's hand to pull herself out of the water. Wrapping the quilt around herself, she hurried back to the cabin, lips chattering. Her body shivered in the soggy clothes. The whole way home she prayed no more angry strangers had found their way to the compound.

Isaac held the door open for her. He had built up the fire and made tea from leaves Little Tom had brought. "Drink it down before you catch pneumonia," he said.

She collapsed on Mammy's bed, still clothed in her wet dress and shift. Goose pimples dotted her arms and legs. Isaac put the cup of steaming hot tea and honey to her lips, but she could hardly swallow. Her eyelids were so heavy.

Chapter Twenty

January 1865

The next thing Dicie knew, she was awakened by the rumble of Mammy and Daddy arguing. Someone had moved her to her pallet under their bed. The room was dark. Had she slept the day away?

"You got to stay," Mammy whispered from over her head. "Anybody what sees you leaving be wondering why. Then they gone be down on us like a duck on a June bug."

"What I'm gone do about this Colt 44?" Daddy asked. "I got to get off this island."

Dicie heard the soft sound of Spanish moss rustling as Mammy turned over on the old mattress. "You got a woman you got to git back to? Ain't no need to worry about that gun. We can bury it in the garden. Praise the Lord you had it. Where you git it?"

"Don't forget the neighbors," Daddy said, ignoring her questions. "Some of them's bound to of heard the commotion."

Dicie shuddered as she relived the cracking noise of Mammy's axe breaking the men's bones. Would that sound have carried to neighbors? Good thing only the brothers stayed in the other half of their tabby.

"They ain't gone admit to hearing nothing, even if they did," Mammy said. "Ain't nobody paying nobody to spy. The chillen and I need you bad till we see what's gone come of this 'freedom.'"

Dicie tried to keep quiet so she could hear more, but her throat was on fire and her head hurt. She couldn't help but let out a cough. It stuck in her throat, but Mammy heard.

"Hush! Girl waking up," she said to Daddy. "That a good sign." She threw off her quilt and dropped to the floor to put her hand on Dicie.

Snatching her hand back, she said. "Lord, this child be burning up with fever. Praise the Lord you done brung that salt. Let me get my herbs and mix her a potion."

Mammy pulled the two bricks out of the hearth and shook dried spirea and pennyroyal out of the paper sack hidden behind the bricks. "Isaac, fetch me the rest of the honey and some garlic buds."

While the spirea and pennyroyal tea steeped, Mammy dipped a thin, worn towel in the water bucket and stepped outside into frigid air. She spread the towel across the bare limb of a yaupon sapling. Once back inside, the sweet smell of mint from steaming pennyroyal cut through the stale smoky odor of the cabin.

Carrying more wet towels outside, she brought the first one in. She laid the half-frozen towel across Dicie's forehead and tucked it behind her neck. "Gus, fill me up a couple more buckets of water," she commanded, while she brought in two more chilled towels to wrap Dicie's chest and legs.

"Lizzie, let me do that." Daddy had gotten out of bed and splashed water on his face. "You mix her tea and say yo' piece over it. I take care of her fever."

He pushed Mammy aside and sat cross-legged on the floor next to the bed. Carefully, he pulled the quilt with Dicie lying unconscious on it out from under the bed. Quickly unwrapping the ragged towel, now hot with fever, from around her neck, he placed a freshly chilled one over her burning head. Her face eased as he patted the towel in place. She lifted her hand to touch his. He smiled and took her thin hot hand in his big one.

For a brief moment Dicie felt his love, and in her fever-induced confusion mistook him for Jesus. "No. It just Daddy," she remembered. "How you get here?" she asked. Before he could answer, she fell back asleep.

He draped another thin, cool towel over her from her shoulders to her bare feet, then stepped outside to hang the ones warmed by fever behind the cabin. "My only girl child," he whispered.

The icy towels tempered the burning in Dicie's body. Daddy's love reawakened her will to live. It didn't take long before she broke into a healing sweat. Coming back in from the cold, Daddy wiped the beads of moisture off her forehead. In his strong, low-pitched voice he sang:

"Little black sheep, where's your lamb
Way down yonder in the meadow
The bees and the butterflies
A-pecking out his eyes
The poor little black sheep
Cry Ma-a-a-mmy."

Dicie hardly heard the words, only the soothing melody. Her daddy was home. Daddy was singing to her. The empty space in her heart filled, blotting out the pain of the invader's fingers digging into her arms.

"Cuffie, why you singing that ugly old song?" Mammy asked. "Don't you know nothing better?"

Dicie opened her eyes, managed a weak grin, and whispered, "No, Mammy. I like that one." She patted Daddy's hand.

"Then you can sip this," Mammy said, holding out a steaming hot tin cup. "Drink up." She held the cup against Dicie's lips.

The hot liquid tasted bitter and sweet at the same time. Dicie sipped, wincing as it burned her tongue. An overwhelming need to sleep gripped her. She closed her eyes. "Please give me my quilt," she asked.

Daddy took away the wet towels and smoothed the quilt over her. Mammy sang:

"De river run wide, de river run deep,
O, bye-o, sweet li'l baby.
Dat boat rock slow, she'll rock you to sleep,
O, bye-o, sweet li'l baby."

"Ain't that a happier song?" Mammy asked, feeling Dicie's forehead. She turned to Cuffie and said, "She don't feel so hot now. Gimme some of that salt."

Cuffie handed her the precious salt he had just given the family. Mammy poured a few grains into her hand, then threw the salt into the fire. Blue flames flared from the red coals. Mammy chanted "sickness burns, health returns" three times, giving the fire her evil eye.

"Wasting salt," Cuffie grumbled.

As the fire blazed bright blue, Dicie fell into a deep healing sleep, holding on tight to her daddy.

Except for restless Isaac, the family stayed inside for the rest of the day. Through the next night, Gus and Rufus slipped back and forth from the other side of the tabby, checking on their little sister as she slumbered, oblivious to their movements.

Everybody but Dicie listened for gangs from the thousand blacks to return, fearing they would come any moment to wreak vengeance. Cold rain fell in misty waves. The axe and all the knives Mammy and the boys could muster lay in readiness. Cuffie cleaned and reloaded his pistol.

Providentially, the compound remained quiet. Dicie slept, dreaming of her daddy and Tom. When she woke, the wintry light in the cabin had dimmed almost to darkness. Little Tom had not come, but Daddy was still there next to her, asleep on the floor on a quilt of his own.

"I love you, Daddy," she whispered. "I wish you always be here."

He leaned over and patted the still damp but warm sheet covering her. "Baby, I love you, too," he said. "If only . . . ."

Chapter Twenty-One

January 1865

L ater that afternoon, Isaac opened the door just wide enough to see out. The family held their breath as he ran his eyes around the compound for strangers who might be looking for the two missing men. Then he slipped soundlessly into the cold rain.

Lizzie read her signs over and over. Cuffie paced nervously around the smoky, cluttered room. Cass tried to stay out of his way. Dicie sat up on her quilt and grabbed hold of Mammy's bed to pull herself up. The room swirled as she worried. Would Isaac meet an angry posse searching for the missing intruders?

At the table, as Lizzie shuffled and reshuffled her cards, she pleaded. "Cuffie, you got to stay." Twice she pointed to thin lines etched on the cards. "This one say good times coming. Ain't no death signs."

"Huh! Maybe you ain't reading 'em right," Cuffie said.

Dicie reached for his hand, but he shook her off and opened the door. Despite the rain and cold, he left, slamming the old door behind him. Upset, Dicie sat back down on her pallet. Why couldn't he and Mammy get along? No telling when he would come home.

The last gleam of weak winter sun barely lit the compound by the time Isaac scratched on the door for Mammy to let him in. He dashed to the warmest spot in front of the fire, shook out his wet clothes, and grinned.

"More preachers coming," he said. "S'posed to be here in the morning. Boys at Hibernia say men up north what call theyselves American

Missionary Board sending all the colored preachers in Savannah out here."

He paused to see what Mammy would say. Her face was hidden as she carefully re-barred the door. Dicie looked from one to the other.

Before Mammy could answer, Cuffie's knock sounded. As he walked into the room, the stink of moonshine overpowered the odor of smoke.

"Tell yo' daddy what you just said," Mammy said.

Looking from one to the other, Isaac continued, "We's supposed to set up a colony. Them preachers gone show us how. They's from a bunch of different churches. African Methodist Episcopal, not just them Baptists."

Dicie watched her parents taking in Isaac's news.

"What about buckra?' Cuffie asked. "They running this show?"

"Them town Geechees say General William T. Sherman of the United States Army s'posed to have all the say so. Savannah buckra done surrendered. They lucky they town ain't burnt like most of 'em."

Daddy nodded. "Saw two big houses burnt making my way here from Darien."

"Wipe yo' feet, boy," Mammy said, handing Isaac an old towel. Mud squished though his bare toes and made muddy tracks across the floor. "You hear anything 'bout what went on here?"

Dicie froze.

Isaac shook his head. "Ain't nobody say nothing 'bout missing any of them thousand niggers. 'Nother boatload coming with them new preachers".

Mammy let out a sigh of relief. Daddy leaned back in the old cane chair, and Dicie felt her stomach ease.

Wiping his toes with the towel, Isaac kept talking, "Them colored preachers and soldiers staying at the old massa's place on Little Comfort. Head soldier giving orders and backing 'em up. Ain't no buckra here 'cepting the Yankee soldiers. Most of that colored crowd camped out in barns near where the soldiers staying. The army done brung food for all of 'em. They eating in the old cookhouse down on Little Comfort, out of this rain. Oowhee! I could smell it all the way to Hibernia. Wish we had some."

Cuffie stood up and moved closer to the fire. "How you know they ain't nosing 'round here looking for trouble?"

"Look like rain been keeping 'em from wandering," Isaac said. "Saw 'em milling 'round Little Comfort barn. Nobody crossed the ditch between here and Hibernia 'cepting me. Weren't no tracks but mine. Ditch full of water."

Still sitting on the bed, Dicie breathed a sigh of relief.

"Told you signs be in our favor," Mammy said. "This island gone see crowd of folk coming like it ain't never seed before."

Cuffie stomped across the room and spit in the slop bucket. "How you know crowd of strangers gone be in our favor?" he asked.

Lizzie gave Cuffie her inscrutable stare. Nobody could say for certain what the signs would mean. Cuffie should have known they had to pray.

Next morning dawned clear. The cold rain had blown out over the ocean. Sun warmed the front of their tabby and rain puddles evaporated, leaving the air wet and heavy.

The storm had erased any sign of the struggle in front of their tabby. No blood or bones were visible. Dicie felt strong enough to swallow a mouthful of grits and sip Mammy's tea and honey concoction. No telling what else Mammy put in it.

Her dress had dried. Once the hot liquid hit her stomach, she sat up to grab the dress off the back of a chair. The smoky room swam, but she pulled the wrinkled dress over her head, then stood while Mammy watched her carefully. At first her steps were shaky, but she opened the door and made her way down the path to the shared outhouse. The fresh smell of wet earth cleaned her nose and throat. In the woods behind the tabby, six deer munched on newly sprouted sweet gum leaves. A buck had jumped the fence surrounding Mammy's garden and was devouring collard greens.

"Git!" she yelled at the buck. Her voice sounded hoarse, but the deer whirled and jumped over the fence, startling the herd. Six tails flashed white as the does followed the leader.

From the top of a tall pine came a shrill, "weep, weep, weep." An osprey was calling her mate to hurry back to the nest with breakfast.

Further up the compound, an old woman, her hair a mass of unraveling grey braids, stood in front of her dilapidated tabby, surveying the rain-drenched surroundings. Without making a sound of greeting, she nodded to Dicie.

A picture of herself as old as the crone flashed through Dicie's mind. Then she thought, "It a long time before I look like her." Gratitude toward Mammy and her spells sent renewed energy flowing through her body.

Behind her from the way she had come, Dicie heard the squeak of rusty hinges on the tabby door. Daddy stepped outside. He watched as she made her way down the muddy path and safely into the smelly outhouse. When she headed home, he was still there. Her heart warmed.

"Got to be on the lookout," he whispered as he closed the tabby door behind her. "Strangers could be hiding, spying on us."

She grabbed hold of his arm and wrapped it around her.

Later in the day, they heard the tramping of boots. Fear gripped the family. Dicie rolled back under the bed. While Lizzie hid behind the door, Cuffie peeked through a crack in the shutters. Soldiers marched into the center of the compound. This time they were accompanied by three Negro men, all wearing Sunday pants and coats and plain white collars that identified them as reverends. All wore shoes, a rarity on the island since the war began.

One soldier blew four blasts of a bugle to summon residents of the compound. Lizzie looked at Cuffie. He nodded and they eased timidly out the door.

White-haired Reverend Houston spoke first.

"God has blessed us. Hallelujah. I bring you the most Reverends James Williams and Garrison Frazier to tell you how we, his servants, plan to implement these blessings. Let us join together in prayer."

"Blessed be our father who has brought us out of bondage and who has heard the great cry of our people for land," the reverend began.

"You think that man for real?" Isaac whispered to Daddy, while Reverend Houston prayed.

"We got to wait and see," Daddy said.

At the close of the prayer, Lizzie boldly stepped forward. "What promise you can give us that our crops and our homes will not be stolen?"

"You may apply for land same as anyone else we bring here," Reverend Houston answered. He stepped back warily, remembering Lizzie and her axe.

"But we cain't read or write," she answered. Best not to let them know she could write in Arabic. Arabic wasn't going to do her any good anyway. "How we gone fill out papers?"

"We will show you. Many more are coming after us to help. They will build a school right here on Skidaway Island. Your children will soon be taught how to read and write. General Sherman has promised."

Lizzie fixed him with her best glare and said, "Can I get yo' personal word on that?"

Reverend Houston took a step toward her. "You the woman who had the axe?"

She stood silently.

"Woman, give me your name," he said.

Mammy kept staring, her lips barely moving. It looked to Dicie like she was reciting a spell, but no sound came out.

Reverend Houston stepped close enough for Dicie to see the threads of black in his white beard. His tone softened. "I come in the love of Christ. I promise I will not harm you or your children. If you give me your name, I will bring you a paper promising no one can evict you from this acre of land." He took off his hat and wiped his brow. As Mammy looked up, he directed a clerical smile her way.

"Lizzie. My name is Lizzie," she said.

Turning to the nearest soldier, the holy man said, "I call upon you to be my witness. I will return with a writing promising that this land is set aside to Lizzie."

Reverend Houston and Mammy touched hands and nodded. "Lizzie, I see that you are a woman of influence on this plantation. Please pass the word to the other people of Brisbane that we plan no harm to any former slaves." The smile he gave her warmed considerably.

She inclined her head slightly.

"By the way," Reverend Houston added, "all you people will have to choose a second name just like white folk. The name will be the same for yourself and for all your children. When I come back with the paper for you, I will add the second name you choose."

He let that sink in, then continued, "You may now legally marry. Once a woman joins in holy matrimony with a man, her last name will be the same as her husband's."

Cuffie and Lizzie stared at each other. Lizzie glanced back at her children. Cuffie put his arm around her.

"Wonder what name Tom going to choose?" Dicie said.

"Why you want to know that?" Isaac teased. "You thinking 'bout sharing his name?"

Dicie stamped her foot and pushed Isaac. Why was he putting his nose in her business? And he guessed right. If Tom picked a last name and they got married, same as the buckra, wouldn't it be her name too?

Chapter Twenty-Two

March–April 1865

Where was Little Tom? Every day Dicie listened for his step on their hidden path, and watched for his tall, thin figure to come bounding up the road. More than a month had passed since he and Dicie watched the thousand freedmen land on the island. Since that fearful day, she hadn't seen him. He didn't know about the two dead men or that Dicie had been sick. What happened? Now it seemed as if he had never been her closest friend.

February and March had been filled with hope and danger. The two dead men never left her thoughts. Even though she could never speak of what happened, every day brought news she longed to tell him.

Across the ditch, mobs of strangers milled around the empty space where Hibernia's praise house used to be. Trampled weeds were covered with tents, some sewn of strong canvas, most a hodgepodge of scraps tied or pinned together. Fresh-cut saplings held the tents erect, but they swayed perilously when fierce ocean gales blew across the marsh.

Memories of singing on the grounds outside the praise house, watching Tom with his father, snuggling next to her own daddy filled her with sadness. The pretty girl who sashayed away from her mammy and plopped down next to Tom in front of all the churchgoers was never far from Dicie's mind. Did the wench have anything to do with Tom staying away?

What if Tom had been hurt or killed? The thought of harm coming to Tom made her shiver, but she pushed it aside. The drum still beat. Tom must be alive and well. Then why didn't he come?

The walls and roof of the old Hibernia master's house, with its hedge of overgrown camellias, bustled with Yankee soldiers. The good, stout overseer's house was occupied by newly freed slaves. Surely some of the thousand newcomers had helped themselves to tabbies in the Hibernia slave quarters. Had any of them ousted Tom and his daddy?

During the last bad storm, the roof on Sampson's ramshackle former headquarters fell in. Just like the abandoned tabbies on Brisbane, Sampson's cabin was full of dead leaves and mildew. Before the onslaught of newcomers, Brisbane had become a silent, peaceful place, inhabited mostly by the elderly and women. Now, bands of the one thousand black men with their women and children drifted aimlessly across Brisbane, looking for something to steal. Newly arrived families from Savannah, homeless and lusting for land, joined them. Hungry men and women lingered behind the tabby where Dicie stayed, looking greedily at Mammy's garden, now planted and sprouting corn, onions, lettuce, and sweet potatoes.

Mammy, Isaac, and Cass took turns guarding their plot. Someone from the family was always outside with a hoe. Dicie was too frightened from the encounter with the invaders to guard it by herself, but she spent most of her days working the rows, not far from her brothers or Mammy.

Reverend Houston's promises of teachers and land did not materialize, even though Isaac again brought news, "Them Yankee soldiers say more church people a-coming. White and colored."

"Then why ain't none of 'em here?" Mammy asked. "All them promises ain't worth nothing."

A month passed with no sign of Reverend Houston and no paper with a promise of land for Mammy. No teachers showed up.

"Done told you how it would be," Cuffie told Lizzie.

At least he still stuck around. Dicie held her breath, but Mammy didn't start an argument.

On a warm day in April right after Dicie turned fifteen, three soldiers came to a halt in the compound and sounded the bugle. Men of the cloth followed behind them, at least ten or maybe more. Reverend Houston, with his full white beard, wasn't among them.

"Interrupting my work to tell us more lies," Cuffie grumbled. His crab traps lay ready to carry to the river.

The first preacher called on everyone to bow their heads for a long, rambling prayer.

"Hope to hell they ain't all going to pray this long," Gus whispered.

The next preacher droned on about a colony run by the thousand colored men who had invaded the island. These men knew nothing about Skidaway Island.

Dicie stopped listening and went back to worrying about Tom. Where was he? Why had he missed his usual trips to see her? Had he gotten hurt?

The pretty girl who used to sit with Tom at Sunday services niggled at her mind. Did the hussy still stay at Hibernia? Tom had never mentioned her, and Dicie was afraid to ask. How much time did he spend with her when he didn't come to see Dicie? Did he tell her how pretty she was, just like he told Dicie?

She squirmed around on her stump and whispered to Isaac, "You seen Little Tom when you been over to Hibernia?"

Isaac frowned. "I'm trying to listen to this preacher. Tom be right where he always at. Who you think beating that drum?"

"I thought it his daddy," Dicie answered. "Did Tom ask about me?" She squeezed her hands into fists, waiting for his answer.

"Hush up," Isaac said. "I didn't get to talk to him. He done took over a lot of the drumming from his daddy. I can't stop him from working. Next time I goes, I can ask that girl, Bella. She spend a lot of time with him."

Bella? Was that the girl who used to sit with Little Tom at services? The one with the flower in her braids? Dicie's face burned. "Who Bella?" She demanded. She knew Tom didn't have a sister.

"Hush up. The man talking," Isaac said again, reaching over and putting his hand over Dicie's mouth. "All us boys knows Bella." He grinned but wouldn't tell Dicie anything more.

After the soldiers and men of the cloth headed onward toward Springfield Plantation to broadcast the news, Dicie's family took a seat in the sun on splintery benches outside the cookhouse.

"I think we should cut and run," Cuffie said. "Them rapscallions what followed the soldiers over here gone be running everything. I sure as hell don't want to have to kill no more of 'em."

Lizzie closed her mouth and narrowed her eyes like he had slapped her. She raised her fist in the direction of the tabby. "We's got shelter. My garden's planted. I got my herbs where I know how to find 'em. Where we gone run to? The war ain't even over. Remember when the buckra shot up Charleston and thought they done finished with the war?"

Cuffie stood and pointed his finger at her. "You think that man's gone bring you that piece of paper? You trying to catch moonshine, thinking he making good. What promise the buckra ever kept? And even iff'n he do show up with it, what good you think that piece of paper gone do you when Massa Warren comes back? Soldiers be gone. He run right over us."

"Better the devil you know than the devil you don't," Lizzie answered. She had that stubborn look on her face. "And Reverend Houston ain't no buckra."

"Same thing" Cuffie said. "Buckra pulling his strings."

Dicie swiveled her head from one to the other. A tear formed and ran down her cheek. Did her daddy mean to leave them again? He had said he loved her.

If Daddy left, would he take her and Mammy and Cass with him? If she left, who would watch this year's newborn minks when they first scampered out of the den? Who would guard the tiny spotted fawns from the rambling, heavy-footed newcomers? What would become of Mammy's garden, already fulfilling its spring promise?

Whether they left or stayed, would she ever see little Tom again? Tom's father might leave and take Tom with him. They were all free now. Negroes were traveling back to Africa. Big Tom knew the language and customs of the land he came from. Her feelings for his son would be hopeless if either family left Skidaway Island. Everything she cared about was falling apart.

"If you got to go, then go," Lizzie said to Cuffie. She was crying now. Dicie got up and put her arms around her mother. Mammy wasn't always easy to be around, but she was the only grown-up Dicie and Cass could count on. Her older brothers helped, but they came and went as they pleased. She might not see Rufus or Gus for days. They were grown men. Even Isaac was hardly around anymore.

"Daddy, please don't leave us," she said. She let go of Mammy and put her arms around her daddy.

He patted her arm, then jerked his body away. Tears stung Dicie's eyes. How could he?

As he turned to leave, wagon wheels creaked. Incoming boot-clad footsteps tramped down the path. Cuffie halted.

Dicie raised her wet face.

Two soldiers approached, pulling a wooden cart loaded with heavy cotton sacks. "Provisions," they said. "Just like the General promised." They rolled the cart to the sagging cookhouse door and unloaded four bags of cornmeal, a barrel of molasses, a bucket of lard, and a side of bacon.

Cuffie's mouth dropped. Lizzie stopped crying. A smile twisted her scarred face.

Dicie wiped the tears off her cheeks with both hands. Offering a prayer of thanks, she jumped up to help stow the provisions inside.

Chapter Twenty Three

April 1865

Over the next month, even more strangers tramped through the Brisbane compound, sometimes opening the door to Mammy's tabby, and gaping at the startled family. Worse yet, when Daddy and the older brothers were out hunting or fishing, interlopers walked right in.

The tabby door squawked one day when Dicie and Mammy were alone tending the garden. Dicie ran to the corner of their home. A man stole out of the door carrying her mother's much-used frying pan.

She screamed, "Daddy," but he wasn't there. How would they eat without the spider? They used it to cook almost everything.

Sharpened hoe in hand, Mammy burst around the corner, screaming like a panther, and swinging her hoe. The man dropped the frying pan and tripped over a fallen log in his hurry to get away. After that, the men in Dicie's family took turns staying near the house, so at least one was always within earshot.

Dicie was too scared of strange men to stay by herself at the hut, but alone in the woods, she felt safe. The wild thickets of wax myrtle and dense canopy of live oaks shielded her. Tall palm trees were silent sentinels standing guard over her. City folks, newcomers to the maritime jungle, stayed close to beaten paths. Whether following the deer to their hidden places under Virginia creeper or walking the shoreline bluff to look for mink's pups, Dicie knew the woods like the cracks in the ceiling of the tabby. But just in case, she kept her ears open for a twig snapped by human footsteps.

With Cuffie home, their farming prospered. He looked at the burgeoning garden and said, "Might as well act like this new thing gone last." He rubbed his hands together and hugged Mammy. "Maybe we can make some money."

Searching the empty barns and corrals for forgotten tools, he helped himself to a plane with a broken blade and a half-buried wrench, rusted shut. He kicked at sweet gum saplings shooting up in the empty corral, and said, "Wish we could get hold of a mule. What happened to 'em?"

Isaac scowled. "What animals Sampson ain't drove to the ferry when he took off, them Johnny Rebs stole. They was using 'em to haul in the cannon works what we made dirt mounds for. Once they hauled all them guns back off the island, we never saw them mules again."

"Damn! Sure could use one now," Cuffie said. "Might as well clear out a piece of woods behind the garden before one of 'em new rascals claim it. Grow us some extra corn and tomatoes to sell in town."

Cuffie and the boys chopped down trees and dug up roots with rusted tools and bare hands. Without a mule, Cuffie hitched the plow to himself while Rufus forced the blade into densely root-bound soil. Dicie and Mammy watched in awe. Alone, the women could hardly have cleared enough for an extra row of corn.

"Bless you, Cuffie," Mammy said.

Drifters wanting to claim Mammy's garden for themselves took a long look at Rufus, Gus, and Isaac, all big hard-muscled men, born and bred on Brisbane and determined to stay. The newcomers passed on to easier pickings in the abandoned cotton fields. Rude shelters made of logs or boards stolen from rotting barns sprouted among waist high weeds. A family moved into Sampson's old house, pulling out broken rafters and patching the roof.

The last of the young ones who lived in the other half of Mammy's tabby had left for the mainland. The old mother had died. Dicie's brothers, Rufus, Gus, Isaac, and Cass cleaned out what was left of it. Now they stored their belongings and slept there. With only Mammy, Daddy, and Dicie living in the original side, the room felt spacious, except when the brothers crowded in for meals. Gus and Rufus sometimes stayed out all night with their women. Dicie didn't know where, but Daddy must have. Some nights he left with them.

When he didn't return, Mammy's mouth turned down, and she muttered to herself. Late at night after Dicie fell asleep, she sometimes woke to the smell of whiskey and the rumbling of whispered arguments.

More days passed with no word from Little Tom. He had to be on the island because the drums sounded every day announcing a new wave of intruders. Dicie worked the garden even harder to keep from worrying about why he no longer came to see her. Did he think about her at all? Or was he spending all his time with that wench, Bella?

Late in March the reverends sent a soldier to announce a date in April when all colored men on the island would elect a governor. Once a date was set, Reverend Houston and others who wanted the job flocked to the compounds, politicking and praying. Each speaker had a different idea about how to run the colony, but all agreed the headquarters were to be on Brisbane.

"I'm sick of them preachers," Daddy said. "They gone be stealing our land. Don't see why headquarters got to be here. They better not make me sorry we cleared space for more garden."

"Our peas and tomatoes growing like lightning. Rosa done told me she'll carry 'em to market soon as they's ripe," Mammy said, flipping through her fortunetelling cards. "Garden got to be tended. Ain't no guarantee them highfalutin city niggers gone stay."

"One of them candidates buying whiskey made right here on this island. He promise a full pint to every man who help him get elected," Daddy said. "Soon's I finish this garden, I'm gone help him."

Mammy rolled her eyes and muttered, "Demon rum. Don't vote for him."

"That's why women can't vote," Daddy said. "They ain't no judge of character."

Mammy gave a loud harrumph as she slapped down her next card.

"Nother thing," he said, "we all gone have to come up with a last name, just like Reverend Houston say. Ain't too many Cuffies, but they got to have a way to figure out if a man named Joe done vote twice. I be thinking 'bout Lincoln. What y'all think of that?"

"I done already told them, my new name be Houston," Mammy said. "Soldier say he gone write it on the deed to my land."

The day came for all the men to vote. The election was to be held at the old cookhouse on Brisbane. The compound was a sea of men, old and young, drunk and sober. Jars of moonshine passed from hand to hand, each man taking a gulp, swallowing and spitting.

Mammy and Dicie watched through a crack in the shutters of the tabby. Cuffie warned them not to go outside, even to the privy.

"Use the chamber pot. Too many men and too much drinking," he said. "Shine'll make a man do things he wouldn't think of without it."

Remembering the strength of the man who grabbed her, Dicie didn't need to be told twice, but Mammy shook her head. She watched a skinny white-haired man stumble and fall, smashing his glass jar of shine in the weeds right in front of her peephole. He lay there in the broken glass moaning, while three other men stepped over him. One let out a string of cusswords as broken glass pierced his bare feet.

"Making a mess for us to clean up. If women be running this here election, it would go a lot better," Mammy said. "First thing I do be outlaw 'shine."

Back in the tabby, Dicie and Mammy listened to shouts and cussing from the direction of the cookhouse. They kept the door tightly barred, except when they recognized Cuffie's loud whisper. He ducked his head in the door every so often but, didn't come home for good until late that night. After he fell into bed in the dark, the piercing rumble of his drunken snores woke Dicie. Mammy didn't speak a word.

Next morning, Cuffie ate his cornbread and greens in frowning silence. Mammy let him sit there until his forehead smoothed. "Lord, I got a headache. Shouldn't have taken all that shine them boys handing out." He gave Lizzie a faint smile. "You gone be happy," he said. "That Reverend Houston got elected governor. Man giving out whiskey didn't make but second place."

Mammy reached over and patted his hand.

A week later more groups of strangers appeared. Two white men, a colored man, and a colored woman accompanied the soldiers. Reverend Houston, now Governor Houston, introduced them with his usual greeting and prayer.

"Today I have good news," he announced. "These blessed teachers are who you have all been waiting for. They signed a commitment with the American Missionary Board to bring reading and writing to Skidaway Island."

As always, Mammy tried to keep from showing her feelings, but a red flush spread from her neck up over her pale, tan face. Looking at the crooked smile Mammy couldn't suppress, Dicie could tell Mammy was the happiest she had ever been.

"It will be up to you to find them a place to stay on Skidaway Island," Reverend Houston said, looking straight at Mammy. "Lizzie, I'm calling on you to help."

To the surprise of everyone, Mammy stepped forward across the trampled weeds and embraced each of the teachers. Tears of joy splashed down her cheeks.

"Praise the Lord. Welcome to this island," she told each one.

After that day, incoming teachers of all races hiked across the island to Mammy's hut. Told about her by Reverend Houston, they came to consult on the number of children living on the island, the distance to other plantations, and the best place to set up a school. Mammy, who had never traveled further from Brisbane than to Hibernia, followed them up and down the island.

"They gives me the taste of freedom," Mammy said. "This be a mighty small island but traveling it remind me how far I come from home." Standing outside the tabby in the warm spring air, she stretched her arms wide.

"Tell me about home," Dicie begged, not expecting an answer. "Where you come from?" She had asked Mammy hundreds of times, but still didn't know anything except that she was born in a place called Mauretania where she spoke Arabic. Dicie hardly understood where Mauretania was. Mammy told her it was many days travel across the same Atlantic Ocean she saw from the edge of Skidaway Island. Dicie and her brothers had never been off the island. Only Daddy had been to the mainland.

Her travels up and back the length of Skidaway Island must have loosened Mammy's tongue. To Dicie's surprise, instead of saying, "Hush up child," she kept talking, so low it almost sounded like she was talking to herself.

"I got carried 'cross hot sand, not like this here sand, but dry. Then through big waves in a little boat." Mammy's face darkened and the scar rose higher on her cheek. Her voice sunk to a whisper, but Dicie heard, "a terrible dungeon chopped out of rock. Then thrown in the bottom of a big ship, like hell but worse. The fever made me disremember."

Dicie hugged her. Something terrible must have happened for Mammy to end up far away from home with her face all cut up. For all the years of Dicie's life, Mammy's past had been too painful for her to speak of.

Mammy blinked back tears and continued.

"When I finally got let out on this Skidaway Island, I didn't know if I would live or die," she said. "To tell the truth, I didn't much care. Then after 'bout four months, I birthed Gus. I knew I had to live. He so little, old women say Jesus gone take him home, but my Mammy done taught me how to make him live, and I did. Fooled them women. My same herbs grow here, in this strange new land, halfway round the world. Everything I need is here. That be a powerful sign."

Tears rolled down her cheeks. Rufus and Isaac put their arms around her. Dicie looked at usually stoic Gus. Tears were in his eyes.

"And now we is finally free. Thank you, Jesus," Mammy said.

When the tears finally stopped, Mammy turned to Dicie. "My Mammy taught me all the spells, and how to root, and how to heal. Now, I got to finish teaching you."

Chapter Twenty-Four

April 1865

As March warmed into April, leaves budded on the vines, yellow flowers glittered in towers of blooming Carolina jasmine, and Mammy kept her promise to Dicie.

"Them yellow flowers sure pretty," Mammy said. "But, lookee. You ain't gonna see no deer nibbling on 'em. That why they growing everywhere. What you think that mean?"

Dicie thought for a minute. "They taste bad," she guessed. She stuck out her hand to pick one of the brightly colored blooms.

Mammy looked disgusted. "Taste bad? You think a starving deer care about how something taste? One bite of them yellow flowers'd strike a deer plumb dead. Even the dumb deer know that. Don't you even think about picking 'em without scrubbing yo' hands good afterwards."

Dicie snatched her hand back. How could something so pretty hurt her?

"However, if, and I do say if, you want to make somebody or something mighty sick or worse, it's handy to have some of them dried leaves. Just be careful you keep track o' what's what," Mammy said.

Further into the woods they passed nasty-looking tangles of stickers. "See them thorns there, all twisted up in the wax myrtle?" Mammy pointed to long green canes bursting upward from a dried-up sticker bush.

The canes were hidden between branches of feathery wax myrtle. When Dicie stepped closer to look, she felt a sting on her leg. Last year's withered gray cane still had sharp thorns. Bare vines ran up the tree, same as the Carolina jasmine but with thorns. A closer look at the new canes showed more thorns, but also bright green leaves and swelling rosebuds. A sweet smell floated around the vines.

"That there is a good vine," Mammy said. "They call it the Cherokee rose. It's good to eat 'long as you don't eat the seeds inside the fruit. Fruit is sweet but kind-a skimpy. Look like a little apple. Best thing about it, the apple be good medicine. Women eat it to help with they monthly bleeding. Men take it when they can't please they women. The roses be busting into bloom any time now. Be careful gathering it. Most of it be too high in the tree to reach and you can't hardly climb the tree 'cause of the thorns. We can get one of your brothers to help. Any flowers left on the vine that turn into fruit, we want to pick. Lot of call for it and folk will pay. Cherokee rose don't bloom but a few days a year."

Dicie wiped a trickle of blood off her leg and stepped back from the wicked-looking bush. "Can we get Daddy to help?" she asked.

Mammy frowned. "If he still be here by the time the fruit gets ripe," she said.

Why did she say that? Daddy hoed the garden just yesterday. He didn't have any other place to go. Mammy didn't make any more sense about Daddy than when she said pretty flowers were evil and dangerous thorns were good. Would she ever learn why grownups said the things they did?

"What's monthly bleeding?" she asked. Mammy never did finish telling her about it. "You mean like on my leg here? Hope I don't get scratched up every month."

Mammy dropped the stem of leaves she had picked and put her arms around Dicie. "Lord, Chile. I ain't used to having a daughter. A woman gets blood every month from where the baby comes out, once she old enough to make a baby. You be getting yours soon. Sometime it hurt your stomach. If it hurt, these here Cherokee rose petals will help stop the pain. I'll make a nice, warm tea for you out of them and show you how to keep yourself clean."

Mammy hardly ever hugged her. Dicie turned her face against her mother's chest and breathed in the warmth of her skin. If only Mammy was like this all the time.

In April the forest animals birthed their young. Her days were busy with Mammy teaching her the roots and herbs and how to use them. While she learned, she hoed the garden and hauled water for unending household chores. When she could, she slipped away to wander through the woods. Tiptoeing past their hiding places, she made sure all the new-born animals were safe.

One afternoon Mammy and Dicie worked side by side digging potatoes for dinner, not speaking, but in companionable silence. A cool breeze cut through the warm sun, blowing away the pesky biting gnats called "no see 'ums." The plentiful winter harvest and healthy shoots of corn popping through freshly turned dirt gave both women hope for the future.

After spying on the sleepy spotted fawns, she felt closer to Mammy. Mammy must love her, even if she didn't always act that way. She had risked everything to protect Dicie from the intruders. She kept Dicie near while she worked. Now she was passing on her knowledge of the super-natural roots. Someday Dicie would have children of her own to protect. She vowed to teach them Mammy's secrets.

When the two women had put enough potatoes in the croker sack and started back toward the front of the tabby, Dicie burst out, "I know where a doe hides her fawns. Want me to show you? It ain't far."

"I'm plumb wore out. Don't feel up to looking for more deer to eat my garden," Mammy grumbled.

"Please, Mammy. They so sweet," Dicie said. "The mother leaves 'em hid while she hunts for food. Then she comes back and nurses 'em."

Mammy smiled, but so quickly Dicie almost hadn't seen the slight lifting of her mouth. "I know how babies look," Mammy said. "God makes 'em like that so they mammies don't think about all the worry and trouble of raising 'em."

Dicie's shoulders slumped. They carried the potatoes inside the tabby and set them on the old wooden table. Each swallowed a dipper of water from the bucket. Dinnertime was two hours away. Unexpectedly, Mammy took Dicie's arm and said, "Show me them baby animals."

Dicie smiled. Together the two women crept silently past the neat garden and into the forest. Following a low path tramped through the underbrush by passing deer, they tiptoed to a pine-needled depres-sion under an old cedar tree. The fragrant limbs almost reached the ground. In the shadows underneath, two spotted fawns slept, unaware of mother and daughter.

"Ain't nothing like a baby," Mammy said. A gentle relaxing of her features smoothed the scarred side of her face. "You was the sweetest little thing."

"Mammy, when you gone teach me to make a love potion where I don't have to give it to the person?" Dicie asked.

"You studying that Tom again?" Mammy asked. "Or you got somebody else you looking at?"

Dicie whispered, "Tom." She turned her head away and opened her eyes wide so the tears wouldn't fall out. "I reckon that last potion you help me make for Tom done wore off."

"Early days yet," Mammy said. "Men be hard to 'cipher. Signs say he coming back, but right now you just got to wait. You still young. Too young, really. While you waiting, you got time to keep learning these herbs. Next, I got to teach you how to say more of the spells."

"Please, Mammy." Dicie clasped her hands together. Tom had acted like he cared about her. He even hugged her the last time they were together, right before they ran back with news of the huge crowd of Negro strangers landing on Skidaway. How could he have dropped her without a word?

Mammy looked at her downcast face and the tears she was fighting to hide. "You need to be learning 'stead of studying some man. Taking care of a baby is hard work." Then her face softened. "I'll think about it. You know, it be a lot harder to root somebody you don't see, than someone who's right there next to you where you can put a little something in they 'shine."

"Tom don't drink 'shine," Dicie said. "He say it make folk act stupid. He need to be sharp to beat the drum."

"One more thing to like about the boy," Mammy smiled. Then, thinking about Cuffie, she folded her lips. Cuffie sure loved his 'shine.

"You didn't save a little piece of him like a hair or fingernail, did you?" Mammy asked. "We could use that. I know you ain't got his footprints nowhere. It more than three months since he been here."

"No, Mammy. I never thought of that. All I got to remember him by is a dried flower he picked off a sweet potato vine and give me."

"Sweet potato flower! That's kinda red. I think it'll do. We got plenty of dried corn husks I done saved. Now here's what you need to do."

When they got back to the tabby, Mammy pulled out her bag of herbs and rummaged through it. All the men, even Cass, were away. She found three dried husks. "This here be plenty. I'll cadge a bit of string what Isaac uses to make his nets."

She twisted and tore the corn husks into a shape that resembled a person, then used the string to tie a neck, two arms, and two legs. Finally, she cut into the trunk of the person and pulled a small bit of husk straight out from the body, right over where the legs began.

"What that for, Mammy?" Dicie asked, pointing to the projection. It looked like an extra arm, but nobody had a third arm where the corn husk man's was.

"You find out all about that if'n this charm works," Mammy said. "Fetch me your flower. We gone put it in a little sack with the man and you gone have to open the sack and say this spell into it three times a day. You say, "Tom, love, love, love. God is love. Tom and Dicie. God give us love."

"How many days, Mammy?"

"Till it works, Chile. Till it works."

Chapter Twenty-Five
April 1865

On a steamy afternoon later that April, Dicie sat cross legged on the floor of the piney woods next to Mammy's garden, chanting the words Mammy used to heal her: "sickness burns, health returns." So many spells to remember. Already that day she had twice said the love spell for Tom. So far it hadn't worked. She wished Mammy could say the spell for her, but Mammy said a girl could only make a man fall in love with her by saying the words herself. Would her magic ever work as good as Mammy's?

The late spring air was still and stifling hot in the shade. Inside the garden where Cass and Cuffie hoed shoots of pesky clover was even hotter. Hardly any breeze stirred.

Suddenly leaves on the big oaks shading the compound began to tremble. Crows chattered. A vulture rose leisurely from the top of a tall pine and made ominous circles in the sky above the garden. Long, slow drumbeats rumbled. Boom! Boom! Booom! Dicie covered her ears, but the deep bass notes penetrated her hands. She rushed from her spot in the shade to the garden to grab hold of Daddy. The drum beat the rhythm of death.

Mammy had traipsed off with a group of white teachers looking for likely places to build the new school. The teachers had already taught Mammy to write her name, "Lizzie." Her excitement lit the tabby when she brought home an old slate and a few pieces of chalk. She wrote "Lizzie" and "Houston" over and over. Every spare minute she practiced writing the English alphabet. Soon as Dicie got through learning the roots, Mammy promised to teach her. Where was Mammy now? Surely the drum didn't beat for her.

"Don't you worry, baby," Cuffie said. "Daddy here. We pray it ain't Mammy. Or nobody we know." They hurried into the tabby.

Isaac had been squatting in the sparse shade of the front of the tabby, knotting a fish net. He dropped the net and sprinted to Hibernia to find out what had happened. A half hour later he came running back.

Wiping the sweat off his forehead with his bandana, he gasped, "President Abraham Lincoln. Somebody done shot him. Headquarters just got the telegram in Savannah. Sent a private out here to tell the soldiers."

"Lord, help us," Daddy said.

Fear gripped Dicie's stomach. She clasped Daddy's hand tighter and put her other arm around him. "What happen now?" Nothing stayed the same from one day to the next.

"We got to wait and see," Daddy said, his hands shaking.

The fear in his eyes scared Dicie even more.

President Lincoln was their savior. Everybody knew that. But colored men and women who came to Skidaway from the outside told stories that struck fear into hearts of the Skidaway ex-slaves. Some of Lincoln's high officials weren't friends of the Negro.

In December of 1864, thousands of desperate men and women followed the Union army as Sherman's soldiers marched to the sea, burning and looting along the way.

Around Skidaway Island's campfires, whiskey flowed while survivors told their stories. The former slaves listened eagerly, grabbing up every scrap of information. Now that they were free, news flashed like lightning around the island. They were anxious to know which side would control their future. Would the promise of freedom be snatched away?

Dicie's brothers listened as a strong dark-skinned fellow with a haunted look in his eyes sipped a cup full of moonshine and recounted his chilling tale. "We was almost to Savannah, when we got stopped at Ebenezer Creek. Them soldiers built a pontoon bridge so all us could get across. The Yankee General Jefferson Davis done told us to wait till the whole army got t'other side, case Johnny Rebs be hiding over there. Them guards pointed rifles at us, making sure us let soldiers git over first. A few of us started to follow the soldiers anyway, just like we been doing all week. Some made it; some they pushed in the creek."

He shook his head at the memory. Smoke from the piney fire swirled around his head bringing on a spell of coughing. He recovered and reached for a piece of cornbread before he continued.

"We trusted 'em. They shared food what they took from white folks along the way. They kept us safe from the Johnny Rebs while we slept at night. But I still be leery. Too many of us."

The men around the fire nodded. "Jest right," several said. "Cain't trust nobody in this world. Nobody but Jesus."

The dark-skinned man kept on, "I ain't see how Rebs could be t'other side of the creek. They been behind us all week. Nothing but trees over there, but the Yanks said Rebs could'a come up from Savannah and be planning a ambush."

He took another bite of the cornbread and chewed before he told more.

"It weren't a wide creek, but deep and running with the tide. Being a real cold day, I figured the noise of t'other army would have reached right back to us if'n they been near."

Gus and Rufus nodded. They knew how easily sound traveled over water. Breathing in the smell of pine smoke, they kept silent for fear the newcomers would run them off. Little Tom sat near them, taking in every word.

The men closest to the fire nodded. "Amen," one or two shouted. "Sho' 'nough. Can't trust nobody."

The storyteller took a big gulp of whiskey and said, "So when I seen the last of them Yanks jump on the bridge, I up and followed. Soon as I got on the bridge, the Johnny Rebs came up behind us, shooting."

Gus gasped. Rufus and Tom held their breath.

The storyteller shook his head. "Yankee soldiers pulled the pontoons away from where I come from. Man jumping on after me fell straight in the water. I heard the splash. That water cold as ice. None of us knew how to swim.

"Them Johnny Rebs charged, mad as everything, and shooting wild at all us poor niggers left behind. Yankee guards turned around and shot at the Rebs. We was trapped in between. Both sides hit them waiting on the bank.

"What be left of the bridge bobbed up and down while the Yanks pulled it to shore and cut it loose. It like to turn over, with all them soldiers scrambling to get up the bank. One of them guards tried to push me off, but I pushed him back and ran ahead."

The men in the circle nodded their heads. Some had been there. The jug of whiskey emptied. "Bring us another," one of them yelled.

The storyteller had tears in his eyes. "Our folks got caught between the Johnny Rebs and the Yanks. Both of 'em shooting. Thousands jumped in that creek and drowned. It was that or get shot. Don't know how many run and hid in the woods. If'n they did, they still ain't got no way to cross that creek."

A shorter man jumped up, silhouetted against the fire, and hollered, "He speaking the truth. I be one left on t'other side of the creek. No way to cross and got shot at by both sides."

Little Tom asked the shorter man in a low voice, almost to himself, "So how you come to be here?"

His words fell into silence. Another jug of shine was making the rounds as men relived that gruesome day. Tom's voice carried to the sharp-eared speaker.

He turned to face Tom. "With the help of the Lord, boy. With the help of the Lord. I run into the woods away from all of 'em. Didn't know if I be going the right way or the wrong way. I slept in them woods two nights, nothing to eat, and freezing cold. Finally, I seen a Geechee woman working a garden. She give me cornbread and boiled cabbage and pointed the way to Savannah. Said the soldiers done took over the town and nobody'd pay me no never mind."

The crowd huddling near the fire came to life. Some had been part of that desperate gang of camp followers. "Amen, brother. Amen," rang out.

Back at the cabin, Isaac wiped the sweat off his face. He scared Daddy and Dicie with the awful story. President Lincoln was dead, and they couldn't trust either side.

"Right now that Yankee General Jefferson Davis what drowned us or got us shot, s'posed to be in Savannah, keeping the Johnny Rebs from taking the city back," Isaac said. He gave a little smile and continued, "Union soldiers s'posed to be hunting the buckra President Jefferson Davis, to arrest him."

"How you know all that?" Dicie asked. Her big brother got around, had his nose in everybody's business, but every story he told hadn't proved to be true. How could a man with the same name be in charge of both sides?

"Tom told me. While he beating the drum. His Daddy sick, so ain't nobody else over there to beat it 'cept Tom. Everybody tell him the news."

His words drove all thought of President Lincoln out of Dicie's mind. Her heart thumped so loud she didn't hear a thing Isaac said after "'cept Tom."

Isaac kept on talking. "Tom be with Rufus and Gus when they heard soldiers talking about all us what got shot or drowned. Some say it weren't right. Some say the Yanks ain't got no way to take care of all us, so they took the easy way out."

Dicie's foot started shaking. Why hadn't anybody told her sooner? The drum beat all the time. How was she to know Big Tom wasn't beating it? Was Tom stuck at home caring for his daddy? Was his daddy the reason Tom hadn't come to see her, instead of that flower-in-her hair hussy, Bella? A hundred questions welled up in her mind. How long had Big Tom been sick? Ever since she and Tom saw the thousand black men and ran to warn their folks?

"How long . . . ?" she started to ask, but Daddy got his questions in first and loudest.

"Who they gone put in President Lincoln's place?" Daddy asked, drowning out her voice.

Isaac wasn't listening to Dicie. "Tom say it got to be the Vice President, Andrew Johnson."

Both men shook their heads. Rosa had long since brought news from Savannah about Andrew Johnson. He was the buckra's man. Word was he was against freeing the slaves.

All the people on Skidaway Island had prayed for the health of Abraham Lincoln. Now he was dead.

Isaac looked up and his face lightened. "Tom told good news, too. He say Yanks celebrating 'fore they heard about the President. The head buckra, General Robert E. Lee, hisself, done give up fighting. Surrendered in Virginia five days before Lincoln got shot."

Cuffie let out a whoop. "'Bout time," he said.

Isaac held up his hand. "Hold on. They say soldiers still going at it out west. The war ain't won yet."

Seeing Cuffie's crestfallen face, he added, "but it look like it be soon."

Good and bad, all mixed together, just like the Carolina jasmine and Cherokee rose Mammy taught her.

Next morning Yankee soldiers marched back to Brisbane. This time they brought along Reverend Houston. The men came to an abrupt halt in front of Mammy's tabby, stamping their boots in rhythm and shifting their rifles.

"Miz Lizzie," the lead soldier hollered.

Mammy opened the door.

Reverend Houston smiled. "Here is your written promise, orders of General Sherman himself, that the United States of America will deed this five acres of land to you." He held out a half sheet of heavy paper.

Mammy grabbed the paper and stared. Words had been filled in on a printed form. Melted red wax embossed with more words clung to the paper below a scribbled signature. It looked official. "Lizzie," with a space after it, shone in the top line of writing. She hugged the document to her heart.

"If you got a pen and ink, I want you to fill in my last name, 'Houston' right there," she said, pointing to the blank after her name. "Same as you." She smiled at Reverend Houston.

The soldier looked at Reverend Houston for approval, then turned to the uniformed man behind him. "You heard the woman," he said. The other soldier pulled out a steel pen and a bottle of ink. He squatted in front of the stump used as a seat and dropped the precious paper flat on the smooth wood. After carefully writing the name Houston after Lizzie, he blew on the paper, waved it in the air to dry, and handed it back to Mammy. "Now you are Miz Lizzie Houston," he said.

Mammy beamed from ear to ear, her scar twisting so far, Dicie feared her face would split. "Thank you, kindly," she said to Reverend Houston. "I pray the Lord to bless you."

Once the soldiers left, Mammy told Dicie and her brothers to grab a stick. Even Cuffie picked up a branch and broke off a sharp-pointed piece. She smoothed the dirt in front of the cabin where she swept away their footprints every night. They all practiced writing the name "Houston" over and over in the dirt. When she finished, Dicie wrote 0 1 2 3 4 5 6 7 8 9 after her name, just like Mammy had taught her.

Later, Mammy used a precious piece of chalk to write Houston on her slate. She set the slate on the shelf over the hearth so anyone coming into the tabby could see. "You is Dicie Houston, same as a white girl," she told Dicie.

Dicie somehow felt more grown up. "Can I write the numbers on the slate?" she asked.

"Go ahead, girl," Mammy said, handing her the chalk. "I want all the boys to learn them numbers, too."

Dicie beamed with pride, but remembering the news about President Lincoln, a stab of fear pricked Lizzie's assurance. Even defeated, the buckra still had powerful friends. Would the piece of paper and the new name be enough?

Chapter Twenty-Six
May 1865–July 1865

B oom, boom, bibbitty, bibbitty, BOOM. Day and night drumbeats relayed the astonishing news. Soldiers marched to Brisbane and handed
precious pieces of paper to black landowners, mostly soldiers from South
Carolina, who tramped wildly across the unplanted cotton fields, searching for the boundaries of their land. Yankee teachers kept busy deciphering
the stiff official documents to the astonished ex-slaves.

"Praise Allah. Thanks be to God. I can read," Lizzie fell to her knees
every time she figured out a new word. Half her day was spent teaching folks to write their names. Instead of wasting precious chalk, she
smoothed and wet a patch of dirt near the cookhouse. New landowners
copied their names from the official documents into moist dirt with a
sharp stick. Cuffie and Dicie took over her garden chores.

Whooping for joy, the lucky holders of official promises moved
women, children, and kissing cousins onto land they hoped matched
their papers. They chopped down trees, built bonfires, and planted seeds
in long unused fields. Nearly a hundred strangers claimed land on Brisbane. All the empty tabbies filled to overflowing. The promisees dreamed
of the day when soldiers would come back with their actual deeds.

The dark cloud hanging over their triumph was how to carry the
deeds to the courthouse. Once there, how much money would white
officials demand to record the deeds and how would colored farmers
get the cash?

The South Carolina soldiers celebrated while abandoned slaves who struggled to survive on Skidaway Island during the lean war years waited in vain for promises. Imprisoned by slavery until 1865, those who had tried to escape to warships had been rebuffed. The ships were full. Hopeful Skidaway slaves slunk back to the island or drowned trying.

What would become of them now? The papers gave growing crops planted by Skidaway farmers to the South Carolina men. The former soldiers were also given rations. Skidaway ex-slaves were doomed to starve.

"Ain't our problem," the newcomers said. "General Sherman give us this land. You better clear out."

"Like hell I will," Cuffie said. "I got land, too. I mean, my woman got land. Them rascals better watch out helping theyselves to my tomatoes." He was mad as an osprey who just had his catch snatched by an eagle. "It ain't as if government ain't still handing 'em rations."

He pulled his gun out from its hiding place under a loose floorboard and began hammering at the pin, trying to loosen it so he could clean the chambers.

"Thank you for running 'em off," Lizzie said. She patted his arm. "Don't know which be worse, the crows and squirrels or them thieving niggers."

"New landowners bringing some fine-looking women out here to help 'em," Cuffie said. "City girls must figure them men what got land, got money. They 'spect 'em to snap they fingers and git a crop."

Lizzie pulled a frown and quoted an old African saying: "Women ought to know better'n to hollow out fried fish till they catch 'em. Take a lot of hard work to make money farming. Doubt some them slackers got it in 'em."

"You got yourself a hard-working man," Cuffie patted her rear end. "I just scared 'nother thief out our garden. Next one gets to see this gun." His bare feet had tracked mud all over the floor.

"Don't I know it. You keep away from them bitches," Lizzie said. It had always been a problem with women chasing after Cuffie. She grabbed a broom and began sweeping away his muddy footprints.

Times had changed on Skidaway. Boats that used to be safely left unattended on the shoreline went missing. Produce was scarfed up by folks who had not planted it. In Savannah, top prices were paid to the thieves who stole Mammy's tomatoes.

"No sense letting them crooks make all the money," Cuffie said. "I'm gone figure a way to carry a load to town myself."

Newcomers and long-time residents who could cadge a bateau or a ride in one joined Cletis and Rosa in carrying produce to City Market. Cufffie managed to find a beat-up piece of boat and dragged it home.

"That thing won't never make it to the mainland," Mammy said.

"Will, too." Cuffie set to work with a bucket of pine tar, slivers of wood, and nails he pulled out of the rotted boards of the cookhouse. He and Rufus tested it in the creek behind the compound. "Tight enough to hold one of us and a hundred pounds of crop," he pronounced.

Downtown Savannah overflowed with soldiers, Yankees, missionaries, and Negroes who were scared to return to their old plantation homes. Savannah's white natives were close to starvation, selling off prized silver, china, and jewelry at bargain prices. Industrious freedmen and Yankee speculators made money hand over fist and spent it freely. Cuffie came home with four dollars and ten cents in nickels, dimes, and quarters, and a length of purple silk for Lizzie.

."Lord a'mercy!" Mammy hollered when she saw it. "What I gone do with this?" Savannah law forbade Negroes from wearing silk, even castoff dresses given to them by their owners.

"Make yo'self a dress and wear it," Cuffie said. "We fixing to get rich. A white man sold it to me for fifty cents. Said he "found" it." Cuffie's expression told what he thought of the man's story.

Cuffie savored his new-found cash. Yankee soldiers had money and didn't mind paying him to empty chamber pots, dig privies, or wash uniforms. With coins jingling in his pockets, he attracted attention. His disdain for the newcomers didn't stop him from accepting a drink and an invitation to sit at the campfire with the new men. Or their women. Sometimes after the boys were safely locked in the other side of the tabby at night, Cuffie disappeared and was nowhere to be found.

Women were no longer assigned to the cookhouse, but men relished building a fire inside the circle of tree stumps and rotting benches where folks used to eat. Moonshine flowed freely.

Some of the new women joined the men and took a drink, ignoring the disapproving glares of old-time females like Mammy. City wenches were bolder, had finer dresses, fancier hairdos, and went to work staking claims on the most attractive men, whether or not the man already had a woman. Respectable women didn't sit and drink with men around a fire. City girls didn't care about respectability.

So, when Cuffie suggested the women get together and make a good time feast for everybody around the fire at Brisbane, Mammy's hackles went up.

"Why you want to eat with them city trash?" she asked. "They don't do nothing but steal from us."

"They got all them provisions from the soldiers. Sugar and tea. Me and two others can kill us a deer to cook. Shrimp and crab be running high," he said. "Some of them new men offered to bring cornmeal out of their provisions and a keg of shine. Why not be neighborly?"

"Thought you wanted all them newcomers gone," Mammy said.

"Now, there, Lizzie. Don't hurt to make friends," he said, patting Mammy on her rear. "Show them city boys how to do the Buzzard Lope. Bet they ain't got nothing downtown like a big old-time plantation celebration."

Dicie watched her parents bicker. Always a nagging worry lingered. She never forgot Mammy putting the spell on Mary after the long-ago bonfire. Then came the news of Mary's death.

Other women in the compound grumbled too. At least ten new families had settled on Brisbane. All the newcomers wanted an old-time country bonfire with circle dancing and a feast. They had hope in their hearts and were ready to party.

Despite her worry about her parents fighting, Dicie clapped her hands when she heard a date was set. How could she forget Daddy in his glory as chief buzzard, out-spinning and out-dancing all the other men?

"Ain't gone be no big celebration like in the old days," Daddy told her. "Just us Brisbane folk."

Mammy's face was sour.

"Come on, Lizzie," Daddy said. "Them young'uns ain't never seen the pea-picking. You can teach 'em."

"Dancing ain't what them girls got on they mind," Mammy grumbled, but she carried her washpot out to the center of the compound on the big day. Cuffie and his friends had caught enough shrimp for everybody. It would take a washpot to cook them, along with hushpuppies from a sack of cornmeal donated by a newcomer.

Despite their disapproval of the newcomers, the long-time women of Brisbane all turned out to help. Seven years had passed since the last harvest celebration. Even the elderly crone hobbled out to offer advice.

"We gone show them city wenches how to party," she said, brandishing her special ladle for pulling shrimp out of a washpot full of boiling grease.

Isaac and Rufus spent hours chopping a big stack of hard, slow-burning firewood. The delicious meaty smell of roast venison and wild boar wafted through the compound. "I wouldn't chop up a sweet gum tree for nothing less than a smoked ham," Rufus said, licking his lips.

"Ain't gone be no big celebration like we used to have over on Hibernia," Mammy said. "Just them folks what been squatting here at our place, and who-some-ever trashy newcomer what call themselves owners here. Ain't worth beating the drum over."

What Mammy said was true. No drum beat to summon anyone from outside Brisbane, so when strangers poured into the compound Dicie wondered how they knew about the feast. Surely all these people didn't claim to own land here. Some came from tents pitched in the cottonfield, but most were folks she didn't recognize from the endless train that crossed and recrossed Brisbane. Would there be enough food?

The long summer evening darkened, the western sky blazed red, the bonfire burned brighter, and folks lined up with tin plates. Cuffie moved from man to man with a jug of moonshine, pouring liberally into tin cups. Mammy, ladling shrimp and hush puppies from the wash pot, narrowed her eyes as two of the city women held out tin cups to Cuffie.

One of the women leaned over and whispered in Cuffie's ear. He busted out laughing, then liberally poured shine in her cup.

Over the noise of the crowd Mammy heard him say, "You know this ain't for women."

The woman pinched his cheek, and moved on, calling back over her shoulder, "Wait till I get you by youself."

The woman with her giggled and pulled her over to where several men perched on fallen logs, eating and drinking. "Come on, Dorothy," she called. "Ain't gone be no more places to set."

Mammy scowled. Dicie's gaze followed the two women while she helped Mammy scoop shrimp from the wash pot. Neither was from Brisbane. How did they know about the gathering? Both wore brightly colored dresses, one blue and the other green. Skidaway women wore rough cotton dresses in dirty-looking shades of grey.

Soon as everyone got something to eat, Dicie and Mammy fixed dinner for themselves and took a seat with the Brisbane women, away from the carousing men. Mammy didn't have much to say. A frown creased her forehead, pulling the scar on her cheek into an upward line.

After they finished eating, Mammy ordered Dicie to gather the family's tin plates and spoons "Time for us to head home," she said. Dicie noticed Mammy had barely touched her food, even though there was plenty for everybody and everything tasted delicious.

Dicie wasn't ready to leave. Nobody had started a ring shout yet or asked the men to do the Buzzard Lope. She wanted to watch Daddy dance, but Mammy's face was grim. She jerked Dicie by the arm, almost causing her to drop the plates. Dicie was too scared to argue.

Mammy didn't bother telling the boys to come home. Cuffie and Dicie's brothers stayed gathered around the fire, Cuffie drinking and talking, his boys taking in every word.

Dicie lay awake listening for drums and fifes, but the music never came, only a few drunken shouts, and the tramp of footsteps leaving the Brisbane compound. Had the newcomers never learned to dance? Much later Dicie heard the old wooden door to the adjoining tabby open and shut as her brothers settled in for the night.

She tried to stay awake until Daddy came home, but he never did.

Chapter Twenty-Seven

July 1865

Every day Dicie repeated the words of the love spell: "God is love. Love for Dicie and Tom, Love." Every day the drums boomed unceasingly, beating to the rhythm of change bounding across Skidaway Island, change to the lives of every poor soul rooted in sand on the fragile wind-swept island. Her brothers assured her the maddening perpetual drummer was Little Tom. She prayed for the silence of the drum. Silence would mean Tom was free. Free to come to her.

Early one hot, dew-drenched morning near the end of July, she hurried outside to check the garden before the heat became unbearable. Always, the garden demanded attention. Today, a buck sporting a heavy rack of antlers had jumped the fence and was devouring their okra. There was no sign of Tom.

"Shoo!" she yelled, clapping her hands. There was a downside to all those sweet fawns. Two more does, each with a little spotted fawn, waited their turn outside the fence. After chasing the does back into the piney woods, she hurled pinecones at the deer inside the fence until it left. Then she squatted on the sunbaked earth to replant what the buck had uprooted but not devoured. How could one deer do so much damage?

Once her loud panting settled into quiet breathing, she had the eerie feeling that something had changed. What was it? Cass was supposed to be watching out for her, but he was still asleep. She looked carefully around, keeping an eye out for approaching strangers. Nobody was in sight but the familiar old woman tending her garden across the way.

The drums! Silence shimmered in the heavy wet air. After all the fuss and commotion, the drums reported—nothing. Was there no news? At least, nothing new this morning? Instinctively her thoughts flew to Little Tom.

As she patted the earth firmly in place around the jerked-up roots of tomato plants and trailing squash vines, Dicie heard the faint slap of approaching footsteps. The sound came from the woods, not from the tabby or from the dusty road that cut through the center of the compound. It was only the gentle sound of bare feet on the leafy path trampled by deer, the path she used to cross the ditch when she visited Tom. Back when the island was almost deserted. Were the pesky deer coming back to feed? This noise was softer than the clatter of hooves.

She stood and peered down the path. Not a deer, but a man.

Tom!

She wanted to run to him. But no. Better wait. Mammy said never show your feelings. Maybe he was coming to Brisbane to see someone else or only passing through to Hampton Plantation. If he wasn't coming to see her, she could hardly bear it.

But, if he wasn't looking for her, why use the deer path instead of the main road? Only she and the deer traveled the low tunnel that was the most direct route to the ditch.

As she waited in the garden not far from the path, watching and not moving, he saw her and hollered, "Dicie!" Breaking into a run, he flung his body over the fence. Dashing through rows of spreading vegetables, he grabbed her and held her in both arms.

She tried to stiffen her body. Why had he stayed away? What would Mammy say about a man touching her? But she was too happy to see him. Her rigid back melted. Her arms wrapped around his bronze muscled chest and strong broad back. Together they held each other and rocked from side to side in the brilliant morning sun.

Mammy had done it again. Her love spell finally worked. Gratitude to her mother flooded Dicie's heart. She couldn't stop tears from running down her cheeks. "What you doing here?" she finally asked.

"I ought not to have come. I can't leave Daddy, but I couldn't stay away no longer," he said. "Miz Laliah offered to set with him for a piece. Today be the first day ain't nothing happening I got to beat the drum for, thank you Jesus. I been dying to see you, but my daddy got sick. Then all them soldiers and preachers kept showing up. Folks got promised land.

Soldiers made a deal with Daddy to pay him to beat the drum, but he took sick. Nobody to beat the drums but me."

Tears continued to seep out of her almond-shaped eyes. "I thought you done forgot me."

"Not much chance of that." Tom smiled down at her and wiped away the largest of her tears with the tip of his finger. "Daddy suffer a apoplexy right after them thousand men come. He can't move his legs or one of his arms. I can't leave him, but he say the drum got to be beat. Miz Laliah be with him now. She's who mostly took care of me when I be too little to go to the fields with Daddy. You know my mammy died when I was born, so Miz Laliah been like a mother to me. She has chillen of her own, and a baby girl name of Bella, born same month as me, so she had milk to feed me."

"God bless her," Dicie said. So many mothers died birthing their children. It terrified her, knowing she could die, too, in the same way.

He put his arm around her shoulders. "Some of them other women been helping me care for him, too, so's I can tend my garden, but nobody can't stay long. Garden's a mess."

She thought of Bella, the pretty girl with the yellow flower in her hair. Was she one of the women? Her smile faded, and she looked away.

Tom saw the shadow pass over Dicie's face. Not sure what was bothering her, he rambled on, "I set the drums right by the house where I can beat 'em and take care of Daddy at the same time. Folks coming and coming to our tabby all time of night and day telling me what the soldiers done and what they hear 'em talk about. So much news, Daddy got me beating two drums at once, my little one and the big one. He say I got to get the message out."

"I know. You got to do your job," she said. Her nose was running, and she had dirt all over her hands from resetting the vegetables. If she wiped her face, she'd get mud on it. If he came to see her again, she promised herself she'd wash her hands and pick a flower to tuck in her braids before she let him see her. Awkwardly, she pulled away and tried to swipe her elbow across her runny nose.

"Here, let me do that," Tom said. He pulled his bandana loose from around his neck and wiped her face. "Let me wipe your hands, too."

He held her close as he wiped her face and then picked up her muddy hand. "What pretty hands you got," he said. Instead of handing her the bandanna when he finished wiping her face, he tenderly wiped both of her hands, then put his arms around her waist.

She breathed in his salty male essence. Her heart raced and a tingling pulsed through her body. She clung to him and they swayed together in the garden, ignoring the sweat pouring down both their bodies.

"We got to get out of this sun," he finally said, guiding her through the vegetables to the shade of the piney woods.

Taking her hand, he led her down the deer path and back into the cool tangle of grapevines and Virginia creeper. They passed the hidden hollow where the doe used to leave her fawn. Now the fawn was old enough to follow her mother, leaving the soft sheltered bed for lovers.

Were the missing mother and baby deer two of those waiting for a turn to eat Mammy's okra? The thought flickered through Dicie's mind as Tom kissed her. Then he eased her down onto the thick bed of dead leaves and pine straw, tossing a fallen pinecone out of the way. His arms held her tight. Forgetting about the fawn, she moved her lips to his and savored the heat rising from his body into hers.

They lay together in the deep shade of the hiding place, his hand stroking her back and shoulders.

"I love you," he said, reaching under her skirt.

Oh, the tingly exciting feeling his hand caused when he stroked her bare legs and the secret place higher up. She reached her hand under his shirt and down his hard body to his trousers to free the huge bulge between his legs. When he plunged it into her, she briefly worried about what Mammy would say. Then she only thought how perfect it felt to be so close to Tom.

Chapter Twenty-Eight

July 1865

"When will I see you again?" Dicie asked when Tom finally moved his arms out from around her and sat up. She held her breath waiting for his answer. She could hardly stand it if he stayed away again for so long.

"Soon, I hope," he said. "Can you come see me tomorrow? I might not can get away, but we stay second tabby from the end, front row. You can see it from my garden."

She hesitated. Since that first time when she crossed the ditch and found him in his garden, she hadn't ventured off Brisbane. After the scare with the strange men, her family never left her alone. Tomorrow, Daddy would be the one guarding her.

"Not sure I can," she said. "Mammy don't hold with me going nowhere by myself with all these strange men wandering the island. Mostly she stay right with me. Daddy be watching out for me tomorrow, 'stead of her." She hugged her knees as they talked. The inches separating them seemed wide as the rushing rivulets that swelled from tiny trickles to rivers as they joined the outgoing tide.

She hadn't told Daddy about Tom, and Tom had not come to see her since Daddy came home. She often thought of telling him, but the time never seemed right. Would Daddy be mad if he knew she was interested in a boy? A man, really. She was pretty sure he wouldn't hold with what Tom had just done with her. She would have to buck up her courage and tell Daddy before she asked him to take her to see Tom. What if he said no?

Would Tom want to be with her if he knew about the man who held her hostage? His hands had been all over her. Her skin prickled with goosebumps, just from remembering. She could never tell him. Mammy always said, "Fool talk much, wise men talk less." Even in these lawless days, the family never told anyone about the murdered men. Their dark secret could get them killed.

Young as Dicie had been, she remembered olden days before slave drivers and buckra abandoned the island. A time when everyone lived in fear. A time when Sampson rode herd over every poor soul, swinging his vicious bull whip at the women. A time when Mammy had to sell her spells and roots under cover of darkness, constantly keeping an eye out for informers.

Even now in the chaos of newcomers coming and leaving, her brothers heard friends of the missing men speculate about why and how they disappeared—the men Mammy chopped up and fed to the crabs. She shivered. It wasn't safe to let anybody, even Tom, know.

He saw her distress and said, "Course you can't come by yourself. I weren't thinking. 'Specially with all them crazy freemen hanging around. I ain't forgot that time Cephus attacked yo' mammy at the bonfire in front of everybody. I sho' don't want no trouble with yo' daddy, neither. Do he know about me?"

"No. I ain't said nothing to him," she said. She tried to picture how she could ask Daddy to take her to see Tom.

As she tried to puzzle it out, he said, "you might not know, but yo' Daddy been spending lot of time over on Hibernia near our place."

She didn't know. "He helps me with the garden most days," she said. She never felt so safe as when her daddy was near. Why was he spending time at Hibernia?

"Ain't during the day," he answered. "I seen him crossing the ditch mostly just about dark. Sometimes he weaving like he had too much 'shine."

She put her hands over her ears to shut out the hateful words. She didn't want to know, but she believed him. Too often she heard Mammy crying because Daddy hadn't come home. It wasn't like Sampson was holding him to work late at night anymore.

"You seen where he go?" she asked, not sure she wanted to know.

Tom looked at her for a moment. "Sometime, I do. Sometime, he pass on through and I don't know where he end up."

Suddenly she had to know. "Tell me."

"Promise you won't say nothing to yo' Mammy?" he said.

What if Mammy asked her? Mammy had an uncanny way of reading her thoughts.

"If she asks me what I know, I got to answer."

"Just say you ain't seen nothing yourself. She know you home at night even if he ain't."

Dicie nodded. She had to hear where Daddy went.

He stepped back and looked her in the eyes, "I won't tell if you don't feel safe knowing."

"No, I want to know," she said.

"Mind you, I don't know what he do when the door close. A woman stay there, name of Dorothy."

She clenched her fists. Dorothy. Dorothy was the name of the city girl at the bonfire on Brisbane the night Daddy never came home. The girl who told Daddy, "Wait till I get you by yourself." Her friend called her Dorothy.

Tom hesitated at the look on Dicie's face, but kept on. "She got young'uns, but her man don't stay with her. I see yo' daddy coming out her tabby right before the sun come up, when I step outside to set my drums."

She winced like the hateful words had struck her.

Trying to make her feel better, he said, "I ain't never seen him go in her door though."

A painful spasm gripped Dicie's stomach. Was she about to lose her breakfast cornbread right in front of Tom? She never forgot the harvest celebration in 1856 where Mammy saw a woman named Mary hanging onto Daddy. Daddy had lied to Mammy to try to stop her from being mad. She remembered the stony look on Mammy's face, and her refusing to acknowledge Daddy's triumph in the buzzard lope.

After that long ago cotton-baling, the last one with Daddy, and a night of sharp words and tears between her parents, she remembered the dark winter afternoon when Daddy didn't come home. She worried and watched Mammy mix her spells, a love spell for Daddy and a poison spell for Mary.

Only a few days later drums beat the message of death. Neighbors whispered a woman named Mary had died. She had looked full of life, smiling up at Daddy. Had Mammy killed her with the spell?

What would Mammy do now if she knew where Cuffie spent the nights when he didn't come home? Lately, she heard angry words again between her parents and saw Mammy's tears.

"A man's got to have some room to hang with other men," she had heard Cuffie yell. But what if it wasn't men he hung with?

Her legs quivered. More family secrets. "Don't tell me anymore," she begged him.

He put his arms around her again and nuzzled her neck. "Shouldn't of said nothing," he said. "Thought you needed to know. Not get caught flat-footed. Prob'bly nothing will come of it. That woman got other men coming and going . Lot of drinking go on."

"Dicie! Dicie, Where you at?" Cass's voice startled them.

"He supposed to be watching me," she said to Tom. "Here, Cass! Coming!" She whirled and ran the short distance up the deer path to the garden.

"Girl. where you been? You like to scared me to death." Cass whipped his face from Dicie to Tom, who was out of breath from running after her. "Oh. It's you," he said.

She saw the puzzled look of Tom's face and tried to explain. "I ain't seen you since it happened. One of them new freedman tried to hurt me. My menfolk been watching me ever since." She felt her face flush.

Tom scowled. "Are you alright? Did he hurt you? What happened? Where he be at?" He curled his fist.

"I'm alright. Daddy took care of him." There was no way she could tell him what really happened. Shivering, she remembered the biting cold of winter air as she waded into slightly warmer tidewater to wash blood and guts off her dress. The memory was too fresh for her to walk to visit Tom without Cass or Daddy. Between her recollection of the two men and the thudding disappointment of not being free to walk over to see him, she started to cry.

Cass saw her tears. "We ain't left her alone ever since," he told Tom.

Tom looked from brother to sister, then nodded his head. "I see. Don't you worry. Reckon I can find someone to watch my daddy tomorrow and come see you, if that be okay with yo' folks."

Dicie nodded her head, Tom gave her a quick hug and headed to the center of the compound and the dusty public track back to Hibernia.

She watched his brisk steps until he turned the corner and over-grown summer foliage hid him. She turned to her brother. Joy and fear fought each other in her heart. The fear she shared with Cass.

"Cass, he tell me Daddy goin' to a woman's house at Hibernia some nights. You know 'bout it? What Mammy gone do if she hears?"

"Now, Dicie, ain't no use to bother your head about what you cain't do nothing about." To cheer her up, he said "Tom looked at you like he wanted to eat you up. You put a love spell on him?"

She smiled. "Course not, Cass. I don't believe in rooting nobody."

Chapter Twenty-Nine

September 1865

"You know what I just heard?" Cuffie was so mad he could hardly get the words out. Wiping the spit off his mustache, he answered his own question. "That ugly, lying United States president done give all our land back to the buckra! The whole Skidaway Island."

Mammy and Dicie had just sat down at the rickety wooden table in the corner of the tabby. In front of them slices of freshly ripe tomatoes were tucked between slabs of cornbread for their midday meal.

Daddy had stomped in, back from Savannah where he sold a whole boatload of tomatoes, okra, and squash from their garden. Even with his pockets jingling with money, he wasn't happy. "Buckra in town having a big ole parade to celebrate. They celebrating cuz they stealing everything we got."

Dicie laid down her chunk of cornbread. Suddenly, she didn't feel like eating.

Mammy's face twisted with shock, then anger. "Signs was right! Near about stepped on a black snake this morning out by the garden. That fool wouldn't move. I knew he trying to give me bad news." Her voice broke. "I ain't getting my deed."

All summer she watched every passing cadre of soldiers, hoping each was bringing the deed she was promised in April. Tears ran down her cheeks, cutting through the anger.

A griping cramp seized Dicie's stomach. She shrank into the corner by the door, trying to hide from the spirit of evil invading the room.

Where would her family go if they had to get off the land? Was Daddy fixing to pitch a fit, lashing out at Mammy like he sometimes did, even though it wasn't Mammy's fault? If he did, would Mammy root him? She wished she could disappear.

"What about my piece of paper?" Mammy closely guarded the promissory note signed by A.P. Ketchman, an officer of William T. Sherman himself. It stayed safe in a metal box hidden behind a brick at the far end of the hearth next to the fireplace, except when Mammy got it out to rub the paper between her fingers and dream. "It no good?"

Cuffie dropped his head in his hands. "I don't know, girl," he said. "I just don't know."

"Knew it too good to be true." Mammy reached for her cards. "They been telling me, but I keep hopin' they wrong." Her voice trailed off as she flung herself face down on the bed, clutching the cards.

After a few minutes of sobbing, she sat up. "What we gone do?" she asked Cuffie.

Dicie slipped out the door to the shady spot where she had been shelling butter beans before Daddy came home. Her heart pounded as she listened to her parents. Did Daddy have a plan?

Everything had been going so well. She wasn't scared of the Yankee soldiers anymore. The freemen stopped stealing vegetables once they saw Daddy's gun and her big brothers standing guard. Tom came to see her regularly. Daddy took the news that she had a suitor better than she expected. Tom and Daddy both had cash money and always brought something special from town. Just last week, Tom brought her a pair of boots to wear when she picked blackberries. Just to see how good they felt, she put them on and went tramping through the briar patch.

Were those good times rushing out with the tide like the chopped-up guts of the two evil men? She kept plopping the shelled beans into the tin bowl so her parents wouldn't look out the door, see her listening, and hush.

"Them freemen ain't gone take this lying down. They's fixing to be fighting going on," she heard Cuffie say. "And I be part of it. Ain't nobody taking my garden."

"Reckon Massa Warren sending Sampson back out here?" Mammy asked.

Cuffie shuddered at the thought of Sampson and his bull whip. "Hope that old bastard done died. No telling. You the one know everything all the time. I'm gone find me a drink." With that he stomped off.

Mammy walked outside, tear tracks still on her face. She stopped when she saw Dicie. "Just when times got to going good. We better pray."

She and Dicie bowed their heads and Mammy recited: "The Lord is my shepherd; I shall not want. Yea, though I walk through the valley of the shadow of death, I will fear no evil, for thou art with me; thy rod and thy staff shall comfort me."

Both felt calmer. Dicie added a silent prayer for herself and Tom: "Please, God, take care of us and let us stay together."

"We gone need him fo' sure," Mammy said.

Mammy plucked sprigs of mint from the tangle on the shady side of the tabby and crushed them in her hand. Then she walked back to the door, chanting as she rubbed the crushed leaves against the door frame, top, bottom, and both sides, moving a stump into the doorway so she could reach the top.

The sweet smell of fresh mint wafted to Dicie. She hoped the spell was powerful enough to ward off trouble.

Boom, boom! Tom's drum signaling danger tore through the hot, sunshiny compound, interrupting the chatter of blue jays and cardinals. The flock of crows perched in treetops near the garden set off their warning caw, caw, caw. Wind picked up. Black clouds scudded across the sky. Her daddy's news must be true.

Cuffie came home before sundown, smelling of whiskey and nervous as a marsh rabbit.

Dicie's heart raced when he walked in. She had always loved his homecoming. Now she was terrified he and Mammy would fight. Soon as she put away the supper dishes, she crawled onto her quilt under their bed.

But this time Cuffie didn't pick a fight. Instead, he passed out next to her with his gun on the floor by the bed. All the men on the island, newcomers and old residents alike, were outraged. Cuffie and Lizzy needed each other.

Dicie lay awake most of the night listening to the sound of Daddy's snores and making sure she didn't roll too close to the gun. The crack of distant gunshots echoed in the darkness.

The family didn't have to wait long for trouble to find them. The tromp of feet and angry voices woke them in the pale light before sunrise. Suddenly the door to their tabby was snatched off its hinges. Dicie stared at the wooden bar, still in place but backed by a rush of cool air and the weak light of early morning.

"Get out! Get out!" A man screamed.

Lurking close behind the screamer, Dicie recognized the stocky, sawed-off body of Cephus, Mammy's old nemesis. Before she could jump up from her bed on the floor, a flash of fire from Daddy's pistol lit the cabin. Its horrific report echoed off the lime and oyster shell walls. The men fell back even though Daddy shot over their heads on purpose.

"Ain't no use Cuffie," Cephus hollered. "We got more men than you got bullets."

Mammy reached for her stash of root hidden behind the brick, and Daddy moved next to the wall where the door used to be.

"I reckon I can first take out who I want," Daddy hollered back. "I don't intend to waste no more bullets."

Isaac and Rufus snatched open the top half of the Dutch door to the other side of the tabby. Gus hadn't made it home last night. "Leave my Daddy alone," Isaac screamed. He and Rufus burst out of the tabby brandishing stout wooden clubs. Eleven-year-old Cass followed, a sharpened hoe in his fist.

Cephus jumped back, stepping on another man's foot. "Forgot yo' boys done growed," he said.

"Come on, man," the freedman whose foot he trod on grumbled. "You say you ain't skeered of nobody. We got twenty head of men done lost ever thing they was promised. He don't even have a promise to this place. Only his woman. I ain't afraid of no woman."

A gaggle of city women hung at the rear of the mob, egging them on. Suddenly one burst forward, pushing and shoving. "That Cuffie you picking on. Leave him alone. He one of us."

The man turned and stared at the angry woman, his eyes bugging out. "Dorothy, you know him?"

"You fool. That be Cuffie what sells my shine for me. Let's go." She grabbed the man's arm and pulled him back from the tabby.

Confused and eyeing the four armed men, the crowd muttered and drew back. As Dorothy hustled the man who wasn't scared of a woman toward the road to the next plantation, she turned her head and hollered. "Why you don't jine up with us, Cuffie?"

Cuffie peered out at the frustrated mob following Dorothy, Cephus, and their leader. He glanced worriedly at Mammy, still in the tabby, roots and cards clenched in her fist. "Thank you kindly," he yelled to Dorothy. "I'll think on it."

Turning to his sons, he thumped Rufus on the shoulder. "Good work, boys," he said. "Hope they won't be back."

He put his arm around Mammy and said, "Good riddance," and sank down on the bed with his head in his hands. "Wonder if them niggers gone be able to change anything?"

"Them dumb troublemakers ain't good for nothing and nobody," Mammy said. "No use to steal from us, who ain't got nothing. We got to come up with a plan. When you reckon the buckra gone come back out here and do what they gone do?"

Cuffie shrugged. "Better read yo' cards woman," he said.

Mammy sat at the table and shuffled her cards. All day long she tried to discern the future, while Daddy nailed the door back on its hinges.

As the sun began to sink in the western sky, Cuffie washed his face and slicked his long black curls.

"Who you fancying up for?" Mammy asked.

"Ain't nobody," he answered. "Just want to see if there be any news."

Dicie held her breath. Mammy didn't say anything. Daddy pulled his battered hat down over his eyes and took off out the door.

All night long Dicie kept an ear out for him, but he never came home.

Chapter Thirty

January–February 1866

A ll of Skidaway Island waited with fear and trembling for the buckra to arrive and reclaim their land. Under orders, Yankee soldiers remained to protect the returning owners. Every day the freedmen watched, peering anxiously at arriving boats and across the rivers, but no owners came.

Mammy prayed and studied her signs; Daddy cussed and grumbled. Mobs organized and dissolved. Freemen from the outside came and went, but most left as they had no permanent place to stay.

Finally, Mammy planted her winter garden. "You do what you want. I ain't gone sit here and starve," she told Cuffie. She and Dicie sprouted potatoes and started turnips and cabbage on a worktable out of reach of critters. Once the seedlings were big enough to plant in the garden, Dicie covered them with deer-proof netting, hand woven by Isaac.

One cold day in January, Tom's father surrendered to his illness. All that day Little Tom beat the message of death. Early next morning he hurried over to Brisbane. Dicie put her arms around him and held him tight.

"He ain't suffering no more," she said.

"I'll never be as good a drummer as him," Tom said, wiping tears out of his eyes. "Hope I can remember all the codes he learned me."

"You the best drummer," Dicie said, comforting him. "I know what you mean. Hope I can remember half the spells Mammy passing on to me." With him in her arms, she felt the heat of his body through his flannel shirt. Blood flowed faster through her own body in response to his touch.

"Least he died knowing we free," Tom said. "That be a powerful blessing. Sometimes he told me 'bout when he used to be free, t'other side of this ocean. How he would run through the forest without asking nobody. Now he and I both can run free."

Dicie listened to his words. Was she free? Maybe, but she couldn't walk alone to the next plantation without fear of the restless, drunken men seeking a place to call their own. How lucky she was to have her daddy near.

Wiping his eyes, Tom settled on the stump by the tabby door. "A great big white pelican be circling our cabin all night while he passed. Don't see many of them, this far from open water. It must of been coming for Daddy, to carry his spirit back to Africa."

Tom buried Big Tom in the graveyard next to where the old praise house used to be. Folks on Hibernia still talked about rebuilding it, but plans stalled when they got the news that they were losing their land. Next to the privy, Tom found a blue medicine bottle one of the soldiers had dropped. He washed it and planted it upside down on a stout stake next to the hole where his father was buried. The blue glass kept evil spirits away from the grave. Reverend Houston himself preached the service. More than one hundred folks from all over the island showed up. Everybody on Skidaway respected Tom, the drummer.

Before his daddy died, Little Tom had found time to plant a winter garden. He gave Cuffie a load of his broccoli and cabbages to carry to Savannah to sell. "Nobody but me to feed now," he said. What he didn't eat or give to Cuffie, he sold to the soldiers.

After Big Tom passed, Little Tom found time to spend with Dicie. As they strolled down the forest path to the edge of the marsh, they talked about what they hoped to do, if they would have land. Since Tom's daddy had never escaped from Skidaway Island to serve in the United States army, he couldn't get one of the written promises.

"We can't count on nothing," Tom said. "Don't even know if we can stay on this island."

Dicie knew what he said was true. She still wished he would say the words, "We will be together no matter what." Once, after they made love, she summoned her courage and said, "I want to be with you always."

She looked at him expectantly. He hugged her tighter. Fleetingly a guilty look crossed his face. Then he buried his face in her neck without saying anything.

Far as Dicie's family knew, Mammy's paper promising her the land was no good. Yet they stayed put where Dicie and her brothers had lived all the days of their lives. They had nowhere else to go.

One day late in February, Tom didn't emerge from the forest path at his usual time. Strong gusts of icy wind blew from the Atlantic Ocean across the gray marsh. The gales blew through the shoreline, rattling palms, and bending cedars almost double. But Dicie knew the weather wouldn't keep Tom away.

Early that morning, distant blasts of bugles awakened her. A momentous event had happened, but what? The chilling blam! blam! of Tom's metal drum followed the bugler's notes. Then the BOOM! BOOM! of his daddy's old hollow log. All day long Tom beat both drums. Isaac ran to Hibernia to find out why.

The buckra had returned.

Soon as Isaac came back with the news, Dicie and Cass hurried over to Hibernia to hear what Tom could tell them. Isaac sprinted to the western edge of the island to watch for incoming boats. Mammy rushed off to find her schoolteacher friends. Daddy, Rufus, and Gus stayed behind to guard the tabby and garden.

Dicie found Tom in front of the tabby where he now lived alone. Someone had built a fire not far from where he sat. A circle of freemen warmed themselves around the fire. From time to time a man stepped forward to relay new information to Tom. Without skipping a beat, he shouted the news as he received it, pausing for a response after each pronouncement.

"Buckra here!" Tom hollered.

"Tell it, brother," the men shouted.

"Freeman Bureau!" Tom said, hitting the top of an empty five-gallon tin can that sat next to his big log drum.

"Amen," the crowd shouted.

"Reverend Houston!" Tom cried.

"Praise the Lord," the crowd responded.

Finally, Tom paused for a drink of water. Despite the cold, he was sweating. He stood, stretched his legs, and walked over to Cass and Dicie. Putting his arm around Dicie's shoulders, he said, "Ain't Massa Warren himself what come. None of the massas be here. They sending the old drivers to tell the Freedmen's Bureau what to say to us."

She steeled herself for more bad news. She never forgot her agony when Daddy got sold away. Or the broken promises that he would be allowed to return to visit. What if her parents were separated again? What if the buckra took Daddy to Savannah? Or Tom had to leave?

"What they gone tell us?"

His face turned stony. "We betting they ain't coming to give us our land back. Don't know 'bout the crops we done planted with none of they help. We don't know nothing for sure. Rumor say they gone offer us to stay, but we don't know what terms. Maybe they give us part of what we grow. They can't keep everything now, and 'spect us to work like we used to."

Cass gasped. "Why should we give 'em anything? They left us on our own to starve."

Dicie turned Tom's words over in her mind. The possibilities were too grim to think about. She loved the forest and the animals, the waving marsh grass, and the glimpse of the big ocean. "Do that mean we gits to stay?" she asked.

Where would they go if they left? How could anyone know they would be better off somewhere else? On Skidaway Island, nobody starved. Nobody froze. God was in the forest. Evil spirits abounded, but so did the spirits of good.

Tom shook his head. "We don't know. How they gone make anything off this land, if'n we ain't here to do all the work?"

Relief that they might get to keep their home flooded her heart, but he frowned and said, "Maybe we gits to stay. Maybe we ain't. But how is us doing all the farming like we always done, and them taking all of the profit, better than being a slave? What in it for us?"

"Better the devil you know than the devil you don't," she said. Mammy said that all the time to Daddy when he talked about leaving.

More farmers joined the group around the fire. "Back to work, man," one of them yelled at Tom. "We ain't paying you to stand around jawing at that pretty girl."

"You ain't paying me neither way," he yelled back.

Out of the corner of her eye, Dicie saw the girl, Bella, step out of a nearby tabby.

She was rounder than Dicie remembered, and there was no flower in her braids, but otherwise, she looked the same.

Tom watched Bella walk toward them. "I got to go," he said to Dicie, squeezing her hand and turning away.

Dicie froze.

Cass pulled her arm. "Come on. He got to beat the drum," he told her. "Let's go."

Reluctantly, Dicie headed back toward the ditch with Cass. Just before they dropped down into it, she looked back to see if the wench was with Tom. He was studiously beating the drum. Bella had stopped to talk with two other men. Dicie could hardly bear to take her eyes off Tom and Bella, but Cass pulled her forward.

What would happen once she and Cass were out of sight?

Chapter Thirty-One

March 1867

"Them lowdown, thieving sumbitches wanting me to sign this piece of paper or git off." Cuffie slammed his fist into the tabby wall, scraping his knuckles. He clutched the paper so tightly, ink smeared, and words blurred. Blood dripped from his skinned knuckles, adding round red smears to the paper.

"God damn buckra want us to work all ganged up, same as slaves. They demanding we 'low them overseers to come back and tell us how to work. Like I don't know how to plant better'n Sampson and the rest of them God damn sumbitches."

"Don't take the Lord's name in vain," Mammy said.

Cuffie looked ashamed for one instant, then his face twisted back into rage. Stomping his foot, he hollered, "Everything we grow the land-owners gits. We ain't git nothin'. Only thing they do for us is lets us stay in these no good, broken-down huts. Oh, and keep our kitchen gardens what they ain't got nothin' to do with. They even want to tell us when we can tend our own gardens and what hours we got to be raising cotton for them to sell and keep all the money off of."

Mammy's scar twisted as she took in the bad news. "What they lost the war for? I gotta go tell Teacher. Them soldiers oughtened allow this."

"Well, they is. They is." he repeated. "I still got my gun. I gonna shoot any bastard what make their X on anything like that. We got to stick together."

Mammy planted herself next to the hearth, listening to Cuffie rage. She had read the whole contract to him four times. There wasn't any sense in telling him again. The landowners could only plant a crop if their former slaves agreed to work. Cuffie's band of freemen had to stay their course and refuse to sign until the buckra made a better offer. Caving in would let the buckra regain slavery's hold.

The crows had been cawing all morning. Nothing was more certain than crows to let folks know hard times were coming. Lizzie could never forget a whole flock swirling around her, cawing up a storm, just before three slave traders, including her own uncle's cousin, seized her and carved up her face when she fought back. And then the image of the knife flashed into her mind. She grabbed the mantel piece to stop her trembling.

"Teacher telling freedmen not to sign," she said to Cuffie when she returned from meeting with the one teacher remaining on the north end of the island. "If y'all stick together, they got to come up with something better. Teacher say buckra gone lose they land if they can't get nobody to plant a crop. They can't pay the taxes 'less they got cotton to sell. They looking to have to sell to the Yankees for no money."

Cuffie spit at the fireplace. "What we s'posed to do while we waiting for them to make us a better offer? Stay here and starve?"

Swallowing her annoyance with him, Lizzie said, "While we waiting, we just keep on working our gardens and fishing our waters. Who gone stop us?"

"I be a man. I can do better off this here island. I got United States money in my pocket right now," Cuffie said, jingling the coins to show her. "Them soldiers'll give me more soon as they get paid."

"We got to pray them Yankee soldiers sticks around," she said. "They ain't gone be here forever. No telling how many folks get murdered once they clear out."

"Reckon they be in Savannah a goodish while, even after they gits off this island," Cuffie said. "'Spect they might give me a job in town."

"We was doing better during the war, when they left us alone," Mammy said. "Ain't nobody gone starve out here on this island. Long as fish be in the sea, berries on the vine, and sweet taters in the ground, we gone survive."

That night Cuffie lit a pine torch and walked to Hibernia to sit by the fire and cogitate with other freedmen while they drank moonshine.

"Y'all men sticking together give us the best chance," Mammy told him when he got ready to leave. "But ain't no need to stay out all night."

During that short, cold afternoon before he left, Mammy and Dicie tried to protect what was growing in the garden from ravenous deer. The deer got extra hungry just before leaves budded in the spring.

Dicie ground seeds she had saved last fall from hot pepper plants. Mammy mixed the powdered pepper in a jug with melted lard and vinegar, muttering an incantation as she worked. They sprinkled the potion on their cabbage and collards. The pungent seeds discouraged the deer from eating everything, and the lard kept the rain from washing the powder off. The smell was enough to run critters out of the garden for a while.

Just to be sure the potion worked, Mammy walked the fence line around the whole garden, chanting her spell, "Ebbtide, keep away, ebbtide, keep away, *aibtaeid*," as she dribbled the contents of last night's chamber pots in the dirt.

Cuffie's gang stuck together. The impoverished and defeated buckra were in a hard place. Their women sold diamond rings and necklaces to Yankee soldiers for just enough money to buy food.

The stalemate continued for the next few weeks. Afternoons, Mammy visited her teacher friend and met with a sympathetic Freedmen's Bureau agent. Nights, Daddy drank moonshine and plotted with his newly freed buddies.

Dicie debated whether she should pull her onions now before the vegetables in the garden were stolen or wait until the onions grew bigger. For the last two weeks, the drums had beaten incessantly. She had seen nothing of Tom. "It's' cause, he's beating the drum," she told herself.

Religious leaders and abolitionist educators who were encamped on Skidaway Island pressured the Freedman's Bureau for a compromise. Finally, the Bureau offered to sell abandoned and confiscated swamp land in South Carolina to the freedmen in exchange for their promised acres on Skidaway. Many potential farm laborers, especially those originally from South Carolina, left, taking their families with them.

"Good riddance to bad niggers," Cuffie said. "Bet the government gone change they mind and take that land away from 'em, too. Hope they don't try and come back here."

Taxes were due. Without crops, the plantation owners couldn't raise money to pay taxes; Without money, they couldn't plant crops. Northern investors circled like buzzards over the dying economy.

When time for spring planting had almost passed, Tom hurried up the road to Brisbane, not on his and Dicie's special path. It was the first time Dicie had seen him since she and Cass left Hibernia.

Without meeting Dicie's eyes, he gathered the freedmen and delivered his news. In desperation, Massa Warren had made the Brisbane folks a better offer. He promised to lease individual fields to any of his former slaves who were willing to work the land and to allow him to sell their crops. He promised that the money from the sale of the crops would be divided. Massa Warren would keep half. Half would go to the man who leased the land and raised the crops.

"He offering us same as white sharecroppers git," Tom said.

"Humph! I ain't never heard of them white sharecroppers amounting to much." Cuffie spit on the ground. "How we gone know how much that thieving bastard gits for our crop?"

"We gone have to trust him," Tom said. "They s'posed to write it down."

Cuffie looked at Lizzie. "Woman, I hope you can read what they write."

"Who gone pay for the seed? "Mammy asked. "We ain't got more 'n what we use for our own garden. What about a mule? The plow we use ain't got hardly nothing left to the blade."

Tom rubbed his hands over the legs of his overalls. "The Bureau s'posed to be working that out. Massa Warren gone let us stay in the tabbies, but you might have to walk a far piece to the land what you get to lease. He ain't offering but five acres each to a man. If he want us to grow cotton, he gone have to give us the seed. We ain't got none."

"Hell, that ain't much of a deal," Cuffie said.

"Freedmen's agent talking about the massas bringing cornmeal, sugar, and tea out here now, to sweeten the deal, along with some pigs we can raise and butcher," Tom said. "He might throw in some dress goods and shoes like he used to do back when we wasn't allowed to have cash money. But he might charge us for that out our share."

The faces of the other freedmen and women still at Brisbane were solemn, as they listened to Tom.

Dicie turned to Tom. "You gone sign something like that?" It was the first time they had spoken. She swallowed hard. It took all her courage to look at him.

Cuffie broke in. "Damn girl, right now we keep everything we raise. Why should we give him half? A little sugar and some tea, we can buy ourself. I brung tea back from town last week. Big old sow over yonder by the creek just had her third litter of piglets. My boys can catch 'em anytime they gits hungry. What we need is milled timber to fix a good pen. We need a mule and a brand-new plowshare."

"Hear, hear!" the man next to Cuffie chimed in. "That don't sound like much of a offer."

Tom scratched his head. "You forgetting Massa Warren can put us off this island, off our land what President Abraham Lincoln done promised to us. Them Yankee soldiers'll help the massas, not us. What crops we got in our gardens'll belong to him, 'less'n we make a deal."

Mammy had held her peace till now. "If they bring us a paper, I'll take it to Teacher."

Tom grinned. "If Teacher say we should sign it, you have to teach me to write my name."

"I'll do more than that," Mammy promised. "I'm gone make Teacher start learning me some 'rithmetic so's I make sure we getting what right outta the sale."

"If'n I decide to stay," Cuffie said.

Dicie's stomach ached from anticipating their fight.

Tom looked from one to the other and said, "I got to run back and see what else news come in." He grabbed Dicie's arm and headed her back toward the path through the forest. Once they came to the low trail that led back into deep woods, he stopped hurrying. "Let's you and me set for jest a little piece," he whispered.

He led her to the sheltered place where the doe left her newborn fawns. The deer were heavy now with unborn babies, but spring had not yet arrived, and the empty clearing had filled with dried leaves and straw. Vines and branches had grown over and around it since last summer when the last of the fawns was old enough to follow its mother. Tom threw aside fallen pinecones and cleared a soft spot for Dicie. Wrapping his arms around her, he guided her down and kissed her softly on her lips.

She tried to hold herself stiffly, but a warm glow pushed Bella right out of her mind as he pressed her against him. If only she could stay in this safe spot with his arms around her, away from all the shouting and quarreling.

"I want you to be my girl," he said, smoothing her long thick hair. "When this mess get straighten out, if I get a place of my own, will you come and live with me?"

"Ain't nothing I'd like better," she said, wrapping her arms around him.

They lay together for what seemed like only a minute before he said, "I got to go. The Bureau agent s'posed to be back with answers. If'n it ain't too bad, I aim to give it a try. Maybe I can save up and move us to the mainland. Long as you here, I want to stay. You go; I go."

Dicie grabbed hold of his arm. She could hardly bear having the warmth of Tom's body snatched from her. He had uttered the words she longed to hear.

He sat up, pulling his arm away. "What I hear, most of 'em say if they lose they land, they leaving. Some men even talking 'bout heading up north. Some say it be too cold up there. Out west, where they ain't many folks, you can git youself a piece of farmland just by working it. Might not be another man for twenty miles beyond where you at. A body can raise a family in peace."

He put his arms around her for one last hug. "I want you with me."

Watching Tom descend into the ditch separating Brisbane from Hibernia, Dicie worried. How could she be sure he really meant what he said? Was his drumming the only reason he had stayed away or was it Bella?

Late that night, her thoughts worried her like a snake playing with a rat. Daddy wanted to go. Mammy wanted to stay. What would her life be like if she lived with Tom? Trying to get to sleep, she twisted and turned so long on her pallet under Mammy and Daddy's bed that Mammy hollered, "Girl, hold still. You got worms?"

She held her body rigid, but she had barely fallen asleep when a rooster crowed somewhere in the compound, and Daddy's feet hit the floor next to her head.

Chapter Thirty-Two

April 1867

Two days later, Mammy and Dicie were alone in their half of the tabby when they heard the tramping of many footsteps. "You wait inside and listen through the crack under the window," Mammy told Dicie. Accompanied by two soldiers and an elderly black man, the Freedmen's Bureau agent halted in front of their tabby.

The hair escaping from under the black man's battered fedora had turned white, and a roll of fat hung from under his shirt. Mammy had to peer hard before she recognized Sampson.

"Miz Lizzie," he said. "I'd of known you anywhere. God bless you."

Mammy's mouth dropped. Five years had passed since Sampson disappeared from Skidaway Island. In all the time he cracked his whip at the women of the compound, he had never spoken to her in such a kindly tone. But it was his same old gravelly voice. She'd never forget the sound. But why the conciliating attitude? He must be up to something.

She closed her mouth and bent her shoulders to the humble position Sampson formerly demanded, but she answered him not so meekly as in the past, "Hey there, Sampson. What you doin' here?"

Out of the corner of her eye she saw other residents of the compound slide into their tabbies and bolt the doors. Nevertheless, they would all have their ears pressed up to the window cracks.

"I come see if'n I can get all us back working," he said, pulling on the brim of his old hat. "Let bygones be bygones. Ever' one of us need to be making money again."

"I ain't never made no money with you," Mammy thought, but she held her peace. It must be true, what they said about the buckra needing workers. Why else would he be acting so slimy? She waited patiently for his next words.

He hitched up his pants until they covered his belly and said, "Ain't you itching to know what gone happen?"

"You want to tell me?" Mammy said. She surprised herself, talking back to him like that. For a minute she held her breath, remembering the big old bull whip he used to carry. But times had changed. She was free. The familiar soldiers were with him, and he didn't show any sign of carrying a whip.

"You and me gone be partners," he said. "Where yo' old man at? He come back home once he be free? Or you got 'nother one?" He gave Mammy the smarmy smile he used to give the woman he selected for "special services" after work.

Isaac and Cass peered out the door of the other side of the tabby. Nobody had asked Massa Warren if they could take over the empty half. Seeing the old overseer, Isaac whispered to Cass, "Run get Daddy and tell him to bring his gun."

Isaac stepped forward out of the door while Cass climbed through the back window, heading to Hibernia where Daddy most likely could be found. "Daddy be here directly," Isaac said to Sampson. He hoped his words were true.

Mammy's heart stopped racing. Her men were near.

"Why, boy, don't you know me?" Sampson said to Isaac. He took a long step closer to Isaac, moving into the boy's personal space, like he used to do when he carried a bull whip. "I be the driver here when you wasn't knee high to a grasshopper. I got business with yo' mammy. Daddy too, if he here."

"What you got to say?" Mammy asked, drawing Sampson's attention away from her boy.

"Massa Warren want you to stay here on Brisbane and work for him. 'Stead of working where he tells you, you gits to farm any five acres you choose out of his twenty-five hundred. What you grow will be half your'n and half his'n. More you grow, the more you gits. If these here boys of your'n want to join up with you, he be willing to lease five more acres to each of them."

"What about the garden behind my tabby? "Mammy asked. "I been tending it all by myself. What it got in it belong to me."

Sampson reached up and adjusted his old, dirty fedora. When he lifted it, Mammy noticed his castor-oil coated curls hadn't just turned white; the top of his head was completely bald. "I'll have to talk to the massa about that. He ain't said nothing 'bout folks keeping extra crops for their own selves. How much you got?"

"Ain't but about half an acre and hardly nothin' in it now, but I be fixing to plant a spring garden. I done already sowed part of it, but if nobody work it, deer'll eat it up in a minute."

Sampson whistled. "A whole half acre. A heap bigger than what Massa Warren 'llowed back in olden times."

A statement, not a question.

"True that," Mammy swallowed hard, hoping her other menfolk were on their way. "But you forget in them days you brung me coffee, tea, molasses, salt pork, cornmeal. You ain't brung me nothing in more'n five years. I'd of done starved."

"I'll speak to the massa about it," Sampson said.

Just then Cuffie strode forward backed by his muscular sons, Cass, Rufus, and Gus. At the approach of the four strapping men, the soldiers grabbed hold of their rifles. Eyeing the soldiers, the men halted a short distance away.

"Hear somebody asking 'bout me," Cuffie growled, stepping forward. "What yo' want?"

"Massa Warren send me to see if you wanna do some farming with him," Sampson said. A placating smile spread across his face.

"Why you think I want to trust a man with my business what sold me 'way from my family?" Cuffie asked, balling up his fists.

Sampson's smile wavered, but he stuck to his mission. "If we don't get some crops in the ground, everybody gone be hurting. He offering you a lot more land than you got now, seed to grow cotton, and half the money when he sell it. Cotton'll grow money in yo' pocket a lot quicker'n a mess of collards."

"I gone have to have it wrote down and have my woman here give it to the teachers to read anything he wants to say to me," Cuffie said, grudgingly.

"You got to ask yo' woman? That ain't the Cuffie I remember." Sampson's voice rose to a high mocking pitch. He pulled a document out of his pocket and stepped toward Cuffie, waving the paper close to Cuffie's face. "I got a paper right here you can make yo' X on, unless you turning into some kind of bitch."

Cuffie punched the paper aside with his fist. "You lying bastard, don't call me a bitch."

Sampson scowled and took a step toward Cuffie.

One of the soldiers raised his rifle and motioned the other to stay back. Holding the rifle high, he stepped forward between the two men and grabbed Sampson's shoulder. In a commanding voice, he ordered, "Halt!

Cuffie took two steps backwards, away from the barrel of the gun.

The soldier told Sampson, "Look here. I know this man. No need to fight him. He's been doing my laundry since we've been billeted on this God-forsaken island. Our whole detail uses him. Leave him alone. He's got a right as a citizen of the United States to have anything he signs looked at." He gave Sampson a sharp shake on the shoulder. "Give the paper to Miz Lizzie and we'll bring you back next week to see what he says."

Sampson looked like he still wanted to fight, but grudgingly he handed the paper to Mammy and stomped off toward the next tabby. What else could he do with the two soldiers there?

"Thankee, man. See you at camp tomorrow. I'll make sure I gets that uniform spanking clean," Cuffie told the soldier.

The soldiers followed Sampson, but before they left, the one who told Sampson to leave Cuffie alone, drew back and whispered, "Watch your back with that one."

"Yes, sir," Cuffie grunted.

The family walked inside the tabby and barred the door. Mammy started reading. "A-r-t-i-c-l-e-s of Agree-m-e-n-t," she sounded out. "It'll take a minute." She shifted the paper further down to where the name Cuffie was written.

"Just look at this," Mammy said. "Says Cuffie got a right for one year, that'd be 1867, to plant the five acres over yonder, way over by the pine trees where the east cotton field used to end and the creek come in, but it say Massa Warren git to sell everything we grow. He keep half the money from what he sells and give Cuffie half. Eighteen sixty-seven nigh half gone, and what s'posed to happen after that?"

Cuffie shrugged his shoulders. He was still mad.

Dicie stepped closer to Mammy so she could see the paper over Mammy's shoulder. The numbers were all there, just like Mammy had taught her. She wished she could read the letters.

"And lookee here. This paper say we got to grow everything under the supervision of Sampson Jones. Is Sampson so high-faluting he got two names now? Done thought we was through with him."

"Woman, you doin' a fine job, reading all that off that paper," Cuffie said. "But you run along and find yo' teacher friend. No telling what massa might of slipped in there to try and juke us. I'll take care of the chores for you today."

Mammy hurried off while Dicie and Daddy trudged back to the garden.

Daddy asked, "How we gone trust that bastard to give us our share. Come to think of it, if Sampson be doing the selling, how Massa Warren gone know he getting his fair share?"

Dicie didn't have an answer. "We gotta watch him," she said. But she could only watch what he took from her family. "Maybe when the time come, you can ask in town what cotton going for?"

"You a mighty smart girl," Daddy said. "I always told Mammy you got a better head on your shoulders than most. Never paid 'ttention to the price of cotton, since I just be selling vegetables. I sho' will listen up next time I goes to market."

In the bright spring sun, the garden made a fine-looking sight. Constant vigilance and the fence the boys put together out of saplings helped keep the critters out. The homemade fertilizer Mammy concoct-ed from ashes and waste, human and animal, worked better than what Sampson used to bring.

Their winter garden was done, all but the onions, whose white bulbs showed sweet and full above the black dirt. Early pinto beans climbed up the trellis Isaac twisted together from bamboo and dried trumpet vines. Popping up beneath another trellis were the first leaves of butter peas. Sweet potato vines already curled upward from roots left in the soil last year.

While Daddy shoveled lush black rows for the squash, cucumbers, and tomatoes that Mammy was sprouting inside the tabby, Dicie walked through the garden, picking newly emerged weeds. Smelling the fresh rows of dirt Daddy turned up, Dicie could almost taste the delicious, juicy vegetables to come.

Later, as she helped Daddy wrestle a tree stump out of a newly cleared strip of land next to the fence, Dicie said, "Good thing Mammy asked Sampson to add our garden to the paper. You and Mammy done worked that piece over yonder since before I was birthed." She pointed to part of the garden in the corner nearest the tabby. There, a bright red male cardinal chased a brownish female around a weathered fence post.

"Lord, that brings back memories," Daddy said. He flashed a grin; then his face grew somber. "I got a chance to get a little real money out of this garden. If that sumbitch tries to mess with my vegetables, I'm out of here."

Dicie twisted one of her curls around her finger. But what about me, she worried silently.

Chapter Thirty-Three

April–August 1867

Mammy strolled back to the tabby with the paper from Sampson all marked up. "Teacher wrote down everything we want," she said. "She say if it ain't wrote down and everybody done put they name on the paper, it ain't no good. Teacher added that part about we get to keep everything in our vegetable garden, and we can use any farm equipment he give us in our garden, not just on the massa's land."

Dicie took the paper from her hand and studied it carefully. Where Teacher had added her writing, it was plain as day. She hadn't changed any of the numbers. Dicie wished Mammy would hurry up and teach her to read the words.

"Tell Tom I'll fix his'n, too," Mammy said.

Dicie hurried down to the edge of the island with a crab trap and a bucket. That night she and Mammy boiled crabs for a celebration. Finally, they could get settled.

"Don't hollow out yo' fried fish till yo' catch 'em," Daddy warned, tossing his empty crab-shells out the door as he repeated the advice folks brought with them from Africa.

"The cards say better times a-coming," Mammy said.

Cuffie grunted and shook his head.

"How 'bout you show me them cards, soon as we finish eating?" Dicie asked Mammy. She had learned a lot of Mammy's magic, but it seemed like the cards always showed something she hadn't learned.

"Any time got to be better'n what we been through," Daddy said.

Another week passed before Sampson came back to the compound. While he was gone, Dicie studied Mammy's cards. Each time she cut the deck, a joker turned up. Not a good sign. Why didn't the cards show good news for her, like when Mammy read them? Days passed and the family despaired of making a cotton crop. The cards showed hard times coming.

Every day disgruntled newcomers trudged down the main road across Brisbane, heading back to the mainland. Men, women, and children carried sacks of their belongings. Few had a cart to pull; none had a mule to pull it. Lean-tos were abandoned and many old tabbies once more stood empty.

"Come out here and look what I brung" Sampson hollered, when he finally returned. He stood outside the tabby door with a box of dried tea leaves, a fifty-pound bag of sugar, four bags of cornmeal, and too many other boxes and bags for Dicie to count. A loaded wagon and mule waited beside him. "Hope you got that paper signed and all ready for me."

For a change Mammy was all smiles. "Good gracious, Sampson, we been looking for you all week. Here yo' paper. Teacher made some changes, and Cuffie signed his name and put his initial "C" there by everything Teacher wrote," Mammy said. "Did Massa Warren agree to me putting on there that I keeps my garden? Teacher done wrote it right here." She pointed to handwriting on page two. Teacher had crossed words out and put other words on both pages.

Sampson snatched the paper, and without looking at it, stuffed it in his pocket. "I got a bolt of flannel for you and a barrel of salt pork besides all them provisions," he said, gesturing to the sacks already unloaded. "Soon as you get the rest out the wagon, I'm gone meet yo' Cuffie over on that five-acre piece down by the creek. I got five acres worth of cotton seed and a new plow blade for him, but he got to get that seed in by the end of this week. Field's done grown up something awful. Cuffie'll need to mend the fence what's there, and build a 'nother one to fence off them sections what connects to the field next to it, soon as he gits the seed in. His five acres ain't the field yo' boys used to work."

Sampson looked around cautiously. Cuffie was nowhere to be seen. "Where he be at?"

Mammy kept her eyes fixed on a squirrel burrowing in the dead leaves next to the tabby. "He ain't home right now. Reckon you can find him over to Hibernia, where the soldiers stay at."

Cuffie didn't make it home to dinner last night. They hadn't seen him that morning either, but she wasn't going to let on to Sampson.

"Have one of your boys find him and git him on over there," Sampson said. "If this seed gits stolen, he gone have to pay for it." He climbed back on the wagon and flapped the reins. "Git," he hollered to the mule.

Dicie began hauling the provisions into the tabby. "Just look at this sugar," she said, dancing around the heavy sack, made of heavy white cotton cloth with blue flowers printed on it. "See how pretty that bag is. We ain't hardly had real sugar since the war 'cept for that little bitty paper sack Daddy brung. The bag be big enough for me to sew a waist and maybe a pair of bloomers out of it, once we eat all the sugar."

Dicie brewed the tea leaves. She and Mammy sat on the bench outside the tabby to enjoy the hot fresh drink, splurging with heaping spoonsful of real sugar instead of just a few drops of aging wild honey. From the top of the big pine tree by the door, a trumpet vine dropped orange petals at their feet. Honeybees flitted in and out of the flowers still on the vine.

"Reckon Sampson gone bring back that paper with Massa Warren's name on it?" Mammy asked.

Dicie took a sip of tea and focused her thoughts on Sampson stuffing the paper in his pocket without looking at it. "Probably not," she concluded. "Will it matter?"

"We have to wait and see," Mammy said. "Least it's buying us some time. Young Massa Warren ain't never been that bad, 'cept he hardly ever be out here, and he let Sampson run everything. I just pray to God we get this crop in and harvested befo' Sampson and Cuffie blow up at each other."

Cuffie and the boys plowed and fenced the five acres. Sampson leased the boys another five-acre plot and supplied them with fertilizer and cotton seed. The five men worked together, weeding and carrying water to the plants during a dry spell. After laying fallow for four years, the field was extra fertile, and the cotton plants grew lush and full. With all the men working, they had plenty of time left to help Mammy and Dicie with the garden. Yellow squash, tomatoes, and cucumbers flourished.

"Lord, we got enough for a hundred folks," Cuffie said. He filled a croker sack and carried it to the soldiers' encampment at Hibernia. Fifty cents jingled in his pocket when he got home. "We got enough to feed us and more coming. I can carry a load to sell in town and spend this here money. What you want?" he asked Dicie and Mammy.

"A new needle," Dicie said. The one she was using had rusted and left tracks on the pretty fabric left over when they emptied all the sack of sugar.

"More chalk," Mammy said. "So I can teach Dicie and Cass how to write they letters. And some ink. What Teacher give me is about gone."

"A knife," Cass said. "All I got is the one you say ain't no good anymore. You done wore it out sharpening."

Next week Cuffie loaded up two croker sacks with yellow squash, butter beans, cucumbers and tomatoes. Each sack weighed forty pounds. "Gone make me some money for sure," he said as he hoisted the sacks on his shoulders.

Just as Cuffie got to the river and dropped the sacks in his bateau, Sampson came running up. Two flunkeys with him flexed their muscles and scowled. "Hey there, Cuffie," Sampson hollered. "Where you goin'?"

"Got business in town," Cuffie said, hopping into the bateau.

"I know you ain't selling no crop. That paper what I brought out here say Massa be only one can sell anything you grow."

"This here be from my garden," Cuffie said. "He ain't got nothing coming to him from the garden. Teacher wrote it out and my woman give it to you."

"Who you think owns land what the garden sitting on? You got a paper says something different?"

"You ain't brung it back after I give it to you," Cuffie said. "You ain't got one I signed without it saying I git to keep my garden."

"Let's see what he got in them bags," Sampson told his men. The two henchmen headed toward the water. One jumped off the low bluff onto the shore, while the other scrambled for the path where Cuffie's bateau was beached.

Seeing them coming, Cuffie jammed his paddle into the sand and gave a mighty push backwards. His loaded bateau shot out with the outgoing tide. The hapless pursuers stopped still, sunk in marsh mud, watching Cuffie slide away.

"Let him go. We go git what's left of his garden and git his money too, when he comes back," Sampson told them. Armed with stout sticks, hidden knives, and empty croker sacks, the three men hurried over to the Brisbane compound where Mammy and Dicie were picking weeds out from under vines loaded with ripe red tomatoes and green tomatoes, soon to turn red.

"Hey Miz Lizzie," Sampson sung out. "I come to git yo' tomatoes so the massa can sell 'em and give you yo' share."

Mammy whirled around "What you mean? This my garden. Teacher wrote it on the paper."

"Heh, heh! You got that paper?' Sampson laughed nervously. He was still a little skittish around Mammy. "I brung some help to do the picking in case you was too busy."

His two enforcers advanced with the croker sacks as Sampson waved his stick toward the tomatoes. "Don't forget them cucumbers," he yelled.

Mammy let out her blood-curdling panther scream. One of the flunkies drew back, but Sampson had heard her scream before. "Done told you she going to do that," he yelled. "You men or not?"

Dicie cowered in the corner of the garden, hoe in hand. Sampson must have known Daddy wasn't there to protect them. She wished he was here with his gun. Where were her big brothers when she needed them?

One of the men set his foot down right on top of her biggest yellow squash plant. All the ripe tomatoes Mammy saved for supper next week were ripped off the vine. Sampson and his flunkies stripped all of the half-ripe ones, too. Next, the robbers headed for cucumbers, yanking up the roots of some of the plants as they snatched all the biggest fruits.

"We leaving you plenty to eat," Sampson said as they tramped across new shoots of okra. He pointed to Dicie. "Just you remember, any extra you got what you don't need to feed yo' self and this girl here, I'll be back for. Once I sell 'em, I'll give you yo' half. You ain't allowed to sell nothing 'cept through the massa. That means me."

Mammy gave him her best evil eye but said nothing. Memories of the beatings he enjoyed giving in the old days kept her rooted to her spot in the garden. Dicie tried to hide behind a trellis of butter beans.

Soon as Sampson disappeared with his flunkies she said, "Lemme run see what Teacher say. No telling what'll happen when Cuffie gets home. I'm taking you with me far as Hibernia. You can stay with Tom."

Chapter Thirty-Four

August 1867

Soon as they crossed the ditch, Dicie's eyes met Tom's. Standing bare-chested in his garden among trellises of butter peas, tangles of tomato vines, and chutes of knee-high okra, his muscles shone, a black-skinned prince. Dropping his hoe, he jumped the sapling fence, nodded to Mammy, then grabbed Dicie's hand.

"Welcome to Hibernia," he said, his brow furrowing. "What y'all doing here?"

Despite Mammy's eagle eye upon her, Dicie reached for Tom's shoulder and pressed her face to his chest. She burst into tears, ignoring Mammy's suddenly sucked in breath. She held her emotions under tight rein during the rape of their garden, and watched silently as evil men threw ripe tomatoes into croker sacks and broke the necks of her prized yellow squash. She wanted her daddy, but trembled with fear. How would Cuffie act when he found out? She cried all over Tom's already sweat-soaked shoulder.

Mammy frowned and muttered under her breath. "Girl, how many times I done told you don't let nobody see yo' weakness?" She jerked Dicie away from Tom and wiped Dicie's tears with the hem of her skirt.

Turning back to Tom, she said, "We got a big problem. Sampson done come and tore up our garden and stole my vegetables. He say we can't sell to nobody. Only Massa can sell what we grow."

Tom patted Dicie's shoulder. Tears dribbled from the corners of her eyes.

"She got a right to cry," he said, turning to Mammy. "Thought you had a piece of paper."

Mammy scowled. "What he say ain't what we put in the lease paper. Teacher wrote the garden only belong to me. Massa selling my vegetables ain't part of the deal. We been selling 'em ever since Cuffie came home."

Tom looked at the two distraught women and shook his head. "What Sampson say 'bout massa signing the paper?"

Mammy gave him a disgusted look. "He ain't never said whether he did or he don't. Just brought out a passel of provisions and said we had the five acres. Now he promising he gone bring back half the money what he gits from selling our garden produce, but we don't look for that. Pro'bly just another lie. I'm fixing to find Teacher to see what we can do."

Dicie stood up straight and pulled away from Mammy. She tried to rearrange her face to make believe she was strong, even though she longed to throw herself back in Tom's arms.

Mammy gave Dicie a stern look and asked Tom, "Do you mind if Dicie stay with you while I hunt Teacher? I won't be too long, but Cuffie went to town, and I'm scared to leave Dicie alone, what with Sampson and his boys on a rampage."

"Course she can stay. I be right here in my garden. We ain't heard from nobody yet 'bout signing no share-cropping paper." He wiped the sweat out of his eyes, and said, "Hope my garden be safe."

"You lucky you ain't got Sampson messing with you." Mammy stopped in her tracks as a thought crossed her mind, "You heard 'bout some Yankee gone buy Hibernia? That what Teacher say."

"Ain't heard nothing for sure or I'd a put it out on the drum. If'n some Yankee buys it, it'll pro'bly take a while for him to pay 'tention to Skidaway Island. If it happen, I'll beat the drum."

He scratched his head and reached for the kerchief around his neck to wipe more sweat. "Wonder what set Sampson off? You think he hear about Cuffie selling produce?"

"Not far as I know," Mammy said. "Course that Geechee got spies everywhere."

She looked over at Dicie, and rubbed the scar on her face, thinking. Wrinkling her forehead, she muttered to herself, "Wonder if he could've seen Cuffie leaving with the croker sacks this morning?"

Just then a pleasantly plump girl, a little older than Tom, strolled from a nearby tabby to the edge of the garden. She had a pink flower stuck in her braids and carried an empty basket over one arm. Bella!

"Tom," she called, "My mammy sent me over here to pick some of your lady peas." She slid the basket over her wrist and twirled it around with her fingers while she stared curiously at Dicie and Mammy.

Tom looked over at Mammy. "This here be Miz Laliah's daughter. Hope she ain't bothering you with her bad manners. Miz Laliah's the woman what saved me when my mammy died. She done just had Bella here and more'n enough milk for two babies. Most folks think Bella my sister."

Tom smiled at the pretty girl and said, "Bella, mind your manners. This be Miz Lizzie and her daughter, Dicie."

Bella laughed. "Pleased to meet you. Some little brother he be. Think he can boss me around just cause he bigger than me."

Dicie stared at the beautiful girl. Like a sister? Was that why they always sat together at the old praise house?

Mammy said, "Miz Laliah? A good woman. When I lost my babies I always worried 'bout what happen if I be the one to go home, 'stead of my baby."

Tom reached over and took Dicie's hand. "Bella, this girl here is Isaac's little sister. You know Isaac."

Dicie's face got hot. She wanted to throw her arms around Tom and drag him away from Bella, but Mammy would have had a fit.

Mammy gave Bella a tight smile. Her scar drew down toward her mouth as she turned back to Tom. "You won't mind then if Dicie bides a piece with you while I run over to the schoolhouse to look for Teacher? I 'spect I be back under two hours."

"Course not, Miz Lizzie," Tom said, eyeing Bella nervously.

Mammy hurried off. Dicie glanced at Bella and picked up the hoe Tom had dropped. Fixing her eyes on the section he had been working, she continued down the row, carefully chopping out the weeds without disturbing the roots of his vegetables.

Bella sashayed over to the lady peas and began picking. Both girls kept their eyes on their tasks, but each snuck peeks at the other. Bella really was pretty. No other girls close to Dicie's age lived in the Brisbane compound, so Dicie wasn't sure how to act towards her. Did the other girl always put a flower in her hair, or did she just do that when she was coming to see Tom? Seems like the flower would have wilted if she had picked it that morning.

Dicie tried chopping weeds faster. She wanted Tom to see how good she was at taking care of the garden. Bella didn't look like she did much farming.

The sun shone high in the sky, and the three young people wilted in the heat. Bella looked like she was feeling the heat the least. Of course. The clothes she wore were so skimpy, they were hardly decent. Even though Bella was old enough to let the hem of her skirt down to cover her ankles, it was hardly longer than her knees. The top of her waist was unbuttoned low enough that her breasts showed.

Dicie wore an old skirt of Mammy's that reached her ankles. Her waist was fastened all the way up to her neck. When Bella looked the other way, Dicie unbuttoned the top two buttons. A slight breeze cooled her chest.

It seemed to Dicie that Bella took more time than needed to fill her basket. A crow let out an annoying caw, caw, the whole time Bella dawdled in the peas. When she finally picked all she wanted, instead of waving goodbye and walking back where she came from, she sauntered over to Tom, smiled at him, and said loud enough to be sure Dicie heard, "I'll see you tonight at supper. You gone love how good these peas taste."

She strolled slowly out of the vegetable patch, glancing back to see if Tom was watching.

He was.

Dicie hit a piece of dried marsh mud with an extra strong whack of her hoe.

Tom dropped his rake and walked over to Dicie. He took her hands and said, "Miz Laliah been fixing supper for me and Daddy since I be born. She brungs me a plate when I'm drumming and can't get away. That why Bella gits free run of my garden."

He looked so worried, Dicie unexpectedly felt sorry for him. Why was she worrying about Bella? She reached out to touch Tom's cheek. At least the wench was gone.

Tom didn't put his arms around her like she expected. He twisted his foot and looked at the ground. "There's something I got to tell you," he said. "Daddy always wanted me to take care of Bella. When he got sick, he made me promise I would stay with Bella. She know that."

Dicie drew back in shock. "But you told me you want to be with me." she said. Tears burned her eyes. How could he have tricked her so bad? He had said he loved her.

Tom looked miserable. "I do," he said.

The tears burst out, but she dashed them away with the back of her hand. What if Bella was watching? "If you gone be with her, don't come see me no more," she said. Her heart was breaking.

By late afternoon Mammy still hadn't returned. Dicie retreated to the shade of a live oak, drinking from Hibernia's well, and trying not to look at Tom. Let Bella chop his weeds.

Tom stayed in his garden, leaning on his hoe, and avoiding looking in Dicie's direction.

Finally, Dicie spotted Mammy trudging up the dirt track. She was dirty and sweating from the three-mile walk from the schoolhouse. Her face was downcast.

"Teacher's gone try to talk to Freedmen's agent, but she say she can't be sure he can help." she said. "Since the government done changed, most of them agents been fired, and the rest side with the buckra. She say the soldiers 'bout to be called back off of the island and won't be nobody left to interfere."

Tom stepped forward. "I ain't surprised. We got to pray, Miz Lizzie," he said. "Maybe Preacher Houston can help."

Dicie felt the pain return to her stomach. Tom was such a polite, helpful man. Just the kind of man she wanted. Now he would disappear from her life.

"Doubt if he can," Mammy said. "Teacher say he leaving us, too. Going to Atlanta to be a bigshot in the legislature." Mammy's foot twitched, and she looked worried. They would be powerless against Sampson without the soldiers.

All were silent for a moment, contemplating the enormity of their loss.

Mammy's fighting spirit briefly returned. "We all gone have to pray, including Sampson, when Cuffie finds out about the garden," she said.

Chapter Thirty-Five

August 1867

Neither Dicie nor Mammy felt like eating that night. The brothers in the adjoining tabby were left to feed themselves. Dicie told them what happened to the garden but kept her talk with Tom to herself. Her grief was too raw to share.

Gus offered to strangle Sampson, but Mammy forbade him. Tired as she was, Mammy drew herself up and ordered, "I ain't gone have no fighting. If you dig a pit fo' him, you dig one fo' yo'self. I ain't gone lose you, too."

All night long Dicie lay awake listening for Daddy's special call, three notes of the great horned owl. Mammy had barred the door, but she lay awake listening, too. Neither really expected to hear from him, but Dicie especially needed him to comfort her.

Next morning her empty stomach growled, getting her out of bed before the sun rose. She cracked open the door and scoured the horizon, looking for traces of Sampson or Daddy. Neither were visible, but Sampson's big shoeprints were smack in the middle of the gray sand in front of the tabby. Like always, Dicie had raked the yard smooth last night before they went to bed so nobody could steal their footprints. Mammy told the boys to rake their side. When her brothers didn't, Dicie raked their side, too.

She tiptoed around the corner of the tabby to check the dirt in back. More of Sampson's footprints, big boots with distinct heels, were pressed into the dirt. Her brothers went barefoot, and Daddy wore slides. Only Sampson's prints were there.

Praise the Lord, Daddy had sense enough to stay away. Dicie hoped he was safe.

She picked a mess of green tomatoes and fried them for breakfast. They weren't too bad with cornbread, but she missed the big red juicy ones she had in mind to eat before Sampson stole them.

Mammy hardly touched the food. Instead, she left Dicie with her brothers and marched through the compound, asking everybody if they had seen Cuffie.

"Probably over to Hibernia," one of the new city girls said. Her hair stuck straight up over her forehead, no braids at all. Smears of red paint dotted her cheeks and covered her lips. Just the kind of hussy Cuffie would know.

Mammy scowled at her. "What makes you think that?" she asked.

The young girl took several steps back. She had heard Mammy wasn't to be trifled with. "Root doctor or maybe a witch," was what folks said.

"You know, 'cuz he do washing for the soldiers," the girl said. She stammered as she spoke. "I gotta go," she said, retreating into her tabby.

Was she one of the wenches Mammy saw drinking moonshine with men at the Brisbane bonfire? She looked like the girl who begged Cuffie for a sip of his shine.

The old woman Mammy occasionally slipped food to hobbled out of the lean-to next to the cookhouse. "Got me something to eat?" she asked.

Mammy stared at her. The woman's thin grey hair looked like it hadn't been combed since before the war, but now she wasn't quite as skinny. When she begged, kind newcomers had shared their rations. Now the newcomers were gone. "I'll see what I can do," Mammy said. "You seen my man, Cuffie?"

"To the side of the river t'other day. I had a crab line, back a little ways from where them bateaux pull up. Sampson and two o' his bully boys raising a ruckus. Cuffie clumb in his bateau, like he trying to leave real fast. I made sure I hid behind a bush so's they ain't seen me.

"What Cuffie do?" Mammy asked gently, before the woman's story wandered away in the mist of her mind.

"I hear Cuffie holler, 'leave me alone. I ain't yo' slave no more.' Then a bunch o' splashing commenced. When I peeked out the bushes, Cuffie done push his bateau off in the water. They try to wade after him, but mud suck 'em down. They cussing up a storm. Something about they want to see what in his sacks."

"You hear anything else?" Mammy asked, scratching a mosquito bite.

"You got anything good to eat?" The woman's mouth hung open and a dribble of saliva ran down her chin. "I be so hungry I can't think."

"I'll run home and see," Mammy said.

Hurrying back to the tabby, Mammy let out a stream of Arabic. "Ahbil!" Stupid!" To Dicie she said, "Now we got real trouble. Found out what set Sampson off. Cuffie can't keep his mouth shut. No telling what else gone happen if he do come home."

She fetched a piece of cornbread from the bread box and took it along with some fried tomatoes back to the old woman. "Come on down to my tabby if you hear any more. I'll fix you a piece of blackberry cobbler if my girl pick enough berries," she said. "Now tell me what else you hear."

The woman gobbled the cornbread. "Sampson too busy trying to haul his bully boys out the mud to do nothing but cuss."

After two more days with no word from Cuffie, Mammy sent Isaac over to Hibernia. "Look around and see if that woman named Dorothy know where he might be," she said. "Don't ask her straight up. Just scout around where she stay and see what's what. Best if he stay over there, if that where he be, till Sampson stop looking for him. Sampson ain't got no right to make nobody do nothing at Hibernia."

The next evening Dicie walked along her trail behind the garden, grieving over what Tom told her the day before, and wondering what she did wrong. How could she have mistaken his feelings for her so badly?

Silently surveying the forest for young deer, she glimpsed a shadow. The shadow moved. Not a deer. Out of the corner of her eye, she spotted the full dark figure of Sampson hiding behind a tangle of vines, sneaking around back of their tabby. She slipped off the trail. Crouching through a low path made by deer, she ran to the front door to warn Mammy.

"Chile, ever since you found them footprints, I felt his spirit circling our home at night," Mammy said. "Let me teach you the spell I'm working on. I has to be careful it don't catch the wrong person. Lucky, he left all them big prints for us to root him with."

Mammy poured a little water in the dirt behind the cabin where Sampson's tracks were thickest. With a flat-bladed shovel, she carefully lifted the dirt under and around the shoe print and laid it on the hearth, still intact on the shovel.

"We let this dry good and hard, then we can save it on a piece of tin from the junk pile. We put a heap of poison on it and say the spell. Then we hide it real good next to where he spying on us."

"What the spell?" Dicie asked. She had memorized more than ten of Mammy's spells. Some made sense; some were just random sounds. Learning another spell would help keep her mind off of Tom's shocking news. How could he have told her he loved her?

Mammy looked around the garden and into the woods behind. "Them leaves got ears," she whispered. "Follow me inside."

She looked under the bed, then barred the door. "It got to have his name in it," she said, referring to the spell. "Now he got two names, it got to have both, Sampson and Jones. You say his name and 'be gone' three times. Then the word 'mawt.' Mean 'die' in my home language."

Dicie nodded, repeating the words to herself. "What you gone use for poison?" she asked.

"Oh, the poison ain't no problem," Mammy said. "He ain't got to actually touch it. Not if the magic be strong enough. Of course, if'n he see this here root and try to pick it up, it'll kill him quick. We can use a rag to strip some leaves off'n that there oleander bush or I can cut some stems off'n the yellow jasmine vine. He ain't gone see nothing 'cept dead leaves. I can use some what I already dried."

"Even the deer know not to take a bite outta them plants," Dicie said, remembering what Mammy had taught her.

"That true," Mammy said, nodding.

The two women set the dried footprint just outside the garden gate where Sampson would likely pass if he was to steal more vegetables. They covered it carefully with dead oak leaves. Mammy said the spell three times with Dicie, then made Dicie repeat it by herself.

They walked down to the edge of the marsh to wash their hands. Mammy carried the cup of lye soap, to make sure poison didn't linger on their skin. "Somebody brung them oleander seeds from Africa," Mammy said. "Some say so they could kill their selves 'stead of going into slavery. A little must of spilled out, cause them bushes be all over, growing wild."

Night fell before Isaac returned. "Daddy safe to Hibernia," he said. "I done told him 'bout Sampson. He be plenty mad."

Mammy and Dice expected that. "He gone 'bide over there?" Mammy asked.

Isaac nodded. "Dicie, he give me this pack o' needles fo' you."

"Where he staying at?" Mammy asked.

"To Hibernia, just like you said," Isaac answered.

Mammy looked at him, expecting more. "That all you gone say?" she asked.

"He brung you back some chalk, just like you asked. Here." Isaac pulled the chalk out of his overalls pocket.

Mammy snatched the chalk. "He staying with that woman?"

Isaac hung his head. "He come out her back door, going to do washing for the soldiers. I didn't ask where he stay. Just told him not to come back while Sampson watching the tabby."

"Harrump! That hussy. Young enough to be his daughter."

Isaac watched her carefully. No telling what Mammy might do when she got riled. "Mammy, I'll help more in the garden" he said. "Me and Gus and Rufus and Cass can tend Cuffie's five acres. We been mostly doing it ourselves, anyways. He be over there working for them soldiers or done gone to town."

Mammy stared at the floor for a minute. Watching, Dicie thought she saw a rare tear roll down Mammy's cheek. Finally, she said, "Thank you, Isaac. If we got something to sell, I reckon you can tote it over to Hibernia. Just tell that horse's ass to make sure he take it out the long way, not through the landing, and make sure he don't say nothing to nobody."

Chapter Thirty-Six

October 1867–December 1867

An aura of sadness permeated the declining compound. As summer ended, more and more folks left Skidaway Island. Half the tabbies at Brisbane were again empty. Storms hurtled over the marsh and across the island, rattling palm fronds in trees near the water's edge. Fallen limbs piled up around abandoned homes with nobody to clean up after autumn squalls. Firewood was easy picking, but dead wood burned fast.

The sadness in the compound reflected Dicie's loneliness. She was glad to be rid of the noisy outsiders who scared wildlife and shot more half-tame deer than they could ever eat, but she missed seeing others her age. Most of all, she missed Tom. Was he missing her, too?

One person remained whom Dicie didn't miss. Like a buzzing mosquito, Sampson's irritating presence made her long for the peaceful times during the war when he was nowhere to be seen. Although women weren't forced to work in the fields anymore, he still came snooping around the tabby, spying on Mammy and Dicie.

"Hey, Dicie," he would sing out and stop to watch her working. "You turning into a fine young lady." His compliments made Dicie blush and look around for her brothers or Mammy.

On Hibernia, where the landowner was dead and the heirs yet to make an appearance, life was livelier. A few United States troops remained quartered in the old plantation owner's mansion. Folks, including Tom, tended their plots and sold the produce to the soldiers or carried it to town. Cuffie, now living on Hibernia, collected a few coins for emptying the soldiers' slop jars and washing sweaty, mud-covered uniforms. The Freedman's Bureau headquarters on Skidaway shut down, but sometimes an agent came to meet with the soldiers and pass on rumors about ever-changing politics on the mainland. Hibernia, with its connection to the outside world, created a stimulating environment compared to isolated Brisbane.

On Brisbane, Sampson ruled. Mammy's spell hadn't worked. When Reverend Houston visited the island, Sampson was all smiles, but Reverend Houston was preparing to take a seat in the new Georgia legislature. If elected, he would resign his job as governor of the Skidaway Negro Colony.

He made the announcement to the freedmen who remained in the Brisbane compound. "It will be a great day for Georgia. If you men vote for me, I promise to work to move everyone in this state forward."

Mammy wasn't impressed. "If'n he gits elected, he has to move to Atlanta. He ain't here half the time now. Sampson just gone git worsen."

The Freedmen's Bureau said nothing about paying someone to replace Reverend Houston as governor. The freedmen had no money to hire anybody. Would Sampson become the self-appointed ruler of the Negro colony on Brisbane? He acted as if he already was.

Mammy moved his dried footprint with its decaying herbs to the other side of the garden, where he often walked. She repeated the spell when he came near, but still he spied on the house and garden, waking them at night with his heavy footfalls, snorting and spitting. There was no way for Cuffie to come home with him there.

"We got to git rid of that worthless nigger," Mammy fretted daily, but her spells did no good.

Despite the risk of running into Tom, Dicie tried to go see her daddy when she had time to spare. While he was hard at work for the soldiers, their meetings were never satisfying. Often, he was outside, tending a washpot full of military uniforms, but barely had a minute for her.

The worst was when Daddy told her to meet him inside Dorothy's tabby. These meetings were filled with unspoken questions and Dorothy's looming presence. And her smell. Dicie could hardly attend to Daddy, for the strong sweetish smell. How could the woman breathe, stinking so bad? What would Mammy say if she knew?

Daddy ought to be home at night, sleeping next to Mammy in their bed over Dicie's pallet. Mammy was sad and grumpy without him.

Finally, as his exile continued, Cuffie passed the word through Dicie for Mammy to meet him over on Hibernia. Dicie walked with her. The two of them stood under the autumn sun, the air drenched with water from heavy nightly rainstorms. Cuffie reached for her hand. "I miss you, Lizzie" he said.

Dicie looked the other way. Embarrassed, she pretended not to listen to Cuffie's declarations of love. She hoped that woman, Dorothy, wouldn't come strolling by.

Putting his arm around her shoulders, Cuffie led Mammy to a bench under a nearby live oak. Brushing a hank of Spanish moss off the bench, he said, "I hope to find a way to get home to you and the young'uns. Soon." He fetched a cup of cool well water and held it to her lips.

Lizzie sniffed and reached out her hand to touch his arm. "I know you can't come home, long as Sampson be watching," she said. "I don't want no trouble for you or for me and the chillen." A tear rolled down her scarred cheek. Dicie shuffled her feet nervously as Cuffie put both arms around her.

"I be home soon as them soldiers quit paying me," he said, pressing a whole dollar bill in her hand.

"Thank you, Cuffie," Mammy said, putting her head on his shoulder.

Cuffie looked over her head and behind her. Abruptly, he stepped back. "Got to get to work," he said.

"I miss you," Mammy said, reaching out to hold on to him, but Cuffie was already walking away.

Dicie grabbed Mammy's arm and steered her toward the path home. A puff of wind blew the stink of an overly sweet perfume past their faces.

After a few weeks of spying, the boys figured out Sampson's schedule. When their garden had enough ripe produce so Sampson wasn't likely to notice some missing, Isaac carried a sack full of vegetables to Daddy to sell. On a return trip Isaac brought cloth or sugar that Cuffie bought in town. But the stealthy loads had to be small. Sampson was always watching.

He and his bully boys raided Mammy's garden again, stealing more than half of the cabbages and turnip greens out of the last big fall crop. Dicie hid in the tabby with her hands over her ears as they whooped and grunted outside. Mammy watched helplessly.

"Don't you worry none," he taunted Mammy. "I's gone bring yo' yo' part." As always, his bully boys tramped off through the harvested section, smashing the remaining greens that the family needed for food.

Two weeks later he returned, a fake smile splitting his face in half. "Got yo' money for you." He handed Mammy fifty cents.

"That all you got?" Mammy demanded. Her voice was shrill. "You took forty head of cabbages and a peck of greens from us. Our half should have been at least two dollar. How much you give Massa Waring?"

Sampson looked at her warily. "Now Miz Lizzie, you know I ain't gone cheat you. I ain't brung no paperwork, but you can trust me."

"Fine. I'll just ask Massa Warren's grandson next time he come by."

Sampson banged his fist on their table. "I said I'll bring it! Ain't no use to bother him."

Mammy glared at him.

Sampson turned and stormed out of the tabby. Two more weeks went by before he returned with a crumpled and torn piece of paper. Numbers covered the back and front, most crossed out and rewritten. "See, it got Massa Warren's bookkeeper's name on it signed by hisself. He got fifty cent too, just like you."

He slapped the paper down on the table. "You can look at it yourself while I go bag up a mess of your collards. You got plenty to sell."

Pulling a croker sack out from under his arm, he strode into their garden and filled the sack with fresh collard greens, including what Mammy had planned to cook for dinner. Leaving the garden gate hanging from a broken rope, he stomped off toward the boat landing on the other side of the island.

Their garden was a mess. Tramping across the onion patch, he flattened slow-growing chutes and mashed the bulbs deeper into the dirt. His bully boys knocked the saplings Isaac had so carefully woven into a tight fence out of the ground. It took Mammy and Dicie an hour to repair the damage and ruined their plans for that night's supper.

Sampson forgot to come back inside for his paper. Soon as she saw he was gone, Mammy carefully folded it and stored it in her hiding place in the bricks behind her herbs, fortune-telling cards, and rooting ingredients.

Chapter Thirty-Seven

January 1868

As fall deepened into winter, Cuffie's five acres lay fallow, but Sampson hounded Rufus and Gus until they ventured out into the wind to cut saplings and replace rotten fence rails around Cuffie's share, a job they hated.

"Wish I could kill that nigger bastard," Rufus said, warming himself at Mammy's fire before he sat down to eat the collards and ham Dicie had cooked. His clothes were wet from the mist blown in off the Atlantic Ocean. "He getting half our crop, but don't do half the work. Them fence rails could of waited till a warmer day."

All that was left in Mammy's garden were onions and collards, but they still caught Sampson snooping around the tabby at night. Didn't he know they saw his big footprints the next morning?

"Don't know why my spell ain't working," Mammy whispered to Dicie that night after the boys had left to sleep on their side of the tabby. "But it ain't. We got to take it to the next step."

"How, Mammy?" Dicie asked. She almost didn't want to know. Rufus brought in a pail of water from the well before he left. If he had left it outside, it would have frozen during the night. She set the pail on the hearth and put an extra log on the fire, even though they had finished cooking. Outside, a broken limb banged against the tabby wall. Thinking about what Mammy was fixing to do gave Dicie chills that had nothing to do with the weather.

"We got to kill something," Mammy said. "Ain't gone be easy with the frogs and lizards sleeping underground in this cold. Sometimes you got to kill something to kill somebody. Sampson got that evil force in him."

Dicie shivered. She knew where snakes slept and where frogs and newts hibernated, but she always silently communicated to the animals that their secrets were safe with her. Every time the boys brought home a deer they killed, she felt guilty. But humans needed meat to survive, and Sampson was preventing Daddy from coming home.

Daddy would never be safe on Brisbane as long as Sampson controlled the plantation.

She would have to help Mammy kill a lizard. Eye of newt was a required ingredient for a death potion.

As the early winter afternoon darkened into night, she followed Mammy into the thickest part of the garden, the part Mammy never allowed anybody to weed. A stiff wind shivered the dried stalks and dead leaves hanging in a thick tangle above the faded stems of summer's poison ivy.

"Good hunting weather," Mammy said, cryptically. The wind moaned through the surrounding forest like an animal in distress.

Mammy never let Dicie work this overgrown part of the garden. Still, she knew where the frogs and lizards hid. Snakes, black racers, king snakes, and copperheads loved to burrow under the concealing cover of dead leaves. Reptiles hibernated in protected spaces where few humans trod. Dicie sensed their presence. She understood their desire to hide from humans. How could she violate their secrets?

Only to bring her daddy home would she sacrifice a reptile. Reluctantly, she pointed out the most likely spots to Mammy. They cleared dead leaves until Dicie spotted the telltale sign of a hidden burrow. With the flat-bladed shovel, Mammy dug deep, then deposited a pile of dirt and a sleepy hidden lizard on the dried leaves. Dicie grabbed the unresisting animal and held it against the dirt while Mammy used the shovel to chop off its head. She couldn't keep herself from sobbing.

Ignoring Dicie's tears, Mammy said, "Bring the head inside and I'll teach you how to get the eyes out. Take a steady hand not to squish 'em."

Before she followed Mammy inside, Dicie covered the lifeless body of the lizard-like newt and said a little prayer, "Jesus, forgive us. Please bring Daddy home safe."

Giving a little pat to the soil over the body and tail of the newt, she said, "God rest the soul of this little lizard."

Inside, she watched carefully as Mammy removed the eyes and mixed them with arsenic from an elixir of Carolina jasmine. Next, she added mustard seeds. Removing some of the dirt from Sampson's footprint, she made a cloth bag for all the ingredients, and said the spell:

> *"Eye of newt and mustard seed,*
> *Flower of death, meet our need,*
> *Make a charm of powerful trouble,*
> *Like a hell-broth boil and bubble."*

Mammy recited the spell three times, then thrice repeated, "*Mawt,* Sampson, *mawt.*" She whirled around each time as she repeated the spell, then tied a string to the bag and looped it around her neck under her blouse.

"Three a powerful sign," she told Dicie, who watched with her mouth hanging open. Dicie drew back, not sure which she feared the most, Mammy or the spell. Never before had Mammy let her watch all of an evil spell.

"This time of year, buckra do they hunting," Mammy said. "If they gits a boar or a deer, it keep mo' better in the cold. No flies around to ruin it. We gone see what we see."

The next morning, water on the ponds was coated with a thin layer of ice, but rays of sun shone through the tall pines. The freezing wind dropped. As the day warmed, an osprey flew from the treetops and dove into the nearby brackish lagoon. Breaking through the ice, it thrust upward with a big fish grasped in its ferocious talons.

Boats full of buckra hunters emerged from the fog hovering over the Skidaway River. The hunters, clad in warm woolen coats and tall boots, pulled their skiffs up on the shore of Skidaway Island and climbed the bluff to Big Ferry Road.

A few hours later a short, stocky, white-skinned man carrying a hunting rifle approached the Brisbane compound with confident steps.

"Howdy there, Massa Warren," Mammy greeted him, her penis bone charm around her neck and safely hidden by her shawl.

"Good morning, Lizzie," he answered. "I'll be staying over at Springfield for a few days but wanted to check on my people. Tell me what's happening. Sampson says your garden didn't do well this year."

Mammy said a little prayer. The man was one of Massa Warren's grandsons, finally come to check on the place. "Just you step around back to see for yo'self while I go inside and git the paper what Sampson say come from you," she said.

Mr. Warren cast his eyes around the greatly enlarged garden with patches of collards and onions surrounded by unused dirt. The big bare sections were weed free and neatly tended. Many collards showed signs of having been trampled and propped up with sticks. Some of the onions were newly replanted.

"What happened?" he asked. "You had wild hogs break in?"

Mammy pointed to the intact fence. "Sampson," she said. "We made a good crop. Sampson took more'n twelve bushels of cabbages out it." She handed him the paper Sampson had forgotten. "He be careless 'bout how he harvest."

Master Warren's lips moved as he twice reread the paper. "Sold, 12 cabbages," he muttered.

Mammy pointed to the empty quarter acre that had been filled with cabbages and the pile of roots and stalks composting outside the garden fence. "Them's the roots and stalks he left behind when he took the cabbage," she said.

"Thank you very much," he said to Mammy. "You will be seeing some changes around here."

He strode purposely back toward Springfield and its intact plantation house.

Soon as he was out of sight, Mammy fingered her potent penis charm and whispered, "Help me, Jesus."

To Dicie she said, "We got to pray, chile."

Only a few hours later Sampson stormed back to the overseer's house. This time two of Master Warren's servants from town were with him. One was mounted on a horse. Both carried guns. The man on foot had his pistol pointed at Sampson. Sampson hollered, "I ain't did it," to the stone-faced men guarding him.

The residents of the compound disappeared into their tabbies. Mammy bolted the door and made sure the windows were latched from inside.

After only a few minutes, Dicie and Mammy heard the guards holler, "Let's go."

Sampson's familiar curses rained down on the compound, but one of the men cocked his pistol.

Mammy peered out through a crack in the shutters.

Sampson faced directly at their tabby and screamed, "Bitch, you gone pay for this."

Pushing Mammy aside, Dicie took her spot at the window and looked out. Sampson held up both hands with his fingers making the sign of the cross, the only power that could conquer witchcraft. He aimed it right at Mammy.

Chapter Thirty-Eight

February 1868–November 1868

"You can tell yo' daddy it look like Sampson done gone," Mammy said to Isaac. A week had passed since anyone had seen or heard from Sampson. His house had been emptied of his clothes and old bullwhip. Rumors flew about his sudden departure. Why hadn't Lizzie heard from Cuffie? He should have come home by now. Tom got all the latest news and passed it on.

The buckra hunters, including Massa Warren, remained at Springfield all week, but on the seventh day the locals hired for the hunt packed the visitors' valises and guns for departure. After the buckra boarded their sleek skiffs and departed, their cook sent leftover deer and hog meat home with the trackers who helped with the hunt. Dicie's brother Gus brought home a ham and hog brains for sausage, along with a bottle of tasty red sauce from Savannah.

Still no sign of Daddy. "Be sure and tell Cuffie it safe for him to come home," Mammy told Gus.

"I sure will, Mammy," Gus said, not looking her in the eye.

Another full week went by without anyone seeing Sampson. Mammy trekked over to Springfield to thank Cassie, the master's cook, for the jar of red sauce.

The big house had already been closed, but Mammy found Cassie at her tabby in the compound. "Umm, umm! That sauce you sent home with Gus sure be tasty," Mammy said. "Do it got tomatoes in it? I ain't never had sauce that good before."

"Massa brung it from Savannah, but I inquired of that uppity Geechee he brung with him," Cassie said. "He say they make it from tomatoes mashed fine, then they add sugar and vinegar. Soon's we get a good crop of tomatoes, I's gone try and fix some."

Cassie glanced out the window. It was still the dead of winter, and most folks were inside their cabins. Nobody was in sight. "How 'bout a cup of tea befo' you head home?" she asked.

Mammy had been hoping for a good gossip. Cassie gestured to an old rocker and two chairs in front of her fireplace. Her tabby was bigger than Mammy's and had a separate sleeping space. "Anything happen I need to pass on to Brisbane folk?" Mammy asked.

Cassie grabbed a potholder and picked the kettle off the iron hanger over the fire. Her face screwed up in thought as she poured hot water into two tin mugs through a strainer full of dried tea leaves. "I gits to bring home what's left over after they done give out the meat to the trackers," she said. "They left a bag of good sugar."

Mammy waited patiently for Cassie to finish straining the tea and adding sugar. Finally, Cassie set the kettle back over the fire and settled her large bulk in the rocking chair. "You knowed Sampson gone, don't you?" she said. "He a hard man."

Mammy nodded and blinked back tears.

Cassie pushed a steaming cup over to Mammy and said. "Thank God he ain't got nothing to do with us. Massa Warren always stay here when he come 'cause he ain't got no house on the island. He told young Willie to run over to Brisbane and fetch Sampson t'other day. I be up to the big house fixing dinner when Sampson come."

Mammy leaned forward. Everyone who worked closely with the buckra knew it was their duty to listen to every word. Eavesdropping was the best source of important news.

Cassie rocked back and forth, then said. "Next thing I know Massa Warren done raised his voice. Sampson too, although it ain't like him to back talk the massa.

"We got out their way fast. I hid in the pantry with that wench they done hired to help me. Never heard young Massa Warren raise his voice before. Sampson hollering he ain't did it, whatever they fussing about."

Mammy pressed her lips together to keep from smiling. He most definitely did it. She remembered Sampson hiding cotton in his own bateau back years ago. It was a good thing Sampson never caught on that

Mammy learned her numbers and how to add when she was a little girl back in Mauretania. "What Massa do?" she asked.

"I ain't see'd him from the pantry, but I heard him holler, 'Git out!' 'Bout an hour later, the wench went out to empty the slop bucket. She seen Sampson push off for Isle of Hope with his bateau all loaded up. Nobody ain't seen him come back."

Mammy nodded. "His place done been emptied of what was his'n." Nobody could say for sure what he had in the house, but nothing was left except old furniture that had been there all through the war.

Mammy didn't share with Cassie the threat Sampson made when he left his house with the armed guards. It wasn't any use to borrow trouble. The women sat together in a companionable silence that only could happen on a bright winter day when no buckra and no overseer were around.

Soon as she got back to Brisbane, Mammy told Dicie and the boys what she had learned. The boys were relieved to be rid of him. "Been a big help these last few days, not having him trying to tell us what to do," Isaac said. "I know Daddy's mind be set at ease to hear he gone." He hurried off to Hibernia to tell Cuffie the good news, in case he hadn't believed it when Gus told him.

When Isaac returned, he was strangely silent.

"I done told him," he said to Mammy. He looked down at the old, scuffed boards of the tabby floor.

"Well, what he say?" Mammy scowled. "Boy, look at me. Why you ain't talking?"

"He ain't said nothing much. Reckon he studying when he coming back," Isaac said. "He say he gone start back helping me and Rufus and Gus at his share, soon as it come time to plant."

"Why ain't he come back with you?" Mammy asked.

"Got to go check my crab traps," Isaac said, running out the door without answering.

Mammy stood there, staring after him.

Dicie rushed out the door after Isaac. "Why you checking crab traps now? It still too cold. You know there ain't nothing in 'em." She had hoped Daddy would walk home with him. She expected him to, or at least to come when he finished washing uniforms for the day. Mammy did too.

Isaac kept on walking toward the marsh. "I found him at that woman's place," he said. "I couldn't tell Mammy. He didn't 'zactly say nothing 'bout coming home. That woman, Dorothy, she standing there listening the whole time. I should of waited till he come outside, but wind blowing too hard."

Dicie fought back tears.

Isaac straightened up and reached for her hand. "I 'spect he be heading this way soon he make it right with that woman."

Goose-bumps popped up on Dicie's arms. She had run after Isaac without grabbing her shawl. Down by the marsh, the wind always blew twice as hard. Even the egrets overhead wobbled as they were blown off course.

Wasn't Daddy coming home? The boys were grown, but she and Mammy still needed him. Didn't he want to be with them? It had to be because of that woman. Evil vibrations had reached out to Dicie whenever she met Daddy at Dorothy's house.

"Mammy's gone find out, one way or 'nother," she said, shivering.

"I ain't gone be there when she do," Isaac said, shaking his head hard. "No telling what she'll do. I reckon she the one got rid of Sampson, even though you and her ain't told me nothing."

He look at Dicie questioningly.

Dicie sank to the forest floor. She couldn't think of an answer. Mammy never said what went on between her and Sampson, but Dicie knew Isaac guessed the truth. She poked through the heavy thatch of dead leaves and pine straw without speaking until Isaac finally gave up and wandered off.

Inside the tabby, Mammy paced around the cramped room. She removed the brick on the fireplace and took out her little bag of herbs, then put the bag back in the hole behind the brick. Dicie listened to her from outside the window. She was scared to go inside, even though she was freezing.

From over on Hibernia, she heard hollering and gunshots, but strangely Tom didn't beat his drum. Why not? Had Tom been hit by a stray bullet? Would her brothers let her know? For the hundredth time she wished she hadn't told him to stop coming to see her. She missed him so badly.

Finally, Mammy left to visit the privy, and Dicie crept inside for her shawl.

Late that afternoon, Isaac came with news. "Them soldiers moving out," he said. "Got they orders today. First, they got to celebrate. You might of heard the whooping and hollering all the way over here. Then they start packing up. You daddy been busy all day, He got 'em a gallon of shine. Now they paying him to carry their gear down to the boats. We was laying low inside the tabbies, afraid to come out."

"What them gunshots about?" Dicie asked.

Isaac shook his head. "That how they celebrate. Wasting ammo and not paying attention to where bullets end up. Half of them gone be drunk before they git to the boat. Tom be too scared to go outside to beat his drums."

The next morning, Dicie got out of bed just as the sky lightened and the stars disappeared. The chamber pot was full, so she wrapped her shawl around her and headed toward the privy. Outside, the weeds around the tabby were white-tipped with frost. The wind had died. Her breath fogged in front of her as she hurried across the compound. A huge full moon in the west slowly slipped toward the horizon. Except for the chirping of a pine warbler, the forest was silent.

On her way back, she heard the crunch of approaching footsteps in fallen leaves. Looking up, she saw Daddy emerge from the forest, heading toward her.

She ran toward him. "Daddy, Daddy," she called, not caring who she woke.

"Hush now, Baby," he said, putting his arms around her. "Don't know when Sampson might pop back up outta nowhere."

He opened the tabby door and they slipped inside. Mammy was building up the fire. Cuffie took her in his arms and kissed her before she could say anything.

"You ready for a man who ain't got no job?" he asked.

Mammy looked like she was about to ask questions, but he put his mouth over hers and kissed her until she forgot what she was about to say.

It was wonderful to have Daddy home. All that day and the next he helped gather and split firewood. He pulled the broken rocker off the bottom of the old rocking chair and whittled a new piece from a fallen oak limb. Best of all he sat in front of the blazing fire and talked to Mammy and Dicie about what he meant to do in the garden once the weather warmed and it was time to plant.

By the end of his first week home the hog meat Gus had brought was gone, and nothing much was left to eat but turnips. All the chores were caught up. Daddy pulled his bag of coins out of his pocket. "Reckon it be time for me to take a trip to town and see if I can round up some more vittles," he said.

"I got fifty-cent," Mammy said. "Reckon you can bring us back a bag of cornmeal? Sampson was supposed to bring a bag the week he left, but I reckon we ain't gone see nothing for a while. Massa must of done forgot it."

"Hate taking money from you, but with them soldiers gone, I ain't sure where more is coming from," Cuffie said, reaching over to get the five dimes from Mammy. "Nothing in the garden to sell, and crab and shrimp ain't coming in till next month. When I get back, I'll shoot us a deer. Maybe Gus can rustle one up, too."

"We gone miss you," Mammy said. "Seem like you was gone forever."

"That puts me in mind of something," Daddy said. "Them soldiers say if I comes to where they going, they might find some work for me. I plan on checking them out while I'm there, and there ain't much to do here in the field or garden. I'm missing they money. Gone set out tomorrow."

Mammy hung her head. "You just got here, Cuffie," she said, twisting her hands together. "Heard lot of talk about you and that wench Dorothy over there."

Daddy eyed Mammy nervously. "Ain't nothing to that, Lizzie." He reached for her hands to stop her from twisting them. "You knows I sell what shine I can get. Dorothy be making it in her hut and I get part of ever' cup I sell. Then soldiers pay good money for hers 'cause it ain't got no dirt and leaves in it. She strain it real good."

"I don't like you doing business with no hussy like her," Mammy said.

"Don't you worry none. I'll be home befo' you can snap yo' finger." He reached his arm around her, patted her shoulder, and gave her a big wet kiss.

The next morning, Wednesday, Dicie watched as her father washed his hands and face and brushed his hair. He hugged her and Mammy. Slapping the boys on their backs, he said, "I'll be back Saturday fo' sho.'" He strode off toward the west where boats to the mainland docked.

Dicie followed him with her eyes as long as she could, then turned and headed south down her hidden path toward Hibernia to see if any fawns had dropped. When she got almost to the big ditch, her eyes must have played a trick on her. The back and shoulders of a distant figure climbing the far side of the ditch over to Hibernia looked just like Cuffie. But when she reached the top of the boundary line, he was nowhere to be seen.

Chapter Thirty-Nine

December 1868

T he sack of cornmeal was almost empty. The family waited anxiously for Cuffie's return. Even though Sampson wasn't there to harass them into doing it, the boys cut fresh rails for the fences around the cotton field. The cold wind blew itself out into the Atlantic Ocean. The days warmed and herds of deer ventured into the compound. With two more months of the worst cold to come before new leaves budded in the forest, the animals were hungry. Gus killed two, and the family feasted on venison.

"Sho' would like a nice hoecake to go with it," Mammy said. Saturday had come and gone but still no sign of Cuffie. She had shaken out the last crumbs from the bag of cornmeal the day before. "Massa Warren done forgot to bring provisions. Almost make me miss Sampson, that sorry nigger. Look like we gone have to hunt up some dried corn and somebody with a grinder we can borrow. If it ain't one worry, it another."

Two more weeks went by before Dicie spotted Daddy trudging up the path from Springfield. He was loaded down with bags and bundles. Breaking into a grin, Dicie ran towards him and grabbed the forty-pound bag of cornmeal resting on his left shoulder.

"Daddy, Daddy," she yelled. "We didn't 'spect you be gone so long."

"Had to make me a little change," he said. "Price of everything done gone up. Found my soldiers, but most of them gone off on leave, so they ain't got much work for me. I just about have to stay over there with 'em to keep earning. I come back to see what work I can find here. Couldn't stand to be away from my family any longer."

He turned his big beaming smile on Dicie. Her doubts about why he stayed gone so long melted away. Her eyes must have been playing tricks on her when she thought she saw him sneaking over to Dorothy.

Dicie patted his arm reassuringly. "Soon we be putting the garden in. You gone have plenty vegetables to sell," she said. "I missed you."

"Missed you, too," he said. "You got that fine boy looking at you. Soon you be gone off with him and forgetting 'bout yo' old daddy."

"Never, Daddy," she said. She couldn't tell Daddy that she asked Tom not to come see her anymore. Not yet. "What you brung us?" she asked.

Mammy, Dicie , and Cass sat around the table while Daddy unpacked the bundles from his shoulders. Besides the cornmeal there was sugar, writing paper, and a sack of peppermint candy.

"Writing paper," Mammy shrieked. "Where you git that?" She hugged the packet of paper to her heart. "Teachers be gone soon now that the soldiers gone. I be wondering how I could git some."

Cuffie leaned over and kissed her. "My smart woman got to have paper," he said.

Mammy grabbed the cornmeal and mixed up enough hoecake batter for everybody. When the boys came in, she fried it up along with the rest of the venison and set out the honey pot. Dicie ate till she was too full to touch another bite.

The next day the boys took Daddy along to the cotton field they worked for Master Warren. A half share of the profit was promised to Daddy, but he had been scared to work it as long as Sampson had been around. Although the dirt was empty of new seedlings, the boys had weeded and smoothed the rows. The fences around the plot were tight. Everything lay in wait for spring planting.

Cuffie admired the newly installed fence rails. "You boys done good," he said.

He strolled back to Mammy's almost bare garden. Scraggly collards and onions were all that was left of the winter planting.

His smile faded. "Ain't nothing needing doing here," he said. "Can't plant till ides of March." He sat down on a stump next to the garden and put his head in his hands.

Mammy stepped around to the back of the tabby and stood over him. "Massa ain't had nobody bring no provisions since before Sampson left," she said. "We ain't getting our cotton money again till next fall. All us could use some shoes. I ain't had a new dress since before the war. Boys 'bout out of bullets. What we gone do?"

Cuffie scowled. "Woman, I'm looking for work hard as I can." He jumped up and kicked at a patch of weeds, sending up a cloud of dust. Finally, he spit out, "I better head over to Hibernia and see what happening. Mebbe Tom know where I can make some money."

The sound of Tom's name pierced Dicie's heart. She still missed him so badly. Running back into the woods helped distract her, but even in the forest she couldn't escape the clamor of her parents' argument.

Mammy pressed her lips together. "Soldiers ain't there."

"Course I know that, Lizzie. Mebbe somebody over yonder got some better idea of how to catch some change than what I get here."

Lizzie could smell that woman, Dorothy, on him. What to do? What to do?

Gus walked up from the edge of the marsh with a bucket full of shrimp. Seeing Mammy about to cry, he told Cuffie, "Don't you holler at my mammy like that."

"Boy, don't you tell me what to do," Cuffie yelled back at him.

Gus drew himself up to his full height and clinched his fists, ready to fight even though Daddy was a good six inches taller and thirty pounds heavier. Setting the bucket down, he said, "Least I'm taking care of her, not running off all the time."

"Gus, don't talk like that to yo' daddy," Mammy broke in, stepping between the two.

"He ain't no daddy of mine," Gus said. "You know that, and he know that. Time to stop pretending."

Daddy shook his head, disgusted. "Who done taught you to catch them shrimp? Nobody but me. Ain't never seen no sorry bastard what fathered you."

Quick as a startled marsh rat, Gus struck Cuffie in the belly. Cuffie steadied himself, reached out, and knocked Gus backward. He tripped over the bucket of shrimp and fell to the ground.

Leaving Gus gasping on the ground, Cuffie stomped off toward Hibernia.

And Dorothy.

Mammy sat wearily on the stump Cuffie vacated and burst into tears. With tears streaming down her own face, Dicie put her arms around Mammy.

Gus got to his feet and scowled at them. "Who my daddy be?" he asked. "I got a right to know. I was just a little thing, but I remember when you first got with Cuffie."

Mammy cried harder for a moment, then gritted her teeth. "Yo' daddy be the slaver what drug me out my house. My daddy's own cousin. He knew I be home by myself. He pulled off my clothes. I picked up a knife to get him off me. He took the knife and carve up my face. He say I won't never be beautiful again. When he got finished with me, he trussed me up and sold me to the captain of the slave ship so I couldn't tell nobody."

Dicie was horrified. She knew something bad must have happened, but she never expected this. She tightened her arms around Mammy.

Hearing the gruesome story knocked the fight out of Gus. He patted his mammy's shoulder. "I'm sorry, Mammy," he said. "I won't fight Cuffie no more. He done his best. I guess that why I got this bright skin instead of his'n."

Mammy nodded. "He just upset 'bout no money and no rations. Mebbe he'll come home."

Dicie hoped so, too. Cuffie was her daddy. Finally, she knew how Mammy got her scars. "Do Rufus and Isaac know?" she asked.

Mammy wiped her face and said, "They don't know, and don't you tell 'em. That man said he kill me if I ever told. He ain't here, but I never said nothing. Telling'll bring bad luck."

After two nights passed with no sign of Cuffie, Isaac ran to Hibernia to search for him. He came back without Cuffie but brought news. Cuffie and some of the other men who had depended on the soldiers were hatching a plan.

"Hope they wasn't drinking no shine when they cogitated that plan," Mammy said.

Isaac just looked at her. The next morning when he and Dicie went to the well, he told her what he heard.

"'Bout dark, Daddy and some of them other men be sitting around a green-wood fire outside the old Massa's house where soldiers used to stay. The fire be smoking up a storm, and wind blowing it in my eyes. I snuck around to the side of the circle and sat down in the shadows away from the worst of the smoke. Daddy couldn't have hardly seen me even if he been looking. I feared if I asked him straight out what he planning, I wouldn't get no true answer, so I commenced listening."

"Was they drinking?" Dicie asked, holding her breath. She knew the answer.

"Course they be," Isaac answered. "I seen a man empty his cup. He passed it to Daddy. Daddy got up, walked to that woman Dorothy's cabin, and come back with it full. He done took a nickel from the man. Then they got to talking money."

An icy blast of wind buffeted brother and sister as they carried heavy buckets of water back to the tabby. "So, he still fooling with that trashy wench," Dicie said.

Isaac nodded his head.

"You got to tell me what he said," Dicie said, "but not here where Mammy might spy us. Once it warms up this afternoon, meet me in the garden."

That afternoon the two of them walked to the little clearing behind the garden near Dicie's secret path to Hibernia. The clearing where she used to meet Tom. The forest was mostly bare of leaves, but the wind had dropped, and sunbeams warmed them.

"I'll tell you what else I saw," Isaac said, "but you can't say nothing to Mammy. She got enough to worry about. She still trying to teach folk how to read, but ain't hardly any learners left. Most outside teachers gone, too."

"'Course I won't tell," Dicie said.

Isaac commenced his story. "Daddy say, 'I got a plan to make money.'"

"'Course all them men listen up. Everybody need money. All the people what had a little change done left. 'Specially the soldiers and the teachers. We depended on them, and they up and left us."

Dicie frowned. It was true. Mammy was left to teach whoever remained on the island with no books, no ink, and no chalk. Weeds grew rankly where tents used to be pitched. Raccoons and foxes took back abandoned cotton fields.

"Daddy say that right after I seen him slip the nickel into the pocket of his overalls," Isaac said. "Everybody seen him. The men around the fire busted out laughing. The man what paid him for the shine say, 'You making money. You just took my nickel.'"

Dicie couldn't help smiling. Daddy hated to be made fun of, but his timing was bad.

Isaac said, "Daddy didn't like 'em laughing at him. He glared and stomped his foot. He say, 'Listen up yo' dumb boonkeys! You think it funny, but I be serious. That nickel belong to my woman not me. She the one making the shine.'"

Dicie shifted her position on the pine straw. "So, he still helping that woman," she said.

Isaac nodded his head, "Daddy stood up. I seen him stumble, but he kept on hollering, 'Soldiers done left. Garden ain't doing nothing till summer. I cain't count on what I be getting outta my share of the cotton, even if Sampson don't steal it.'

"Daddy was spitting mad. He say, 'Sampson ain't brung me hardly nothing last year. My family need clothes, shoes, sugar'"

Dicie nodded, "All that be true."

"Daddy finally tried to sit back down but he couldn't find the stump what he been sitting on. I's afraid he gone fall."

Dicie nodded. She loved her daddy, but she knew he loved his 'shine.

Isaac swallowed and went on with the story. "Man drinking Dorothy's 'shine commenced telling him, 'Cuffie, watch yo' mouth. Making money easier said than done.' Course Daddy weren't listening to him. Finally, the man saw Daddy 'bout to fall. The man, he jump up and caught Daddy."

Dicie caught her breath. How could her daddy drink like that?

Isaac saw Dicie's expression. "No way I could of got him in time."

He continued, "'Nother man with a bum leg slapped his hand down and holler at Daddy, 'Shape up man. We all trying. I be hauling oysters all day up Wilmington River to Wausau in this cold. Like to froze to death, but we gotta praise the Lord. He put them oysters in our river.'

"With the man's help, Daddy sat back down and rested his head on his knees. I feared he was gone cry. Didn't want him shamed in front of his friends."

"Did he see you?" Dicie asked. Much as she hated hearing about Daddy drunk, she had to know.

"He never seen me," Isaac said. "Dark done come, and I stayed in the shadders. After a short piece, Daddy lift his head and say, 'Yeah, that our river alright. One of them redneck buckra tried to mess with me just this week when I paddlin' my bateau back home. The bastard knew I done had money. He wanted a piece for me pulling up my boat. Hell, the river belongs to ever'body.'"

"'Ain't it so,' all them drunks said.

"'Or do it?' the man who helped Cuffie sit on the stump asked. 'Buckra claim they own the marshes. Ain't they rice fields full of river water twice a day? Once high tide go in there to flood 'em, do the river belong to them?'

"'Mess with they Carolina Gold and they tell you real quick who the river belong to. With the working end of a shotgun," another fellow, also drunk, chimed in. 'Yassir, you mess with they rice, and you find out real quick who own the river.'"

Dice thought for a minute. The rivers always belonged to everybody. It was an interesting idea, but Isaac kept on telling the story.

"Daddy struggled to his feet. 'You just said it,' he said. "We own this river. Ain't we the freemen colony General Sherman hisself ordered us to make? They done took everything else they give us, but we still govern this colony. Let's show 'em. Make 'em pay us to use our part of the river.'

"The crowd commencing yelling, 'You crazy, Cuffie. How we gone do that?'

"Then Daddy say, 'Let me tell you.'"

"Oh, no." Dicie held her breath. She didn't want to hear the next part.

"Smoke blew right at me when he commenced telling 'em how." Isaac said. "Liked to choked me to death. I got up and snuck out the back way. No saying what them drunks gone try. Mammy would have a fit if I got caught up in it."

Brother and sister walked back to the tabby, dreading what the next day might bring.

Chapter Forty

December 1868

Next morning Dicie and Mammy were putting away the breakfast bowls when Tom came hurrying across the compound to their door. Dicie opened it, her heart pounding. Was Tom coming to see her, in spite of her telling him not to?

"Y'all seen Cuffie this morning?" he asked, all out of breath. He barely spared a look at Dicie.

Dicie's heart pounded. She shouldn't have got her hopes up. Why did he want Daddy instead of her? Was Daddy already in trouble? Even though Isaac hadn't said anything more, Daddy had to be sinking deeper into whatever crazy scheme he hatched.

"Didn't come home again last night," Mammy said. "Ain't he over to Hibernia?"

"He there last night with the other men, but I seen him leave early this morning heading this way." Tom stepped away from the doorway, kicked at a scrubby yaupon bush, and muttered to himself, "Must of passed through without stopping."

He closed his mouth and looked back at Mammy. Dicie couldn't tell if he had finished speaking or was trying to decide how much to tell. He stepped across the threshold into the tabby and held out his hands toward the fire. "Cold outside this morning," he said, still not looking at Dicie.

"Out with it, boy!" Mammy said. "You ain't come all this way so early in the morning not to tell us nothing."

Tom stared at the floor. A cockroach slid behind the bag of corn-meal Mammy used to make the mush that morning. "Maybe I shouldn't of come," he said. "I hoping to find Cuffie and see if'n I could talk some sense in him."

Mammy's light-skinned face grew even paler. She collapsed into a splintery chair. The chair creaked. "Tell me, boy."

"They be drinking," Tom began.

"I know that," Mammy snapped.

Tom turned around, walked the two steps to the window, undid the latch, and looked out. The hinge on the wooden shutter creaked loudly in the small room. Cuffie wasn't in sight.

Tom's breath came out in a rush. "They talking about barricading the river, charging a toll on all the buckra and white trash coming through," he said. "They say ain't hardly no other way to make money. Skidaway River belong to us."

"Lord, save us," Mammy said. "Hope they don't try it."

"I hope they don't neither," Tom said. "No money better than getting shot."

An icy draft blew through the window Tom had left open. Dicie walked over and closed it.

Tom continued talking. "They speculating 'bout taking over one of them old earthworks down at Modena and charging a toll. Think they can keep who-some-ever they want from passing through the Narrows, lessen they pay."

Isaac appeared in the doorway. "Been listening from my side," he said. "Heard some talk myself last night, but I left before them drunks got crazy. You talking 'bout them earthworks soldiers liked to killed me, making me put 'em up?"

"The same," Tom said. "They had me hauling dirt myself. Then no-body never used 'em for nothing."

"How Cuffie gone stop 'em from passing through?" Mammy asked. "Lot of fishermen take that short cut. Cuffie gone be outnumbered."

"Muskets," Tom said. "They think they can stop 'em with muskets. Cuffie calling on ever'body what got a musket to join 'em. Bullet'll reach from behind them earthworks easy over to the narrows."

The three listeners were stunned into silence. Finally, Mammy said, "Somebody gone get killed."

Nobody disputed her.

"So, what can we do?" Dicie asked. The thought of Daddy being hurt or killed was too much for her to bear. She couldn't stand by and let it happen.

"If'n Cuffie passed by here without stopping, I reckon he heading that way," Mammy said.

"Maybe the four of us can talk some sense in him if it ain't too late." She fixed Tom with her eagle eye. "Where he spent the night last night?"

Tom hesitated, then said, "I reckon he stay with that Dorothy. He sells her shine for her."

No use in denying it. Now Mammy knew for sure.

He held his breath. Isaac and Dicie did, too.

Mammy snorted, but didn't say anything for a minute. She reached up to the peg by the door where they hung their winter clothes. "Lemme get my shawl. It still freezing outside," she said. "I may have to kill him myself, before the law gets their chance." She put her hand under the bed for Daddy's pistol.

It wasn't there.

"Praise the Lord," Dicie said to herself. "Daddy must of taken it with him. Least Mammy can't shoot him with it." Her stomach twisted. Pain shot through her body. She'd do anything to keep Mammy from hurting Daddy. She'd have to warn him not to leave the gun where Mammy could find it. But how could she go against Mammy?

Dicie wrapped herself in her shawl. Out of the corner of her eye she thought she saw Tom cast a guilty look at her, but she ignored him.

The four of them set out for the northern tip of the island. Closer to the river, freezing wind whipped up, blowing Dicie's shawl off her head. The gale carried voices of men shouting. A musket blasted.

Mammy broke into a run toward the edge of the river, and the others followed. Dicie hid behind a big oak where the maritime forest met the beach. She peered around its enormous trunk. At least six men, including her daddy, were arguing. She heard," cain't reach from there" and "we gotta launch a bateau."

The man who shot the musket was about to send another ball toward the water. "Y'all see that? Y'all see that?" he shouted, pointing to a spot in the marsh, more than two hundred yards down the river.

"Yeah, but how you gone collect his toll?" another one asked. "He supposed to throw it back at you from middle of the river?"

Mammy gave her panther scream. The wind picked up her shriek and carried it all the way across the water. Startled, a flock of seagulls eating fiddlers on the opposite shore rose into the air, flapping their wings. The piercing sound scared all the men except Cuffie. They all whipped around to stare at her, including Cuffie, who recognized the scream.

"Lizzie, what you doin' here?" he yelled, running toward her.

"You fools gone get us all killed," Mammy shouted back at him, hurrying forward to meet him.

Cuffie said, "How else I gone get money? Selling a bit of 'shine to folk what don't have no money neither? Ain't nothing in the garden to sell."

Mammy stopped in her tracks and glared at him. "Where you getting 'shine to sell? Where?" She stomped her foot. "From that bitch, Dorothy?"

Dicie and Isaac looked at each other. "I didn't tell her," Isaac whispered.

"Me neither," Dicie said.

Daddy looked at her, stone-faced, not answering. The men on the shore stopped talking to each other and fixed their eyes on Cuffie and Lizzie.

"That bitch, Dorothy," Mammy screamed. "You think I don't know? She put you up to this?"

An osprey perched on a nearby treetop flapped its wings and crossed the river to get away from Mammy.

Cuffie said nothing.

Finally, he took a step closer to Mammy, "Lizzie, we talk about this tonight. You don't want ever'body knowing our business."

Mammy clenched her fists on her hips and scowled. Her face was so fierce, the scar almost disappeared. "You coming home tonight?"

Cuffie stepped closer and turned his back to his listening co-conspirators. "I be there," he whispered.

Mammy's scowl eased. Dicie heard her mumble, "You better be," before she wheeled away from Daddy and marched to where the young people waited anxiously.

Dicie cast a pleading look at her daddy, but he was hurrying back to the river's edge and didn't see. She shivered and followed Mammy back down the path toward home.

By the time Cuffie stepped over the threshold to their cabin, the weak winter sun had set. Mammy had fried his favorite black drum, and Dicie mixed hushpuppies from cornmeal, onions, and dried peppers.

Heat from under the spider kept the cabin warm and cozy. On the back of the fire, dried green beans simmered.

Dicie heard her daddy's hand on the door and ran to open it. She hugged him hard, savoring his smoky outdoor odor.

"Umm, Umm! This smells good," he said, casting an anxious glance at Mammy.

"Set yo'self down and grab a plate," Mammy said. "Soon as them beans get soft, we be ready to eat." Tracks of tears still marked her cheeks, but Dicie sensed her relief that Daddy had come home.

He gave Mammy a big kiss and took a seat at the table. She handed him a plate and spooned fried fish and golden-brown hushpuppies out of the hot bacon grease.

"This'll keep me warm on a cold night," Daddy said.

"That what it s'posed to," Mammy said, reaching for the pot of beans. "Now you home, you can stay nice and warm."

Daddy eyed her cautiously. "Soon as I eat, I be heading over to Hibernia," he said. "We got lot more planning to do before tomorrow."

Mammy halted with the pot of beans in her hand. "What you got to go back out fo'? You ain't spent a night home all week. Too cold to sit around outside, even if you got a big fire."

"Ain't outside. They gathering up at Doro..," " Cuffie started, then shut his mouth. "Inside somebody's house tonight to git things together."

"What you say? Whose house? Don't tell me you staying with that ho' again?"

Daddy rose to his feet. "Now Lizzie, ain't no need to get all riled up. I make us money, real gold this time. Gone be other men there."

"Dorothy!" Mammy screamed. "Dorothy! You spend last night with that Dorothy again." Now it wasn't a question.

She flung the pot full of boiling water and beans at Cuffie. He dodged the pot, but beans and boiling water hit the plate she had made for him. Drops of water soaked his shirt, the plate cracked, and fish and hushpuppies went flying.

Dicie threw herself across the room to grab her mother, just as the door slammed behind Cuffie. "Daddy," she screamed. "Don't go."

Too late. He was gone.

Dicie put her arms around her mother. Tears ran down both their faces.

"I don't care no more. Let the militia kill 'em all," Mammy said. "I don't care."

Chapter Forty-One

December 1868

After a good cry, Mammy turned to the fireplace and pulled out the bricks concealing the hole where she hid her voodoo fixings: mostly leaves, herbs, bits of broken glass, and coins as well as her thin wooden cards. Dicie dried her own tears and watched. Was Mammy intending to put a spell on Daddy? Or hurt him?

Laying the leather bag on the table, Mammy carefully pulled out her conjures. Dicie sucked in her breath when Mammy removed the bundle of dried Carolina jasmine. Arsenic, she remembered. Poison. Mammy never let her make a spell with it.

What could she do? Grown men were scared of Mammy and her witchcraft. "No, Mammy!" she cried, without thinking of anything except her daddy. She dashed to the fireplace, grabbed the crumpled jasmine, and threw it in the fire. She had to save her daddy.

Mammy grabbed her wrist and delivered a hard slap to Dicie's face, but she was too late. The fire blazed up soon as the dried jasmine reached it. Dicie's face stung.

"What you done that for?" Mammy yelled. "I cain't git no more till spring."

Dicie burst into tears. "Please don't hurt my daddy."

"You ain't gone tell me what to do," Mammy shouted. "That man need killing."

Dicie threw herself onto the bed, her tears wetting the quilt she and Mammy had pieced together out of old flour sacks before the war.

The memory of Daddy shooting the men who tried to hurt her flashed before her eyes. She had to save him.

Mammy stomped back and forth across the small room. Her angry footsteps shook the old planks covering the dirt floor. After casting angry looks at Dicie, Mammy finally relented. "Hush them tears. I ain't looking to make you an orphan," she said. "We gone do what we can to help them fools. First, we pray to God. Then you and me practice reading the cards. You know 'em 'bout good as me."

Pulling out the worn wooden squares, she arranged them on the table face-down and flipped over a random card near the middle of the pile. A faded circle filled the center. Tiny crescents flanked either side of the circle. The crescents pointed in reverse directions from each other.

"Sign of the moon," Mammy said. "Mean them men don't know what they dealin' with."

Fear gripped Dicie. "Daddy. What gone happen to Daddy?" she asked.

"Lemme try 'nother one," Mammy muttered.

She shuffled the cards back and forth and in and out of each other without turning them over. Finally, she stopped shuffling and planted the first finger of her right hand on the back of one, this time a card a little off-center.

Dicie held her breath. Mammy turned the thin square of wood over to reveal carved lines filled with traces of black paint. Lines on one end made a triangle. Dangling from the triangle was a stick body. The triangular head hung sideways from a wavy line. Mammy gasped. "The hanged man," she whispered.

Dicie's blood ran cold. Only the freezing wind stopped her from running out of the tabby and over to Dorothy's cabin to warn Daddy. That and the thought of confronting Dorothy. Would Daddy even listen to her?

Turning the card back face down so only the blank side showed, Mammy ran her hands over the jumbled mass, almost instantly restoring the neat pack. She dumped the cards into the sack and pulled the string tight.

"Bedtime!" Mammy ordered. "We go back to the river in the morning and see what we see.

It be cold tomorrow. We'll wear our shawls and carry a blanket to cover up. No more talk."

After banking the fire, Dicie rolled herself in an old blanket and got under the quilt with her mother. Neither hoped to get much sleep. Mother and daughter tossed and turned uneasily throughout the long night.

Next morning, Mammy rose with the late winter sun. "No use to start out too early," she said. "Them fools ain't gone start nothing till that woman feeds 'em, and they drink a little courage."

What she said made sense, but neither woman felt like doing nothing. Dicie fidgeted and stepped in and out of the door so many times, Mammy asked, "Girl, you got ants in yo' pants?"

Well before noon they closed the door and began their walk to the east bank of the Skidaway River. As they neared the edge of the island, they heard shouts, then gunfire. The thick growth of trees, vines, and shrubs concealed the men from view, but the report of muskets propelled Dicie and Mammy's steps to the top of the earthen barricade that Confederates had forced slaves to build. Dicie flinched at the blast of each shot.

A jumble of men and muskets gathered on the wide sandy shore. Dried wrack deposited by last year's storms formed a barrier between the sand at the edge of the river and the earthworks holding back the forest. A bonfire blazed on the sand, dangerously close to the tinder-dry wrack. Clouds of smoke blew erratically up the beach and across the earthworks. None of the men seemed to be tending the flames.

Downwind away from the bonfire, Mammy and Dicie picked their way carefully to the top of the embankment. The tide was low, leaving the river only a narrow ribbon of water between two expanses of marsh mud. In the mud flats, sea gulls pecked at fiddler crabs.

Three bateaux and a line of shrimp boats were being held hostage in the channel by a boatload of Skidaway Island men armed with muskets. Shouting, Cuffie stood in the bow of another bateau. Manning one of the halted bateaux were two dark-skinned freedmen from Tybee. All the other sailors appeared to be white.

Mammy and Dicie lowered themselves back down from the top of the embankment, leaving their heads barely visible from the water.

Looking at the pale-skinned sailors, Mammy's lips made a thin line of disapproval. "White trash, he hope," she said. "White trash what ain't toting guns."

"That Daddy waving a musket?" Dicie asked. "Wonder where he got it?"

"Damn fool! He gone get hisself shot." Mammy said.

They watched silently as the men with Daddy rowed closer to the nearest halted bateau. Cuffie was talking to the white man in the front of the boat, but his words were too far away to reach the earthworks. After a few tense moments, the white man reached inside his pocket and handed something to Cuffie. Cuffie made an exaggerated bow and motioned for the boat to pass.

Dicie and Mammy looked at each other in astonishment. "Can't believe he got away with that," Mammy said. "That man ain't no buckra."

Dicie couldn't believe it, either. But what would happen when the tide came in and the river widened? Would Daddy really shoot a white boatman to prevent him from passing? The two women stayed frozen in their positions as the scene was repeated with the next bateau.

After successfully receiving two tolls and handing them over to one of the oarsmen, Cuffie leaned forward for a brief word with the next bateau in line, the one manned by colored fishermen. He waved them through without exacting any money.

"Fool probably thinks they ain't got no money," Mammy said.

No more bateaux were in line. The tide was rising as the shrimper approached. Their boat was bigger, with outrigging projecting from both sides. Shrimpers worked in crews and likely carried guns. Dicie held her breath as the big craft approached her daddy. Following it, shrieking flocks of seagulls waited for cast-off fish.

The boat stopped right in front of Cuffie. The sail went slack in the narrow channel. The shrimpers had no choice. The tide had risen, but the river was still barely wide enough to accommodate the boat's outrigging. Cuffie and his oarsmen had solidly planted their bateau in the middle of the strip of water. Dicie watched an angry shrimper come to the bow to holler at Cuffie.

The shrimper shook his fist. Cuffie raised his musket.

After letting out a loud, "You thieving nigger bastard," that even Dicie and Mammy heard, the scruffy-bearded white man handed over what looked like a fistful of coins to Cuffie.

The men manning Cuffie's bateau rowed to the shallows and allowed the shrimp boat to inch through the channel.

"He did it." Dicie sighed with relief.

"Lucky," Mammy said. "Ain't no telling when that luck gone run out. I say, let's head for home befo' his luck turn crossways." She gave Dicie a shove toward the bottom of the embankment.

"No, Mammy," Dicie said, digging her heels into the steep slope, surprising both women. How could she abandon her daddy? "You go. I ain't leaving. If'n Daddy git hurt, maybe I can help. I'll come when they shuts this thing down."

Mammy put her hands on her hips. "What come over you, girl? You ain't never been out by yo'self since that time the man grabbed you, and yo' Daddy had to kill him. Don't you know you could git hurt?"

Dicie hardly knew herself what had come over her. Nobody stood up to Mammy. But something inside her had changed. She wasn't that scared little girl anymore. Daddy had saved her. Now she had to be there for him. What if he got shot? "I'll stay hid," she promised Mammy. "Most likely Isaac or Tom be along shortly. I promise I'll let them know where I be."

"Hard head make a soft back," Mammy said, shrugging and continuing down the embankment.

She meant Dicie was likely to get into trouble, but Dicie couldn't leave. She moved down the earthworks to where scrubby oaks had taken hold. It was harder to get a clear view, but harder for any of the men to spot her. Besides they weren't looking her way. All eyes were focused on Cuffie in the rickety boat, bouncing on the incoming tide.

Her legs ached from squatting on the slope. Where was Isaac? If only she hadn't told Tom not to come see her anymore, he would have been there with her.

By the time the sun dropped toward the horizon, her feet were numb with cold. She hadn't had anything to eat since their hurried breakfast of leftover cornbread. Isaac never came. She would have to make the long walk home all alone.

The tide reached its full height, forcing the men on the shore closer to her hiding spot. Soon the river would reverse course, heading back out through the mighty Wilmington River and Wassau Sound to the mouth of the Atlantic Ocean. The chilled oarsmen struggled to hold the bateau steadily blocking the rushing river.

Finally, for over an hour no more boats rowed toward the narrows. The shadow of the forest deepened over the river. The oarsmen hollered to the crew on shore. The waiting gang hollered back. The wind blew their words in her direction. Everybody but Cuffie agreed it was time to come in.

"Jest one more minute," Cuffie kept saying. "Bastards hiding 'round the curve, waiting fo' us to quit. Passed this way this morning; they gotta come back this way tonight. Lessen they want to spend all day going round and cross over to Savannah River."

Maybe Cuffie was right. Or were the deepening shadows and icy wind that sprung up as darkness fell a sign from the spirits? Dicie felt a chill from more than approaching nightfall. Was the absence of river traffic a sign that something cruel was waiting to happen? Were the white boatmen plotting to bring disaster upon the Skidaway pirates?

And where was Isaac or Cass? She had expected to find Tom lurking behind the breastworks. Why hadn't they come? Hopefully one of them would appear before she had to walk home alone.

She watched the tired men plead with Cuffie to come in until a big man on shore shouted, "Cuffie git yo' ass here now, or we ain't splitting the take with you."

Cuffie sank down below the gunnels with his head in his hands while the rest rowed the bateau back to Skidaway Island. As they neared the shore, Dicie saw Daddy raise a half-empty bottle to his mouth and take a long drag.

The waiting crew rushed forward to beach the bateau. The keeper of the tolls lifted the sack with the take over his head as several men helped him onto the sand. "Hosanna!," he yelled.

Others in the group hollered "Hosanna" back.

The chant and response of the men had begun.

A leader sang in a deep, piercing voice, "We go down to the river."

Another improvised the next line just as loudly, "River give us life."

Men pulled out jars of shine. Soon all of them took their turns shouting and responding until their song reflected the day's triumph. Eight quarters and a nickel for each man!

"Ain't nothing to what we make tomorrow," Cuffie shouted. He had the full attention of all the men. No way Dicie could drag him away from his admirers.

She eased down the embankment and headed for home all by herself, racing ahead of nightfall.

Chapter Forty-Two

December 1868

B y the time Dicie reached the tabby, the last gleam of sunset barely lit the white sand path.

When she unbarred the door, Mammy scowled. "Lord, chile, it nighttime. I done sent yo' brothers out hunting you. Where you been? Don't you know witches be riding after dark? Owl been hooting last hour, and you know what that mean."

"I'm sorry, Mammy. Daddy ain't come off the river till just before I left."

"You come home all by yo' self? What got into you, girl? Lemme call Rufus and Isaac. S'prised you ain't run across them." Mammy opened the door and gave her panther scream, followed by "Isaac" and "Rufus" so loud a woman three tabbies down opened her door to see what was wrong.

The boys came running. "What happen? You alright?" Isaac asked Dicie. "Who looking out for you?"

Dicie stood straight and looked at him. "Course I'm alright. I'm a woman grown now. I can take care of myself. Daddy alright, too."

She wasn't about to let him know how scared she got when darkness fell. Or let Mammy find out either. She had run most of the way home, zig-zagging to avoid shadows and places where somebody or something could be hiding.

"Why you so late then?" Isaac asked. "What you doing by yo'self?" He gave Mammy a puzzled look. They hadn't left Dicie alone since the island was first invaded by freedmen and the man had snatched her.

She dropped her eyes to the muddy floor and said, "Boats stopped coming up the river, but Daddy wouldn't quit. Men finally made him come in. Then they counted up the money. Everybody got more 'an two dollar."

Isaac whistled.

"Did he pull out the shine?" Rufus asked.

She nodded, peeking at Mammy to see her reaction. "Daddy say he going back tomorrow."

"Damn fool," Mammy said. "You boys don't go near northwest end of the island. I mean it. I done showed you the hangman card. If'n Cuffie taken down by this foolishness, we gone need y'all even more."

Looking at Dicie, she added, "Tom, too. I told him this morning when he come looking for you. He ain't going over there, neither."

Dicie stared at her in surprise. Tom hadn't come looking for her since that awful day when he told her he promised his daddy he would marry Bella. Bad as she missed him, it was for the best. Why had he come looking for her now, after he had kept away like she told him to? She got goose bumps, thinking how happy she would have been if he had crawled up the battlement and kept her warm.

She questioned Mammy with her eyes, but Mammy looked away.

Later that evening, Cuffie stumbled to the door of the tabby and pushed it open with one hand. In the other, he held a tin mug full of liquor.

Dicie waved her hand to dispel the smell of alcohol. "Daddy, you home," she said, steering him to a chair. What a relief to see him!

"Had to come give my family some of what my plan got us," he said. Reaching in his pocket, he handed Mammy four silver quarters. "Miz Liberty sitting down," he told her. "I be bringing you some more tomorrow." A happy smile lit his face.

Mammy gave him her inscrutable stare. "Thank you for the money," she said. It wasn't any use to try to talk sense into him, but she couldn't help herself. "I'll put it to good use. You ain't got to go out there again."

Cuffie's elated expression faded. He took a sip of the 'shine.

Were there words she could say to convince him not to go back? Tomorrow his crazy stunt would be even more dangerous. Boatmen and shrimpers had been warned. Tomorrow, their own guns would be loaded and ready.

She reached for his hand. Holding it gently so as not to make him mad, she said, "Don't go back no more. Signs say it ain't gone work again."

"Woman, don't tell me what to do," he said, banging his mug on the table and sloshing out most of the remaining liquor.

"Cuffie, I read the cards. Stay here tomorrow," Mammy pleaded.

"I gotta go get me some more shine. I done spilled all this," he said, pushing his chair back.

The door slammed as he staggered out into the darkness, heading toward Hibernia and Dorothy.

Dicie froze in her corner of the room. He hadn't even told her goodbye.

Mammy shook her head. "Please, Lord, look out for him." Turning to Dicie she said, "hope he don't pass out before he git over that ditch."

The next morning dark gray clouds hung heavy, blocking the sunrise. Mammy kept the kerosene lamp burning till way past breakfast.

"Look like rain," Mammy said. "Cold as it is, I hope you ain 't planning to walk back down to the river."

"Mammy, I got to," Dicie said. "I'll stay hid. Please lemme take that piece of oilcloth."

Mammy pulled the oilcloth off the table and handed it to her. She reached into her sack of roots for a charm made from a penny tied up with blue thread and tied the thread around Dicie's ankle.

"Least you can do is wear this," she said. "Keep it on your leg and stay hid. If they start shooting, run fast as you can to the woods."

Dicie gulped. She hoped it didn't come to that. Maybe Mammy was right. She shouldn't go. But if trouble came, maybe she could help Daddy. Swallowing her fear, she looked away so she wouldn't see the worry in Mammy's eyes. After she wrapped the oilcloth around her body over her shawl, she opened the door. Outside, rain spit and wind whipped at the oilcloth, but she walked doggedly down the dirt track leading northwest.

Once she reached the muddy earthworks, she saw more men striding back and forth on the beach than the day before, all hoping to cadge some of the money. Despite the damp, a big fire blazed on the beach. Cuffie bobbed up and down in a bateau in the middle of the river, shouting at the newcomers. She waved to him from the top of the barricade, but he didn't see her. Last night, neither she nor Mammy told him Dicie had been watching. No use giving him more worry.

Unlike yesterday, Daddy's boat was alone in the river. No shrimpers and no bateaux. Misty fog covered the far ends of the river both ways, but still, she should have been able to make out a mast or hear the chants of oarsmen.

Surveying the area for Tom, she couldn't see any man who could be him. She knew it was best that he obey Mammy and stay away, but part of her wished he would come. She would have felt safer knowing he was near. Finally, she gave up searching for him and settled down on the oilcloth. Spreading it over wet sand just below the peak of the barricade, but close to the top, she could see and hear her daddy without being seen from the water. Cold rain began to fall. She pulled half of the oilcloth over her as best she could.

The Skidaway River remained eerily empty. Surely rain and cold wouldn't stop a fisherman. Were they expecting the storm to worsen? But that could hardly be. The weather was too cold for a hurricane. Besides, hurricanes never hit in December. She reached down and rubbed the charm on her ankle for good luck. Gradually the wet sand under her warmed, and Dicie almost drifted off to sleep in her oilcloth cocoon.

The crack of a rifle jerked her wide awake. The rifle shot was immediately repeated. One! Two! Three! Four! Who could reload and fire so quickly? Not even Yankee soldiers had rifles like that. Throwing the oilcloth off, Dicie stared at the river. A steamship almost too big for the channel bore down on Cuffie's bateau, firing bullets right and left of his little craft. Black smoke billowed out of the steamship's tall chimney. The men on the ship wore black uniforms, but Dicie couldn't tell what the uniforms meant. They weren't blue or gray like soldiers from the war.

The Skidaway men on shore rushed toward the woods, swarming over the earthworks not far from her hiding place. She heard them yell, "Militia!" "It militia!" "Run!"

The oarsmen on Cuffie's boat dug their paddles in hard and slammed the bateau into shallow water covering the marsh on the far side of the river. A dinghy filled with soldiers launched from the other side of the steamer and headed toward the gang of men on the beach below her. Any second the panicked freedmen climbing the beach side of the breastworks would trample her. Their fire blazed unattended.

Dicie kept her eyes on Cuffie as long as she dared while she slid backward down the breastwork. She glimpsed him roll out of the bateau, and wade through marsh grass toward dry land before her sightline was blocked by the earthen mound. Then she ran as fast as she could into the woods.

The sound of men's screams and repeating blasts from rifles followed her. When she reached the thick forest and glanced back through a screen of Spanish moss dangling from an old oak, she saw a black man atop the earthworks fall to the ground. Blood gushed from his body. She offered up a brief prayer to Jesus, then, terrified, she pressed herself through the palmetto scrub and away from the river.

Chapter Forty-Three

December 1868

"Yo' cards done tole it," Dicie gasped to Mammy, soon as she caught her breath. Her hair and shawl dripped water all over the floor. She dropped the cumbersome oilcloth on the floor in front of the hearth. "Militia come and shot 'em up."

Mammy fell back in a chair and grabbed her chest. "Cuffie?" she asked. "You telling me Cuffie got shot? Where Cuffie be?"

Dicie wrung her hands and gulped. Fear choked her voice. "I don't know. Them soldiers come charging at the men on the beach just below me. I had to run." Mammy looked so scared, Dicie's heart twisted. She had to offer Mammy hope.

"Ain't none of them heading to far side of the river where Daddy went." Maybe Daddy got away. "Them men carrying Daddy rowed into the marsh where soldiers' boat too big to go. I seen Daddy roll out the bateau and him lying in the grass. When I got to the woods, he weren't there no more. Maybe he done jumped up and went running, but I can't be sure."

Mammy nodded her head. She looked relieved. "Be just like Cuffie to have a plan."

Dicie remembered her moment of panic. "Them men on the shore run right at me. Soldiers firing bullets at 'em, blam, blam, blam. No reloading. Then soldiers jump off the big boat into a little boat and headed after 'em." Dicie burst into tears. She could have been killed.

Tears ran down Mammy's cheeks. After a minute she sat up, wiped her face on her apron, and said, "We got to straighten up. If they come here looking for Cuffie, we got to make 'em think we don't know nothin'."

"How? Where we gone hide? It still raining and too cold for us to work the garden," Dicie wrung her hands again. "What if they be following me? They bound to see my clothes all soaked through. That oilcloth weren't much good for running." She was done for.

"Hush up now," Mammy said. "Take yo' clothes off and hang 'em in front of the fire. I'll mop up this wet floor and get out my quilt pieces. We can tell 'em we been sewing all day. If'n they come. Maybe they don't know Cuffie be the one out there in the river."

Dicie hung her skirt and waist to dry like Mammy said and settled down in her nightdress with needle and thread. More than an hour later they heard men's boots tramping into the compound.

"Open up!" a male voice demanded.

Trembling with fear, Dicie snatched her nearly dry clothes from in front of the fire and stuffed them under the pile of worn-out fabric she was using to sew quilt pieces.

Mammy walked to the door. "Coming!" she called, making a big noise of unlatching the bolt, pulling it uselessly back and forth to give Dicie time to hide her clothes.

When Mammy finally opened it a crack, the uniformed man at the door said, "We come to see Cuffie."

"Cuffie ain't here," Mammy said.

"We heard this criminal act on the river was his idea," the soldier said. "Where is he? We have a warrant charging him with piracy."

"I don't know," Mammy said, still holding the door almost closed.

The man gave the door a big push. The sudden gust of wind from the door opening made the fire blaze. He pushed Mammy aside and strode into the room, followed by three uniformed men. One looked under the bed. The room was so small it was obvious only Mammy and Dicie were there. He stared at Dicie, who was cowering in her chair, mismatched squares of cloth covering her lap. "Where you been all day?"

She was so scared she could barely mumble, "Quilting." She gestured at the quilt squares. Her hand shook and squares tumbled to the floor.

The man grabbed her shoulder. His hand burned her skin through the thick flannel. Her nightdress was dry. "Thank you, Jesus," she tossed up a silent prayer that rainwater had evaporated from her hair and skin. She smelled a rank, musty scent coming from the soldier. His hand groped her breast. Would her nightdress be ripped off at any moment?

Mammy put her hands on her hips and scowled at the man, letting him know he wasn't supposed to be touching her daughter.

Finally, the man let go. "If you see him," he said, rolling his eyes and pulling down his mouth to show he didn't believe they didn't know where Cuffie was, "Tell him if we catch him in the river again, we'll shoot him. We'll be watching."

With that, he summoned the other men and marched out of the tabby into the cold rain.

Mammy re-barred the door and collapsed on the bed.

Kneeling next to Mammy, Dicie patted her shoulder. "You reckon they'll come back?"

"Probably not. They can see he ain't here," Mammy said.

Dicie sighed with relief. "How you stay so brave? I liked to pass out when he touch me with that big old white hand. Thank you for scaring him." Even after three years, every strange man who came near reminded her of the freedman who had held her hostage.

"I ain't brave. Sometimes you just got to do what you got to do. Don't want to ever see you end up like me, with your face all cut up," Mammy said. "Least we know now Cuffie got away. They wouldn't be hunting him if he been caught."

Mammy was right. Dicie breathed a sigh of relief as she reached to pick up the quilt squares. Would they ever have enough to sew a quilt? She dreaded the thought of sitting still for hours, smelling the stink of the tallow candle as her needle jabbed in and out in the endless task of making a new quilt.

"Them ain't the soldiers we know," Mammy said, picking up her tin cup to measure cornmeal for supper. She sighed. "Them United States boys been real good to us. Must be that new militia they let the buckra make. S'posed to be some of our boys in it, but I ain't seed any. Them buckra sound just the same as befo' the war."

Dicie threaded her needle. Would it have made a difference if the soldiers had been the Yankee men Daddy worked for? She wished Mammy had been able to convince Daddy not to go back to the river. Her heart ached at the thought of him leaving them again, only God knew for how long.

"Mammy, I heard some of them men with Daddy holler 'militia.' Didn't know what it meant." Buckra militia chasing Daddy couldn't be good. "What Daddy gone do now?"

"Don't you worry none. He just like one of them cats what come off the ships. Throw 'em every which way and they land on they feet. Cuffie be alright if'n he git to Savannah. He know folk there. He gone take care of hisself, one way or the other."

But would they ever see him again? The longer he stayed away, the shorter he stayed when he came home. Her mind shifted to Dorothy. That scheming wench had more hold on Cuffie than she did or even Mammy did. She didn't dare mention Dorothy. Much as she disliked the woman, she didn't want to remind Mammy to kill her.

Dicie couldn't help yearning for Tom. Maybe somebody would give him the news. Tom had filled his Daddy's shoes. All the latest happenings reached him, and his drumbeats spread the news throughout the island.

But now Tom didn't come, and the drum didn't beat. What was going on? Had the militia arrested Daddy? That night, even her brothers stayed away from the cabin. Dicie and Mammy were all alone. Outside in the darkness, an owl hooted and dead sticks cracked. Raindrops continued to fall, and the wind howled.

Try as she did, Dicie couldn't complete even one quilt square. Finally, Mammy banked the fire and checked the bolt on the door. She and Dicie climbed under the covers, but both listened restlessly for footsteps all through the night.

Chapter Forty-Four

December 1868

Two more days went by with no word about Cuffie. Her brothers' half of the tabby stayed cold and empty. The drum remained silent. Dicie was scared, too scared of encountering more militia to venture outside to hunt for her brothers. Finally, on the third day Gus and Rufus hobbled in, wet and dirty. Isaac and Cass weren't with them.

"Got any hoecake?" Rufua asked. "I'm hungry enough to eat a whole possum by myself. We been hiding in the woods, 'fraid to make a fire. "Cuffie's plan went bad. Real bad. Jim got killed." A tear ran down his filthy cheek. "Couple more got shot. Militia's been all over this end of the island. Lot of Daddy's friends got arrested and hauled off to Savannah. No boats done come, so nobody even had a chance to collect."

"We ain't heard nothing," Dicie said. "'Cept what we heard from them militia what came here looking for Daddy. Nobody here come out they door, 'cept that one old crazy woman. Chamber pots got to be full. I ain't even heard the drum."

"You ain't heard it 'cuz it ain't been beat. Nobody know where Tom at. We been hiding down island ourselves, in case militia come here. Nobody down there know nothing."

Dicie felt the blood drain out of her face. Tom? Mammy told him he wasn't supposed to be anywhere near the river. She turned to face Mammy.

"You seen Tom?" Her voice quavered. She wanted him so bad it hurt.

"You know I ain't seen Tom. I'd a told you. He'd of come see you his-self." Frowning at her boys, Mammy said, "Militia done come. Dicie and me still alive, no thanks to you."

"Mammy, you done told us to lay low and stay 'way from the north end of the island," Rufus said, grabbing hold of Gus's arm for support.

"Never mind that, boys. You reckon you can find out where Cuffie end up? They must not of had him when they came here." she asked.

"Or where Tom at?" Dicie asked.

Rufus grinned at Dicie. It was the first time he had smiled since the boys came in. "Now why you so interested in Tom?"

Scowling, Dicie turned her back to him. She wasn't funning. Of course she wasn't interested in Tom anymore. She only wondered why nobody had beat the drum.

If Rufus had heard and seen what she saw at the river, he wouldn't be teasing her. Bullets going off one after the other, no stopping to reload. A man with blood gushing from his chest. Sights and sounds that filled her with terror. Even though she hadn't seen Tom, could he have been caught in the melee of men fleeing?

"You wasn't there," she snapped at Rufus.

"And you oughtn't of been," he told her.

She stamped her foot. A hundred times she had asked herself if there was any way she could have stopped Daddy from going back out on the river. Why hadn't she tried harder? Even if he had just pushed her away, told her to go home, she could have warned him about the hangman card.

Now all she could do was wait and worry. The weather stayed cold. A heavy fog lay across the island even though the rain had fizzled out. Not even foxes and squirrels in their thick winter fur showed themselves.

The next morning Dicie ventured out behind the tabby. The winter crop of onions and turnips lay silently in the cold mud. No work for her there. No need to do anything but make sure no hungry animal had breached the fence.

As she paced along the border, worrying about Daddy and Tom and checking for loosened fence poles, she heard a dead stick crunch in the woods beyond. The sound of someone or something breaking an-other stick made her look up. Was it a doe, maybe heavy with an unborn fawn? But no deer darted off with a flash of white tail. Although deer blended well with the brown and green winter landscape, her eyes were trained to tell the difference between dead leaves and tan deer.

She froze as a footstep sounded, further away this time, and hushed as though the walker didn't want to be heard. Looking in the direction of the sound, she glimpsed a broad back topped by kinky white hair, hurrying away from the garden. The figure looked like Sampson, but it couldn't be. Nobody had seen or heard from him since his argument with Master Warren. Not since the day Mammy showed Master Warren Sampson's receipt. As she stared in his direction, the figure melted away into the forest. Nobody lived down that way. Between their garden and the marsh were only deep woods.

Had the fog made her mistake a bounding deer for a man? She was sure she had seen a head of white hair, not a flashing white tail. A deer that tall would have lost its spots. Daddy's hair was still black. Maybe a soldier from the militia was watching to see if Daddy came home? Bad as she missed him, she felt a burst of relief that Daddy stayed away.

Hurrying back around to the tabby door, she saw Gus and Rufus still inside with Mammy.

"Just saw a man in the woods," she said. "Look like Sampson used to, sneaking around back in the woods when he spied on us, trying to catch Daddy."

Mammy looked startled. "Pray it ain't so. Sampson been gone almost a year."

"Couldn't be Sampson," Gus said, looking up, and reaching for the poker to stir the fire. "His house been cleaned out. Man from Carolina fixing to move in."

"I seen a man with white hair," Dicie said. "Ain't nobody but Sampson like that 'round here. Not many newcomers since the soldiers be gone. It ain't planting time yet."

"Probably one of them militia, spying on us," Mammy said. "How 'bout you boys staying close for a few more days, just to be on the safe side?"

Gus looked doubtful. "My girl expecting me over on Springfield while there ain't much work to do here," he said. "I'll check in on you. Rufus can have the tabby to hisself."

Rufus nodded. "I got a job down on Delegal Creek. I'll check on you when I can. Isaac and Cass be here."

Mammy pinched her lips together and put her hands on her hips to let the boys know she didn't like their answers, but what could she say? They were grown men. Dicie's heart sank. Isaac and Cass weren't likely to be around, either. Both had women friends. Neither had been home during the anxious nights before. Dicie was the only one with nobody to love.

After wolfing down all the leftover hoecake and turnip greens, Rufus and Gus retired to their half of the tabby to rest up before heading back out. Isaac and Cass finally came home but left to fish the high tide.

After Mammy and Dicie finished cleaning up the dishes, Mammy turned to Dicie and said, "Be careful, girl. Far as I know, Sampson ain't on this island, but he could be out there somewheres. Don't trust him no more 'an any other snake. He got to be mad as hell 'bout Massa Warren catching on to his tricks. I ain't see how he could blame it on me, but I ain't surprised that he do."

Dicie pulled the loose brick out of its place on the hearth and reached inside for the cards.

"That my girl," Mammy said. "Let's see what they say."

Dicie shuffled the cards, then laid them face down in the pattern Mammy had shown her.

Mammy reached out a skinny arm, hesitated a minute, then grabbed one and turned it over.

Both women stared at the upturned card, Dicie horrified; Mammy resigned.

"The serpent," Mammy said. "You was right. We got to keep the door barred."

Two more days went by with no word from Daddy. The brothers came and went. A few times a white-skinned stranger tramped through the compound, but no more militia banged on their door.

The next day was Christmas. This year there was no Daddy to bring the red and white striped peppermints Dicie loved. It hardly seemed like Christmas, but Gus shot a deer and skinned it. Mammy helped him butcher the meat. Dicie soaked the venison in salt water and vinegar to get out the wild taste, then boiled it in the spider with onions and turnips till it was almost cooked. Mammy roasted the half-cooked venison on the spit over the hearth with some of the new sauce she got from the cook at Springfield. Sighing about Christmases past, Dicie slowly savored the meat, while her brothers reached for seconds, found a gallon of moonshine, and acted the fool with the only other young woman left in the compound.

That night the family sat around a bonfire and sang hymns with their few remaining neighbors. Mammy handed out left-over venison. Others roasted potatoes to share. Dicie watched the full moon rise until it lit the entire compound, making deep shadows for creatures to hide in. She pondered which she wanted most for Christmas—to see her former lover, or to see her daddy?

Daddy might not come home, even if he had made it safely to Savannah. How could he, until after the militia stopped looking for him? And what if Tom had already married Bella? Why had Tom promised his daddy he would marry Bella when he said she was like a sister to him? Bella didn't act very sisterly, far as Dicie could see.

And why did Tom tell her he loved her when he was promised to another? With her daddy and her brothers gone, and Tom marrying Bella, all she would have left was Mammy.

The next morning gray clouds covered the sunrise, and a cold wind blew. She hotted up the fire and added another log while Mammy slept. Remembering her worries of last night, she reached behind the brick for Mammy's cards. Laying them on the table, she began pulling out the sacks of dried herbs stored behind the cards.

"What yo' doin' with my herbs?" Mammy asked, throwing back the three quilts on the bed she again shared with Dicie. She got out of bed and ran her hand through her meager curls.

Now, seeing her in the daylight before she put on the rag that usually covered her head, Dicie was shocked by how much of Mammy's hair had turned gray. Her scalp showed through bald patches. Mammy had always been skinny. Now she had become an old woman.

Dicie's heart jumped, but she held onto the sack in her hand. Looking straight at her mother, she said. "Mammy, you got to teach me everything. What if you not here no more? I got to learn now. And how to read. You ain't taught me nothing but the letters."

"I done taught you most of my spells. All but some of them evil spells. Think you old enough to use 'em right?"

"Mammy, teach me." Suddenly, it seemed urgent that she know. Everything. The most powerful spells. How to kill a man. Or a woman. Before Mammy herself passed on to the next world.

Mammy gave Dicie a deep piercing stare. Her scar pulled upward until her eyes looked almost closed except for a malevolent gleam. "*Allah Yakhthek*," she pronounced in a deep sing-song voice. "Means I wish somebody dead, in my language. Don't ever say it until first you think about what might happen. To your enemy and to you."

Dicie drew back. The look in Mammy's eyes scared her. All her life she had listened to Mammy muttering in Arabic. One word sounded familiar. "Allah?" she asked. "That be your name for God?"

"Yes. You listen good," Mammy said. "*Allah yakhthek* means same as 'may God take your soul' in yo' talk. In Africa the words have a secret meaning. You must say the person's name with it. Be careful who name you say. The magic go straight to them."

Dicie screwed up her face trying to memorize the strange words. "Sampson, *Allah yakhthek*," she whispered.

Mammy shivered. "Reckon not wrong to name that one," she said. "'Fore you gets that powerful, first, offer 'em a drink of honey and strong spirits. Lace it with these here dried petals if you can. Oleander or jasmine: don't make no difference. I got some more in my sack, but they been there a long time."

Dicie thought about years ago when Mammy had been furious with Daddy and the woman named Mary died. "One time I seen you make a little straw person," she said.

"That little figure called a doll. Doll'll help, too." Mammy said. "Works best if you can make something to look like the person you want the spell to work on."

If Dicie couldn't bear to kill an animal, how could she kill a person? Then she remembered the two men who tried to carry her off. Daddy and Mammy had been strong enough to kill them. She thought about Sampson. How he threatened to get even with Mammy.

"How we can make a doll like Sampson?" she asked.

Mammy furrowed her brow. "We got to git some old pine straw, what turned black. He dark. And some cotton fo' his white hair. Fo' a man, you got to tie a little stick in between the legs. I got plenty of vine to tie the parts."

"Show me," Dicie said.

"We got everything except old pine straw," Mammy said. "Let me go fetch some from under the wood pile. Sampson done got so fat I better fetch a heap. I be right back." She carefully slid back the board that barred the door and opened the door a crack.

Leaning against the side of the tabby, just beyond the open door, stood Sampson.

Chapter Forty-Five

December 1868

M ammy screamed and tried to slam the door. Sampson caught it with his ham-like hands and held it open. Dicie jumped to her rescue, but Sampson was too strong. Veins bulged in his forehead as he pushed both women back into the tabby and forced his way in. Dicie crashed against the table, knocking Mammy's precious magic root fixings to the floor. Sampson gripped Mammy's neck with his swollen fingers. She flailed against him, but he grabbed her arms with one hand and squeezed her neck with the other.

"Yo' man Cuffie ain't coming back, and yo' boys ain't here," Sampson said. "I been watching you all night. I ain't afraid of yo' so-called magic, and that wench of yours ain't got nothing to stop me. I know you got me fired from the massa."

His breathing grew louder. As Mammy struggled, a coughing spell wracked his body. The hand on her neck slipped, but he didn't let loose. Shifting his position, he tightened his hold on her throat to keep her from kicking him.

Mammy tried hard to breathe. Her light-complected face turned purple. "Let go," she tried to say. Her voice came out in a tiny squeak.

"You and yo' witchcraft ain't gone stop me now," he said.

Dicie bounded from her position on the floor, dried oleander leaves in one hand, shrieking *Allah yakhthek*! With her other hand, she snatched up the long knife Mammy kept sharpened to cut their cornbread for breakfast. She tried to screw her face into the malevolent expression Mammy wore when she taught Dicie the spell. Too bad they hadn't had time to make the doll.

Sampson leered at Dicie, his mouth hanging open. "What we got here?" he demanded. "A little new witch? Girl, I done knowed you since you birthed. You can't scare me with that rooting shit."

Dicie gripped the knife harder and screamed "Sampson, *Allah yakthek*" again as ferociously as she could. His eyes bulged out at the sight of the knife. Jerking his hands off Mammy's neck, he pulled her drooping body against his fat stomach to shield as much of himself as he could from Dicie's gleaming weapon. Mammy wasn't much of a shield. When both stood tall, she barely reached his shoulder.

While Mammy struggled to catch her breath, Dicie let out a good imitation of Mammy's panther shriek, followed by the words of death, "Sampson, *Allah yakthek*." She raised the knife so Sampson couldn't miss seeing it, being careful to avoid cutting Mammy. Sweat poured down Sampson's face and dripped onto Mammy's hair. After flinging the stems of poisonous oleander at his head, Dicie grasped the knife with both hands, ready to plunge it into his unprotected face.

Suddenly, Sampson moaned and grabbed his chest. Mammy slid out of his grasp to the floor. Dicie screamed and jumped back, scared he would try to seize the knife.

But Sampson didn't reach for the knife. Instead, he leaned forward and vomited an explosion of partially digested tomatoes and rice.

The acid stench drove Dicie back another step. She was pinned against the table. Mammy rolled sideways, covered with stinking stomach contents, as Sampson's planted his swollen legs between her and Dicie. Now space opened directly between Dicie and a heaving Sampson. She screamed again, "Sampson, *Allah yakthek!*" Her voice mimicked Mammy's exactly, down to the Mauritanian accent. Dicie scared herself. How could she sound so fierce? She brandished the knife.

Sampson wobbled dangerously, erupted another deluge of vomit, then fell to the floor, landing partly on Mammy. The nauseating smell of fresh excrement filled the room.

Both women froze. What had happened? Mammy was stuck between Sampson and the fire in the hearth. She couldn't move either way. Sampson's weight was crushing her. Flames blazed only inches from her thin slave-cloth skirt.

Dicie steeled herself to plunge the knife into Sampson's fat chest. Would Sampson have hesitated if the situation was reversed? Of course not. His vomit had splattered on her bare feet. If she lunged forward, would he reach out and grab her ankles? If she tripped, it wouldn't take him but an instant to wrest the knife from her.

Sampson didn't move while she tried to judge the best way to attack. His chest didn't heave. The labored breaths he had pulled from his lungs had ceased. Except for the watery bile oozing out from under him, no part of him stirred.

Mammy tried to slide backward out from under him . His big body lay still on top of her like a butchered hog. Pinned, she shot a questioning look at Dicie.

Dicie peered wildly around the fetid room. Seemed like the best plan would be to get out of the tabby. But how? The only way to escape was by stepping on his big body. She listened intently for the sound of breathing. His mouth was open, covered with remains of vomit, but the tongue didn't move.

"The spell," she whispered. "Did it work?"

"He dead, ain't he?" Mammy's voice was loud and sure. "Now get his fat ass off'n me."

Dicie reached for the leg nearest to Mammy and lifted it. The weight was hard to hold, like a half-full bag of cornmeal. Dicie tried to fling it off to the side, but the leg just flopped back on Mammy. Sampson didn't react at all.

"Hurry," Mammy said. "He crushing me."

Mammy was trapped in the narrow space between the fire and the rest of Sampson's huge frame. Dicie took a deep breath, planted a foot on his torso, and hopped over him.

"Hang on, lemme open this door," she said.

A gust of freezing but fresh air swept some of the stink out of the room. The fire blazed dangerously near to where Mammy was pinned. Dicie took a deep breath and pulled Mammy's shoulders toward the open door with all her might. When Mammy slid backward across the floor, Dicie went limp with relief. She let out her breath and helped her mother stand. The two women scurried out of the tabby.

"What we gone do 'bout this mess?" Mammy asked. "Where our men when we need 'em?"

Dicie wondered the same thing. She hadn't touched Sampson. She still held the knife, but there wasn't a cut on him. Was the spell so powerful? Guiltily, she hid the knife under the doorstep.

"How we gone get him out the house?" she asked. Mammy was so frail, the two women alone could never lift him.

Footsteps approached. Dicie whirled to see who was coming. Tom! She let out a little shriek of joy. Forgetting she had told him never to come see her again, she ran to him.

"Where you been?" she asked, tears running down her cheeks. Every worry of the last few days crashed down on her. Now, at least, she knew he was safe. Even if he had married Bella, she still loved him.

"There, there," he said. "Why you crying? I's here now."

Through her tears, Dicie managed to choke out one word, "Sampson." Bewildered, Tom looked at Mammy. Mammy, a slight, aging woman without the head scarf she always wore, stood silently watching Dicie and Tom. The few tufts of hair on her scalp were mostly gray. What had happened to the powerful witch everyone feared?

Mammy saw Tom's questioning look and nodded her head. "Sampson," she said, waiting for Dicie to tell their story.

Dicie swallowed hard. "He dead," she said, pointing to the open tabby door.

Tom stuck his head in the doorway and quickly drew it back. "Phew," he said, gasping. "He dead alright. How come he in yo' house?"

Dicie said, "He been watching us. He knowed Mammy and I be all by ourselves. That same day Massa Warren had him carried off, he told Mammy he gone get even with her. That was nigh a year ago. We ain't seed him since. Then last week, once Daddy be gone, I seen him in the woods."

Tom raised his eyebrows and his eyes got rounder. "How you kill 'im? He a mean sumbitch. Cuffie leave you his gun?"

"Tom, I promise, we ain't touched him," Dicie said.

He looked at Mammy. She nodded her head in agreement.

"Watcha gone do with him now?" Tom asked.

Just what Mammy and Dicie were wondering. Neither woman answered. Then Mammy said, "Can you help us git him outta the house?"

Tom tied his handkerchief over his nose and mouth and approached the door. Sampson's head lay not far from the door. He reached his hand under one of Sampson's armpits and motioned to Dicie to grab the other. Together they dragged the reeking body to the threshold.

"See, they ain't one mark on him," Mammy said. "Do we got to tell somebody?"

Tom and Dicie looked at each other. They had no idea.

Mammy looked around. Most of the tabbies in the compound were empty. Stubborn little oak shoots sprouted where folks used to sit to eat dinner. "Who we gone tell?" she asked. "Reverend Houston done gone. Soldiers done gone. Sampson used to be in charge. Now he gone."

An elderly lady poked her head out of a tabby across the way. "Hey there, Miz Susie," Mammy called. "See here, old Sampson done died right here in my tabby."

Miz Susie jumped back inside, pulling the door behind her. They heard the thump of her barring her door.

"Look like it up to us to bury him," Tom said. "Reckon yo' brothers be coming 'round soon?"

"I sure hope so," Dicie said.

Mammy grabbed a broom and the water bucket. "The two of you go fetch more water and let's see if'n we can get this mess outta the tabby."

As Tom and Dicie walked toward the well, Dicie asked, "Where you been?"

Tom smiled and looked at her. "Been with yo' daddy," he said.

"Daddy?" She couldn't believe it. "Why you ain't told me? I looked for you at the river, but I ain't seen you. I seen Daddy running into the marsh, but ain't nobody with him 'cept the boys rowing the boat. Where was you at?"

"I hid upstream by the Wilmington River," he said, putting his arms around her. "I expected trouble. When them soldier boys turned up into Skidaway River toward Cuffie, I knew trouble had come. Nobody could stop Cuffie, but I figured I might help him get away to town. I took my boat upriver and cut back into the creek where he be headed.

Dicie looked at him like she could eat him up. How could he be so smart? "Did Daddy see you?" she asked.

Tom nodded. "He clumb in my bateau covered with mud. We pulled up at the freeman colony on Grimball Creek, and I walked him to Savannah."

"You did?" Dicie went cold with fear. "You and him both could of been caught. Mammy done told you not to go near that mess. Why you took a chance?" How could he have risked his life and his freedom like that?

Tom smiled down at her. "I done it for you. I know how much you love yo' Daddy."

Chapter Forty-Six

December 1868

I saac hurried up the path to the tabby just in time to see Tom kissing his sister. She had both arms around his neck, holding on tight.

"Oooh! Oooh! Kissy. Dicie and Tom in love," he sing-songed. "What Mammy gone say?"

"Hush up, Isaac," Dicie hissed. The two broke apart hastily. Her face was burning. She stared at Tom. "Can't believe I done that. What Bella gone say?"

Tom wouldn't let go of Dicie. "I ain't promised to Bella no more," he said.

"What?" Dicie asked, stepping back to examine his face. She couldn't believe it.

Isaac looked bewildered. "Bella?" he asked. "Hear tell she got herself a Savannah man."

"Never mind that," Tom said to Isaac. "Where you been? We got work to do."

Dicie ran back to where Mammy was sitting on a stump, rocking back and forth, her hands covering her face. She steered Mammy over to a bench where she couldn't see or smell the dead body and sat down next to her. Together they watched the boys try to figure what to do with Sampson's corpse. Already buzzards circled in the sky, attracted to the smell of death.

Motioning to Isaac to follow him, Tom led him to the open tabby door. "Ain't none of you boys here when they needed you."

Isaac caught a glimpse of the swollen body wedged against the threshold and let out a loud scream. "What the hell?" he yelled. He peered wildly around the compound, looking to see who might be watching. "What you gone do now?"

"First of all, I'm gone get you to help me lift him over this doorway and down the step so we can get his puke outta the house," Tom said. "He too heavy for me and Dicie to lift."

"I ain't touching that sumbitch," Isaac said.

"You want yo' Mammy and yo' sister sleeping in the house with the body?" Tom asked, as Isaac started to walk away.

Dicie leaned forward to see what Isaac would do.

At Tom's words, he stopped and pulled his face into an enormous scowl. Then, he reached for the kerchief around his neck and pulled it up over his mouth and nose. Gingerly, he walked back to the tabby and squared his shoulders. Together, he and Tom lifted Sampson's swollen body and dragged him out of the tabby to the edge of the woods.

"Ain't no preacher at Hibernia," Tom said. "Most everybody done followed the soldiers when they left. Nobody in charge. Reckon it a waste of time to send a message to yo' Massa Warren. He ain't dealing with Sampson no more. We can leave him out here for the buzzards, or we can bury him ourselves like the Christians we is."

Isaac looked over at the body. Wind was already blowing the fetid smell in his direction. "I'm fetching a shovel," he said. "Rufus and Gus should be here any minute. With all us shoveling, won't take long, even for his big, fat self."

Cass trudged up the pathway with Gus and Rufus. At almost twelve years old, he was nearly as big as a man and strong like Cuffie. He had helped repair the fence around Cuffie's share. Tired as the boys were, each grabbed a shovel as soon as Tom told them what happened.

"Roots so thick, we can't hardly dig," Rufus grumbled, as he pounded his shovel into the vegetation threatening to take over the proposed burial spot.

"Sampson ain't never made nothing easy," Isaac answered. "I'll fetch the axe."

Even though Sampson had been hated or feared by all the family, Dicie said, "We Christians. It ain't right not to let God know he coming."

So, Gus said the words Geechee reverends always said when they preached over the deceased, "Rejoice, you is going home." Mammy said a prayer in Arabic, followed by "Allah, thank you for sparing me."

Mammy, Dicie, her brothers, and Tom sang:

Oh, the sun done quit shining,
Works over for the day
Time for me to go home,
Jesus, show me the way.

It was a lot to do for someone who had made their lives miserable. Dicie would never forget her terror or the blood when Mammy birthed her last baby and Sampson wouldn't give Isaac a pass for a midwife. Or her outrage and helplessness when Sampson and his bully boys ransacked their garden. Then there was Sampson keeping Daddy from coming home after he saw him heading to Savannah to sell vegetables. Without Sampson's threats, maybe Daddy would never have stayed with Dorothy. At least now they knew he could never hurt them again.

When the last shovelful of dirt filled the space over Sampson's body, Tom took Dicie's hand and asked her to walk with him to their secret spot.

Dicie stiffened. "What happen 'tween you and Bella? I got to know. I ain't gone be the one you take, cause the one you want got away."

Tom reached to put his arms around her, but she backed away, even though she wanted nothing more than to have him kiss her again.

Still holding her hand, he knelt down. "Dicie, you the one I want. Always been. I never forgot you from the time you was a little bitty thing. How pretty you be. When my daddy got sick, I didn't know how to tell him no. Bella heard him. I finally told her that I still loved you. She been seeing that man she gone marry the whole time Daddy was sick. She mad at me now, but it for the best. I ain't never loved her like I love you."

Tom looked so sad and scared of losing her, that Dicie's heart went out to him. "I know how it is to love yo' Daddy," she said.

The day was cold, and the woods bare of leaves except for the sparse evergreens of winter, but pine straw and Spanish moss piled soft and deep in their hidden clearing.

Tom's body over hers was warm and comforting. He put his hands under her dress and caressed her legs. She lifted her head to meet his mouth in a long kiss. After they had each fulfilled the aching need of the other, Tom said, "Think we can find a preacher?"

"We already done buried him," Dicie said.

"For something different," Tom said. "How 'bout you and me getting married? A real marriage with a preacher."

Dicie could hardly believe what she was hearing. "You mean it?" She squealed with joy. "You and me git married?"

She had loved Tom ever since she was six years old and saw him beating a tomato can drum next to his daddy. She remembered admiring him again when she was eight, the night his daddy saved Mammy from Cephus.

"I hear Preacher Williams s'posed to come out here Sunday after next. Reckon you and me might get hitched while he's here? He s'posed to marry Bella and her man that same Sunday."

"Yes, yes," she said, burying her face in his chest.

"How you feel about us asking preacher to put us down as Mr. and Mrs. Williams? I never did git a second name. We got to have one to put on the marriage paper. I hear Reverend Williams a real good man, coming all the way out here when can't nobody hardly pay him," Tom said.

Dicie thought about her own daddy. Would he keep the name "Houston" now that he was no longer with Mammy? What second name would he take? How would they even find him without knowing his last name?

"How you gone ask my daddy if it be okay for me to marry you?"

He held her tight. The smile faded from his face. "I didn't want to tell you, but Dorothy done left Skidaway Island, too. Yo' Daddy staying with her over in Savannah."

Tears sprung to Dicie's eyes. Her chest heaved with sobs. Good news mixed with bad.

"I should have guessed," she said. "Don't say nothin' to Mammy. Think he'll ever come home?"

Tom kissed her cheek. "Not while them soldiers hunting him. Shrimpers he took money off of got kin in the militia. We got to pray for him."

What Tom said was the truth. Dicie knew he was right. Memories of her parents spun around her head. The nights of Daddy and Mammy arguing while she lay under their bed on her pallet. The boiling pot Mammy threw at him while she screamed Dorothy. Green beans spilled all over the floor. And long ago, the dead Mary. Always, she was haunted by the lurking fear that Mammy would use her evil spells against Daddy.

She must hold fast to the sweet memories of good times. The times she sat in his lap and pressed her face against his flannel sleeve. She would never eat another red and white peppermint again without missing her daddy.

On the way back to the cabin to share their news with Mammy and her brothers, Dicie noticed buds on the leafless Carolina jasmine vines. Shining yellow flowers would soon arch over their secret bower, beautiful, but poison for all except those who knew how to use their power.

As they approached the compound, Dicie ran to her mother. Holding Mammy's hand, she said, "Tom asked me to marry him. I'm gone be Mrs. Tom Williams."

Mammy straightened up. Her eyes had some of the old fire."Bless me, Dicie, night's a shadder, day's a shine. That's what the old folks in Africa used to say. I never would have believed you could grow up so quick. You saved my life today. Tom's gitting a good woman."

Dicie hugged her. "Thank you for learning me all them spells and roots," she said. Dicie wasn't used to sharing words with Mammy, but her heart overflowed with gratitude. What if she hadn't known the spell? Would Sampson's powerful hands have strangled Mammy? Much as she loved all living things, she didn't regret sending Sampson to his death. Life was for the living. Living would be much easier without Sampson.

"I promise I'll use what you taught me to help us what's left here on this island," she told Mammy.

Mammy sat bent so low on the bench, Dicie could hardly hear her. "I know you will chile," she said. "It yo' time now."

The End

www.ingramcontent.com/pod-product-compliance
Lightning Source LLC
Chambersburg PA
CBHW061433030726
47503CB00005B/1386